Four Stories High

A collection of short stories

By

Leon Gratton

Grosvenor House
Publishing Limited

This book is published by
Grosvenor House Publishing Ltd
Link House
140 The Broadway, Tolworth, Surrey, KT6 7HT.
www.grosvenorhousepublishing.co.uk

This book is a work of fiction. Any resemblance to
people or events, past or present, is purely coincidental.

A CIP record for this book
is available from the British Library

Paperback ISBN 978-1-83615-401-3

GOLDEN TONG

Carl Jenson rose from his slumber and sniffed. The last few days were a blur he had been guarding a Saudi Arabian oil tycoon. The money wasn't great but it kept the wolves from his door and helped with his gambling debts. He reached over to the nightstand and opened a pack of cigarettes, drew one out and lit it with a quick, fluid movement on his zippo. The last two nights were a blur for the reason that he had been drinking. He knew he shouldn't, but it was a habit he couldn't shake off. Anyway, he looked at his watch and blew some rings whilst the cigarette burned slowly. He had a feeling that there was a great change in the air.

The phone rang, it was his boss, "You got another job, just came up".

Carl snarled quietly and thought 'Pig fucking knows I need a break. But I need the money too'. Carl smiled in sarcastic sly way. "Who is it?" He asked the head of his security company.

"It's your old pal Kirri Motto."

Carl breathed, this could have come at an easier time, but he knew that sods law was the way things worked in his world. "Okay. Where and when and for fuck sake it better be a quickie?" He replied.

The boss smiled, "He's only here for two days, he's got a prototype chemical cooling system that he has to show to the affluent Brit's. But he has the only formula and let's say he's been getting the usual threats".

Carl smiled and said, "Fucking bollocks. I know Kirri I'm practically family".

The Boss sneered down the phone. "Exactly, he asked for you by name."

Carl smiled and replied, "I take it his son and his school buddies will be here?"

The boss smiled and said, "of course".

Carl went to the fridge and opened a carton of apple juice, his upper body flexing as he carried on drinking straight from the carton. He then went into the bedroom and got out his .357 Magnum and his Tanto. The Tanto was wrapped in a gold cloth and he remembered receiving it at a ritual that he had been at, it was a great honour and great blessing as he was passed the small teacup to turn and drink. This had been because he had saved both Kirri and his infant son from a Triad trap.

The two vans had screeched to a halt and out jumped the balaclava wearing men. He covered over the young child and his father, opened fire on the rest whilst all he could feel was the sting of the vest he was wearing. It was an uncomfortable way; he was hit directly in the back by two scorpions fired instantaneously at him. They ripped into his back as he covered the small child. Then Kirri shot one of the men in the face, disintegrating it to mush. He was using flat pounder bullet's, the ones that, well they were messy. The other man with the other scorpion aimed at Kirri but Jenson had him cold with a single shot to the last place that was armoured his groin. This busted him like ripe fruit being smashed with a hammer. Carl remembered those days. He had been younger, leaner and more, hungry for action.

He smiled and put on his leather biker Jacket. And put the Tanto into his right pocket. And headed down the stairs to His BMW S series, it was practically a tank. He smiled and headed towards the five star hotel where Kirri was staying. As he arrived, he noticed the five Suzuki Katana Motorcycles. The bikes were all black and had a Man in black tight leather on each. On their backs each had a Katana blade. Jensen went up the stairs and straight to suite that Kirri was staying in. He knocked on the door to the suite, it was the penthouse suite.

Kirri smiled knowing that knock all too well. Carl waited. Kirri crossed the floor and opened the door. His torso was naked with the large dragon tattoo on his back and chest. He smiled humbly at Carl who looked at the man who was just as lethal with his hands and feet as any pistol or gun. Carl bowed then extended his right hand to clasp on to Kirri's hand. They shook, then released and smiled.

"Been a while Jenson San," He said with an oriental accent. Kirri looked over his shoulder and said, "I will be two three minutes whilst I get organized".

Carl looked down the hall as the Japanese gentleman prepared himself. The lift and the stair doorway were opened simultaneously. It was a hit, one that had been in the planning for two days. There were seven men in white tong masks, all armed with small arms. And two with long chains with spiked weights on them. Carl Jenson went straight into a crouch aiming at their kneecaps. Nothing put the fear into a tong more than a bullet through his kneecap. He fired and they began to flip around running up walls and getting closer. The two with Kasiriwaza chains moved forward. He got two just before they encroached on him. They fell bleeding in the hallway. And suddenly he was in a close quarters fight with his Japanese dagger.

Just as he began to dodge and duck and use his weapon to its fullest. He slashed one of the masked men along his throat. Kirri on the other hand heard the commotion and immediately went for his Katana, he unsheathed it and as he did so his dragon on his back rippled and growled and then breathed fire. The fire was the key component of his discipline; he was an expert Iiado swordsman and was quick. He took the head off of one Tong straight away. The other four were running out of options. Kirri carried on forward showing no fear. But his upper torso was twitching as the Oyabun (Japanese godfather) carried through with his golden Katana. The Bodyguard Carl was just about to open fire again when the Yakuza boss sliced down two of them and the other two were met with gunfire. Their bodies exploded as Jenson shot one twice in the chest the other got it in the Hari (abdomen).

Carl smiled and reloaded his six shooter. It was a specialist weapon. He then wiped the blood off of his Tanto and counted how many quick loads he had. He had four and that was six in each that gave him twenty-four shots. He had shells in his car in the boot. He had at least Two boxes with fifty shells in each box. He wasn't running out for a long while. The katana wielding Ninja got round to keeping up the rear of Kirri and Carl. As they drove to a safe house in the pleasant suburb of Strepford. It would be a safe haven providing that Kirri's ninja were up to the task. He knew Tongs only let things settle in order to spring a new trap.

They got into the large, detached villa with its own orchard of apples and cherries. Jenson keyed in the pin number on the alarm and then opened the door. They entered, whilst the ninja set up a watch, the five of them immediately hiding in the shadows of the Orchard. They smiled and were only visible to each other or so they thought. Kirri produced the briefcase with the chemical cooling formula.

Jenson smiled. "So, this is the new wave in chemistry" He said then smiled and looked at the formula that was broken down mathematically into a basic chaos algorithm, which only professors in both math and chemistry could decipher. Carl Looked at the numbers and started to feel very old, he was no whizz at maths but knew whoever owned this briefcase was a wealthy man. Carl began to feel the pressure of the chemical in his hands. But no, he was no sell out. Kirri and himself had battled too long to let money come between their honour. It boiled down to respect and that was something they shared between them. He smiled and sat down as did Kirri, Jenson was no fool and knew that the Tongs would be hot on their trail. Kirri then stood up and went upstairs to put on a shirt. He came back with a tailor-made shirt. He had dozens of them, costing at least three hundred a shirt.

Carl began to fill his quick load rounds for his .357-calibre Magnum. He smiled at Kirri who was watching his dear friend load and put them into a pocket on his body armour. He had several of these pockets and they were all, in reaching distance. He worked left to right and that was a simple measure of skill. He was a very competent marksman and had won several trophies. All for the best marksmen. He never cracked under pressure and never missed a shot. He mainly shot for his targets head, but when the opportunity arose, he would aim for the heart or the throat. He was a split ender, which meant that he shot the last two bullets into the targets, chest. This was an elite skill he had picked up in the special forces. He had grown fond of the Magnum .357 as he was gently eased into the Body guarding game. He spent years watching the rich as they alienated themselves in a fool's paradise. Jenson carried on making quick loads. Kirri admired the man, the sheer killing power and energy of him was a force to not take lightly. Many a would-be assassin was struck by the sheer killing power of Jenson. Any one of them realised, but realised too late, how skilful Jenson was. He could nail a fly through its heart at ten paces. This was attributed to his calm demeanour. He had it nailed and nailed cold. His skill was unrivalled.

He had a thing about knives. Razor sharp blades. But seldom used them as he loved the power of the .357, it was one of the most dangerous guns on the market. It was known to crack lorry engine blocks. It was a stopping power that couldn't be beat. I mean the Magnum .44 was the big guy on the block or was until the Desert Eagle .50 surfaced. He wasn't a man to rely on power, no, the .357 was just right. He knew for a six shooter it was deadly and accurate. He carried on feeding loaders shells. Then he got up stretched his legs and arched his back until it cracked. Then drew out his Tanto and showed it to Kirri.

"I see you still have my gift."

Carl Jenson smiled at him and bowed his head slightly. Letting his hair cover his eyes. "Yeah, I like the Tanto it shows a classy side to my abilities."

Kirri smiled and replied, "You must let me teach you Iiado".

Carl nodded and said, "You know when this is all over, I'll come over to Japan and well train, I'll teach you small arms tactics you can show me the way of the Katana".

Carl sat down and Kirri poured him and himself some room temperature Saki. They sat for an hour or so conversing mainly about how this new invention would revolutionise the chemicals that were delicate and needed to be kept cold for long periods of time without refrigeration. It would revolutionise transplant transportation. Organs such as the heart, would be sprayed by the chemical then warmed by its other part that took away the chill leaving a healthy heart with no signs of decaying. It was a miracle chemical. One that would change the face of medicine. The Triads wanted it badly, it was a game changer. A modern day marvel that had just been discovered. It was a cash cow and was only needing the basic formula to come into their possession then they would own the most significant of inventions. It would change modern science as it was known. The way in which the organs could be stored cheaply and efficiently. Giving the organs the longer lasting freshness without the tissue damaging becoming prevalent in the organ transplant.

It was years in the making and some might say it was a godsend. Kirri was onto a veritable medicine miracle. He smiled and after explaining the details to Carl he continued to drink his Saki. Then all of a sudden, the back porch door was shattered. And in walked a huge Chinese man with two scimitar blades, he began to circle the blades in a web of death motion. Jenson was quicker and flew across the room with his Tanto gleaming as he struck and took the Tongs head off. It was an impossible move on Carls part, yet he did it anyway. The large carcass of a man fell to the floor pumping blood from his neck all over the floor. He then spat on the corpse of a Tong. Kirri who had a split second to react had drawn his Katana. And went straight out into the garden and saw the gruesome sight of his son and the foot of his ninja. Hanging from the trees by chains. They had killed five Ninja and hung them from the large Oak and conifer trees.

He bowed his head and sighed, "This was not supposed to happen".

Carl looked at the cascade of corpses. "They must have been outnumbered," He said then began to heave the heavy corpses down through the trees and onto the soft bracken of leaves and twigs. Kirri walked up the dead body of his son and took the patch off him. It was the seven-star shuriken and only the very noble and affluent of Ninja were given the honour of wearing it. He handed it to Jenson who smiled solemnly and put the patch into his jacket pocket. Kirri smiled back then walked straight back into the safe house. Carl knew the man said little in the way of words, but his silence said it all. Carl knew that the rest of this would be a brutal protection, a hard fight. He had a solution, he would call his old Sargeant Major who was a special forces sniper, His name was Darren Chord, he was a crack shot and known to make targets that were impossible. He was a miracle man in the special forces, escape, evasion and inversive tactics. He would sneak up and infiltrate enemies, by either being captured or getting into the local areas without being detected.

He had a whole heap of medals and earned every one of them.

He was a marine commando, old school, who you just didn't try to fool. His marksmanship was unequalled. And Carl was sure he was the best person to get him through London with minimal casualties, and without drawing attention to himself by either the police or paparazzi. They would need to be silent and they had just lost the upper hand that the Ninja clan that was led by Kirri Mottos son gave them. He knew that the police and the newspapers would love the outcome to favour them. But this couldn't happen as the prototype chemical was still needing refining and it would take a few days to be fully functional and ready to use. He smiled as the sniper answered the telephone promptly (Three rings).

"It's Carl," He said and the sniper smiled down at the telephone and said, "I had a feeling you might call."

Carl grinned and responded, "well how long is it gonna take you take to dig out your weapons?"

Darren Chord smiled down the receiver and said, "I'm way ahead of you soldier". It took him three minutes as he always kept things to hand. Then about fifteen minutes later he was at the safe house. He had two major weapons when going on an urban excursion one was the Browning automatic pistol the other was a Skorpion, not the conventional one, but the Hekler and Koch slightly heavier and sturdier one. He was also in a full flak jacket, back and front covered. Oh and of course down his boot was his commando dagger. As he liked to get close to the bigger targets, showed aptitude, showed courage, showed lethality and ferocity and the remainder of their troops knew they had been in a fight that was for sure. He liked to get up close and personal. The more the merrier. He loved combat stealth; sniper cover, a rep as a soldier with no conscience. He listed his kills in an open firefight as forty plus, judging by the amount of ammo he had expended and what he had left. Him and his squad were undefeated in areas of Lebanon, Libya and various other desert war zones.

Jenson smiled as he entered the house, his stoney Joe face with pock marks from a severe acne problem. He had handled it well by setting about the first kid who commented on the problem. He knocked the kid out, the kid was twelve and in primary seven, he was in primary three. Six years old, nobody messed with him, he made friends with a kid from Finland whose family were descendants of Finnish royalty. Enough said as they had a lot of dick measuring with each other, both proud of their countries, neither would back down. They stayed friends all through primary and through secondary schools. They sported themselves with weapons The Finnish kid liked to collect knives like Darren, he was at an urban school and like I said no fool. He knew the cosh and the chain. They were inseparable at one point. And knew they could count on each other. Anyway Darren left school and went straight into the navy traversing one of the hardest courses in the world, the commando course. One in a hundred conquered the course and that was sheer determination. The Finnish kid, well he went on to be a hells angel, also not to be sniffed at. They were a brotherhood after all, like the wolf shirts of Scandinavian countries.

They had each-others backs for many years. But Darren became a true nomad living in the army and honing his skills. Becoming more deadly, no, if there was anyone befitting this job with Kirri Motto and Carl Jenson it was Darren Chord. He became a Sargeant Major but felt no need to leave the armed services, no he was hoping to make full blown Colonel. But that was years down the road. And he would have to earn his stripes many times over before getting his wish granted. He had the wife, the mistress and two kids. It was a simple life, married life, but it suited him down to a T. But the army was a calling, a strong disciplined calling and his soul and heart were in love with it. He had a good call to duty, but this was like going back to the old school gang days where you relied upon each other not to let anyone get close and if they did they would have to be dealt with terminal force. No if's, buts or cracks, you relied on your fellow soldier and as he had been a foot soldier of the gangs in London, he had become renowned up and down the country.

He had been involved in certain criminal gang violence but decided to put his thinking gear behind the courage he had and joined up when he was seventeen. Now thirty and still a specialist, he finished off his tours (For the meantime anyway) with a stint in the Engineers.

He was fast becoming a Sarge Marj. His gillie suit was a prize that he earned, even his weapon was earned and treated with respect, his tattoos from friendly artists around the world, he was covered. Wings and everything. His build was stocky and short but not too short no he was deceptive in his build, showing nothing that could be used in the covert way. No tails just an average Hooligan/come pedestrian come businessman. He made covert silence a piece of art. No, he was unrivalled in most areas of soldiery. Even the jungles of Cambodia became his playground. He had a knack of arriving in heavily out-manned areas and setting the facts straight. British intelligence was the best. And he was right hand to Queen and country. Of course, he was depended upon by various Dukes and Ministers and occasionally came to the Aid of Carl Jenson. And they were the only times he and Carl got to be straight with each other and these times were few and far between.

He smiled and shook Kirri Mottos hand who smiled back and sheathed his sword. "Where are we heading?" Asked Chord.

Kirri smiled. "Clear across the other side of London," he said as the sword snapped in the sheath.

Jenson smiled and placed his Tanto into the inside of his leather bomber Jacket. He smiled as he did so and reloaded his .357 Magnum. Carl pocketed the quick loads in and around his person. He holstered the weapon softly and began to put on his bullet proof vest, Kevlar from Kosovo. They took the headless corpse out of the house, then put in the call for the cleaner. They arrived two minutes after as the Vauxhall Laguna left, they had to get to the chemical warehouse and laboratories. And they needed to put the formula in the hands of the head technician of Cal Tech.

They would use offensive tactics, relying a lot on the break and clutch. They knew they were going to encounter a lot of resistance as the Triad were lying in wait just around the corner from the traffic lights that were leading onto a dual carriageway where they would encounter the majority of resistance. Darren Chord was driving as he split the pedals and shot the car forward, gaining momentum, then shifting up gear and settling into a cool momentum, tricks that he had learned as a forces driver shuttling various brass and dignitaries around London. He had been ambushed several times and knew the need to put offensive techniques into play. This was a pincer trap and relied on two cars coming straight for them and one behind. That would offload its ammo at the Laguna. The Laguna had reinforced bullet proof metal and windows that even the heaviest mini gun would have trouble breaking through.

Chord smiled and slammed the foot brake and pulled on the hand brake. spinning the car one hundred and eighty degrees. Then he shifted gear again and followed through. The Tongs in the car that were closing up the rear were suddenly made to swerve and the choice was simple, left hit the pincer on the left or right hit the pincer on the right. Either way it was crash and burn time baby. And the other side went smashing into the concrete sidings of the hard shoulder. Losing all control as the other two smashed head on into each other. He spun the wheel again and turned on a dime and went back through the smoke as the three car pincer was left desolate and in flames. Chord smiled as he looked at the wreckage and began to speed off. Knowing their next move would be at the Junction before the tunnel. It would present itself a very tough and non-negotiable challenge, kill or be killed.

He heard the motorcycles revving up in front of him this was going to be tough. Chord smiled turned round and said, "relax Its just starting". He then opened the window and cocked his Skorpion machine pistol. Then he heard the three Bikes screech their tyres and let rip. Darren laughed this was textbook stuff to him. They were using tactics that he knew all too well. As they drew closer, he let off a short burst at the leader. Who decided to show some grit and popped a wheelie. Darren smiled looked at the bike and aimed for the petrol tank. It didn't take much of an aim as Darren's reach was steady as a rock. The bike lit right the way up sending the rider straight back and leaving a big puddle of fire that the other two had to navigate around. They got closer and Darren began to shift up gears again, and again he let off a-small-arms burst of bullets. This one copped it right in the face, blowing the riders head into several pieces. The other bike came gunning going through the gears sizing up the car. The Tong on the last bike took aim and looked the devil right in the eye, he was unnerved by a quick smile and a single shot from Jenson with his revolver and the Tong flew back as his chest exploded and he went scraping along the tunnel. His leathers being insufficient as he went straight through the Petroleum puddle and lit up like a dry bush with a naked flame. Darren carried on driving through the tunnel he sniffed and slowed down to watch the fire. "No problem to me," he said then broke into a small grin.

Kirri looked at the carnage and smiled then said quietly, "So it begins".

Jenson smiled and followed through with the thought, "Yep so it begins".

Kirri smiled, knowing he had one of the worlds, best marksmen leading up the charge. They carried on through the tunnel heading directly to the chemical labs with the documents and files on the new freezing chemical that was years ahead of itself. It was a great advancement. Kirri's company had got the thing whilst looking at molecular break down. In other words, they had found something that was a great benefit to mankind whilst researching a chemical weapon that broke the human body down on a cellular level. It was a great advancement in the fields of molecular chemistry. Kirri's technicians had all popped corks of champagne and celebrated, especially after the trials on various tissue samples and pieces of animal organs. But someone had leaked the finding of the chemical to the Chinese who were desperate enough to hire as many Triads and Tongs to capture it and at the same time take out the head of the Motto enterprises. But he wasn't going to just roll over and die. No, he would guard the chemical formula with his life. And seeing as they had killed his son, he would certainly want revenge. He smiled as they went through the heart of London and headed to the northeast side.

They needed to make a couple of stops on the way to the Chemical refinery, mainly to make sure they didn't alert the police too much. So, they turned onto a side street that was upper class tenements. They entered the second safe house and began to check their weapons whilst Darren Chord watched from a window down on to the quiet street.

"It's to fucking quiet," said Darren.

Jenson's face was set, stoney and impassive. He reloaded his revolver. Darren reloaded his Skorpion whilst looking out into the Neon buzz of the street lights. Whilst doing so he again remarked, "It's too fucking quiet".

Carl scoffed and said, "Yeah, why do you think they are best assassins in the world?"

Darren smiled, "I've killed better".

Jenson flicked his barrel wheel back into the revolver. He then went and joined Darren at the window and looked out onto the street, watching for anything that could tell the tale of Tong advancement. This was a very difficult thing to do as they could pretty much turn invisible and advance on the three of them. That's when it happened, a flash and a large bolt action rifle fired in the distance. The bullet went straight through the window and missed the two mercenaries. Darren stepped back and Jenson switched off the lights knowing that this would confuse the sniper. But the Tong had a set of night scopes and were using them to full advantage. He fired again and Jenson hit the floor feeling the bullet going whistling by. Darren hit the stairs and went running keeping to the shadows as much as he could. He thought he saw a flare of muzzle flash and headed in the trajectory of the bullets.

The sniper thought he had all the time in the world but Darren had him sussed, He moved around the sniper knowing exactly what to look for. He saw the snipers hunched shape and circled drawing out his commando dagger out of his boot he barely breathed as he drew closer to the Chinaman. Next second, he was in top of the sniper drawing his razor-sharp dagger across the man's throat. The blood splashed all over the hill that he was settled on. He stripped the man's weapon, it was a SIG SSG-3000, Swiss made with a five round magazine, he had used three. And the other two were just left. Darren headed back to the safe house. He was slipping in and out the shadows as quickly as he could, he knew that there were more heading in his direction. He made it just as the shadows began to take shape. It was going to be a struggle to get around and out of the vicinity. Kirri opened the door to Darren who sniffed in a military way.

"I got the dink," he then made his way back to the window, smiled and donned his jacket. Jenson went down the stairs where he was greeted with revolver fire. And Beretta fire. He ducked and aimed his revolver in the direction the fire had come from. He aimed and listened doing everything he could in the dark. He fired. Three shots of his six-shooter Magnum .357. Two hits and one miss. He looked at the darkness but knew he had hit something. There were at least three of them and they weren't waiting for an invite. They came at him and they came at him hard, no warning, nothing. They came at him shooting and swinging their Knives, half knives and tong axes. But Jenson was up for it. He started to bounce on his feet knowing that it was harder for them to hit a moving target, he spun out a couple of kicks, mawashi geris. Then aiming at one of their midriffs. Knowing that he had balance and the right strength he caught two of them in the belly with slugs from his revolver. He quickly put the quick loader into his revolver and was good to go. He aimed at the triads that were trying to confuse and beguile him throw him off centre. He took aim and closed one eye using the barrel sights on his revolver. This had given him ideal opportunity to squeeze the trigger at just the right time. He caught one in the neck the other was hit in the chest, this gave him ample opportunity to face down the last three Bang! Bang! Bang! The last three shots claimed their mark; three white Tong'd masks were hit as Jenson blew the masks that they each wore to pieces and disintegrated their faces.

Jenson spat on the pavement. "Not good enough," He, said and reloaded another six quick reloaders.

Jenson walked back up the stairs and Darren was looking out over the battlefield and all its bloody glory. "That's thirteen," he said as Carl entered the apartment.

Jenson looked at the Yakuza boss and said, "You're just in luck, we have to get to the other safe house". Jenson knew if they headed straight to the Chemical laboratories, they would be cut down by a sizeable force. It was best to take the side route knowing that safe houses were positioned in tactical ways so as to keep the clients safe and give the bodyguards the advantage of position. But these were Tongs and had been the most lethal of killers since before Christ, since the dawn of time even. They had grown in strength and grown lethally through Shaolin days and before. They had seen China grow and grow and still no one had defeated them, no one had gotten to the Golden Tong. But do you know what, Kirri Motto was sure going to try. Jenson smiled and took the two quick loads that he had emptied and filled them again. He was back to full strength. And that was just as well, as the nearer they got to getting to the laboratories the more heat they would draw. But they had to get to the next safe house and sure firing hell there would be more snipers and more Tong hit teams.

Jenson was just getting warmed up. Kirri sat in the back seat whilst Jenson sat in the front passenger side and Chord took the driver's seat. He spun the steering wheel and did a smooth three point turn, faced off with the road and headed into the urban jungle that led to the second safe house. They arrived at the second safe house untroubled by the Triads. But that only made things more creepier, quiet, and ominous. Chord was ringing and cracking his knuckles gently saying a buddha mantra to settle him into a calm yet ready mood. He knew these things as he had been a survivor in the Indo China wars. Korea, Vietnam, South Korea. He had also been responsible for a number of failed tests on nuclear weapons. He had been applauded by various ministers and royalty. Given numerous medals and ribbons from both the British consulate and American government. And he was still one of the hardest S.A.S. Soldiers to grace the earth. He popped up on some of the European most wanted, listed as pass without trace. That meant that he was treated as armed and dangerous and was giving all rights to pass through unmolested and unobserved. They knew he was a serious hombre and to be allowed to pass freely. He smiled and carried on the silent murmur of a mantra. Kirri exited the car as did Jenson. They headed up the stairs and onto the balcony and watched as they were needing to settle for a while, the adrenaline settling down in the three of them.

Darren Smiled as he walked up the stairs and entered the small but plush flat. It had been used only two or three times in this Governments leadership. No, the place was again a tactical advantage with good routes for them to escape from going north, east or west. South wasn't option, well not one you could make easily. Darren ungloved his Browning Automatic and set about loading a few more magazines seven in total each magazine loading Thirteen rounds and easy to slip in the handle of the weapon. He loved his Browning treated it properly and after every mission he slid the thing apart and cleaned it thoroughly. He also kept a box of shells close by as you never know, one of the magazines may jam. As was common with short recoil weapons. But proper maintenance was the best way to avoid jams and he was averse, to leaving the muzzle dirty and the rest of the thing unoiled. It was a nice pistol and was a craftsmen choice when it came to pistols. He really loved the thing like any military artist. He could paint and preen a beautiful tapestry of death. And this was why he was such an efficient warrior.

On his right shoulder he had a Cobra snake coiled around the Commando Dagger. On his left he had Wings either side of the Commando Dagger. He had earned both tattoos. And always remembered their codes. He who Dares Wins. And Carpe Diem. He was covered with various skulls and dragons He had done tours with Gurkhas and various Indochinese rebels. That's when he grew fond of tattoos. He began to appreciate the Oriental way of life, becoming friends with various tribes in Indo China. He kept faith in what he knew and what he could do. He was well respected. And a constant source of tactics and power moves. He was also undefeated in the martial arts world, studying as many as he could. His favourites were Judo and Karate. But he had a working knowledge of Gung Fu and Wu Dang Tai Chi. He had also dabbled in various styles of Jujitsu (Including certain styles of Ninjutsu). But he was sworn to secrecy in all applications of his arts, especially unarmed combat. Jenson had stayed true to The Japanese style of Bu-jitsu. He had studied others but found them boring and hard to apply into the game of martial science. He also studied Russian Sambo. He was an expert through and through. But Darren Chord made him look like an absolute beginner when they had studied and had a trade-off. Each of them being a true adept in the martial arts ways, and they had lots to trade, style wise. They kept a lot of secrets in all their styles.

Darren smiled and carried on reloading his magazines for his two primary weapons. He brought the shells out for his Skorpion and these were 20 rounds per magazine. Again, he had seven magazines strapped around his Kevlar body armour. Each with a pointed slug that would rapidly destroy up to two inches of metal. They sat back after checking their weapons and making sure they were all armed and good to go. They began to discuss tactics and the best way to trade blows with the Tongs and the best escape and evade tactics. They knew one way and that was to face them head on and was probably the best way the old Samurai tactic in which they saw the target and didn't deviate from taking the target. Samurai wisdom states that, "one who is engaged in combat will not deviate from the target it has first seen".

As they finished their discussion Carl decided to kick the armament up a notch and went and got the safe houses weapons supply. In it he found a Parker Hale 85 Sniper rifle in tiger stripe green. It had the case and in it was the disassembled Rifle and four 10-round magazines.

Darren Chord smiled as he looked into the case. "Nice one!"

Jenson sealed it shut and replied, "That's in case we need to get the advantage over them." Darren smiled and slid his browning back into its holster. "Never can be too prepared," he, said.

They then headed back down the stairs and into the car. This was a sure-fire bet that they would need all the fire power they could get. And Darren was prepared for anything. It was going to be a hard couple of days as sure as apples was apples, they were walking into a trap and a bloody difficult one at that. But they were prepared for anything and it was going to be some showdown. They would need all their skills, and sure as sure could be they were heading into the direct firing line of the Tongs. And they had a nice little army of about forty to forty-five trained assassins, all with combat pistols and sharp razor like knives (Oriental Style). They were expecting anything. And Jenson was of the opinion that he couldn't let any of them get close as they were unstoppable at close quarter combat. And Jenson was wary of any of them closing the guard. It was just before dawn on that humid muggy morning late august and they could feel the energies of the Tongs all around them. They were outmanned to say the least. And the Chemical Factory where the new innovation was to be left was just opening up for the day. If they lost this next battle then they would be dead and all the glory would go to the Triads. And well, death was something that Carl and Darren dealt in, and they knew the risks were always against them. But the two of them thrived on combat, breathed the air of combat were always prepared for combat. Leaving the dead under their boots was satisfaction enough. No money, no political power felt as true as the ends of combat. No, it was an adrenaline rush and gave the two of them a great feeling. It was something that was bred into them, army, navy air force. No, they had each earned both stripes and respect. Then they were soldiers of fortune a mercenary strike force working all over the globe. Sometimes killing sometimes guarding and sometimes sent into jungles to rescue rich oil barons from capture.

This happened a number of times, well more than the government cared to let loose in the papers. Carl readied his revolver and pulled it from his shoulder holster. They were just rounding the corner that led into the Chemical distillery. The front entrance was the only entrance and this proved an ideal place for an ambush, but Jenson and Chord knew this. Kirri was preparing for anything as were Chord and Jenson. They all began to exit the car and Chord gathered the Parker Hale 85 sniper rifle from the boot of the car. They then entered the Factory's front door. That's when the first of the Tongs struck.

The building's layout was deceptively large and gave the Tongs advantage over them, but this was closed down by the superior Marksmanship of both Jenson and Chord. They nailed one Tong each, Jenson hit his mark on the white masked faced man in the face. While Darren hit his in the chest. Both knowing they were through playing games with the Tongs. There was a sudden turn to the left and it was being defended by three more white masked men. They let off a spray of rapid fire at Jenson and co. Who had the advantage of seeing the three Tongs first. This had aided Kirri, Jenson and Cord. Jenson ducked and fired off a well, aimed shot at the light bulb that sent it into semi darkness. The three Tongs began to use the limited light as an advantage, but that was a big mistake as Darren saw their pattern of placement and knew the small arms they had were as much blinded for them as it was for them. They let off another couple of sprays from their UZI's counting on holding the three men in place but Jenson smiled again and aimed his large calibre Magnum. He saw one of them duck but wasn't quick enough, Jenson shot him in the hip which blew apart The majority of the hip splaying and destroying the man's midriff. The other two looked at the ghost like man and realised that it was only a matter of time for them. They sprayed the hallway again, both of them this time nearly depleting their ammo. But they were still in control of the hallway. Then suddenly Kirri was in play, a ghost-faced killer had come round behind them and was about to finish them off. But Kirri with catlike reflex's leapt, sending the Tong staggering backwards. As he sliced the man's head clean off.

Kirri then told the other two, "We're getting sloppy".

Jenson let off another shot at the two Tongs. While Darren smiled and said, "Fuck it" and let off a small spray from his Skorpion He caught the one closest to the hallway and his bullets went ripping into the man's chest. "Stupid fuck should have worn a vest."

Jenson ran slightly towards the junction and rested on his knee. With one leg straight out as the third Tong went to shoot. Jenson fired off one diamond of a round and blew his neck and head to pieces. That was it, they were all quiet for the meantime. They headed further into the chemical plant, knowing that the people they were dealing with were being held hostage. But Kirri had a thirst for revenge and knew that they were walking into a trap. Kirri decided to keep a close eye as they moved forward into the factory. There were various laboratories and testing points but no one around. It was spooky, especially at the rear and that was why Kirri was checking the rear as often as he could. Chord smiled and produced his Browning Automatic, he checked that he had one chambered and let his Skorpion slide down into its holster. This was going to get personal.

They wanted a proper go, well now they got one. He was readying himself holding the pistol in front of his Hari knowing that the split second he was saving was ample as some of those mad Tongs threw a nice dagger. And they seldom missed, but then neither did he. Not with the browning. He had earned his Browning, knowing and keeping it at optimum level. His Sergeant had given him top marks for cleaning and maintaining his field side arm. He then went on a small arms course, learning the newest variants of the Skorpion and Hekler and Koch sub-machine guns. Then as his career advanced, he went onto sniper and distance weapons but in his heart was the commando dagger and the years of discipline in both bladed and unarmed combat. He smiled slightly as he walked cautiously down the corridor. Remaining quiet yet ready, he barely breathed. He was so gone on chi. This had taken years to master and only came at times of great strength. He didn't flinch as he came to the end of a junction. He stopped and Jenson hit the corner adjacent the laboratory, number five. He waited until the chi swam and turned him quietly, aware not breath not even a fly could be more ready. He looked into the darkness of the Lab and listened. Knowing with his keen sense that there were two or more Tongs in there. He smiled and said to Jenson It's wedding time. Then dropped to his knee and aimed his pistol Jenson did the same. Kirri stayed back at the corner still watching their backs. Then they let a sudden burst of ammo as the three Tongs gained a slight advantage. They threw up a quick spray of Uzi nine millimetre bullets, enough but to high, as they did so Jenson cut down two with his revolver and Darren got one in the face and two in his body. The three Tongs fell with a thump. It was a quiet thump but one that settled the debt. And it was a steep debt at that. Jenson stood up slowly and cautiously and Darren did the same. Kirri came round the corner and looked at the three Tongs.

"Not so Hard Jenson San".

"Not with how hard a blow that Chord can deliver."

Chord gave a small inner sigh and carried on walking taking point. Jenson smiled, he loved his old sarge, some days he could give him a sloppy wet kiss. But that was out of the question. Jenson followed through and carried on walking behind his sarge. His face was stoney cold almost Sicilian. Jenson had Italian in his D.N.A. but it just made him a better lover. And more exotic the country got the more he was hot to trot. Chord he was the same as Jenson, a man's life flowed through his appetites, they made him that bit more honourable. That bit more Mysterious.

Darren smiled as they turned another corner to yet another laboratory. There in the shadows were several ghost-faced killers, all ready to take it down to the wire and Chord liked that he smiled just as the trap they were in sprung. Three Tongs sailed through the air and landed in striking distance; Chord let the grin shine all over his face.

"That's more like it," he said then lifted his foot and retrieved the commando dagger. Jenson produced his Tanto and they went to work using all their close quarter combat techniques.

"I'm game," said Jenson and he began to close the guard on the Tong who had a Chinese Sai. The other two had long curved half knives. These were ideal for Kirri with his katana. He smiled and confronted the one that had sailed past Jenson and Chord. Kirri stood iron armed and ready as the Tong took the challenge and ran slicing at Kirri. Kirri defended and defended well. He cut through the man missing by a hair breath. Then as he pivoted and sliced, he caught the Tong with upper iron arm that sliced and burst him like juicy fruit. Jenson was battling one of the other Tongs who had a set of wicked metal Dragon chucks. He was spinning the chuckies around and occasionally sending a flick of dragon steel at Jenson. But Jenson could see right through his strategy. So, he waited weaving and bobbing like a proper Boxer and saw his chance. As the flails went to his left he pushed through with his Tanto and skewered him through the throat. Darren was having a little bit of a struggle with the other Tong who was keeping the sniper at bay by swinging what is known as a web of death. Every so often he would attack, driving Darren back with wicked reflexes. But Darren smiled then after a minute or two he grew bored and drew his Browning and blasted the Tong in the chest.

He stood over the crumpled dead Tong, smiled and said, "They always play themselves out, you know that Jenson".

Jenson laughed. Kirri walked forward. Looked at the three dead Chinese and laughed at the whole situation. "They are always eager to please," said Kirri.

Jenson smiled and replied, "Come on we got a long way to go and the more of these Tongs that come at us the more we get, the more we are safe".

Kirri looking humble smiled at this and replied, "Yes Jenson San. But the closer we get to the prize the more they will send at us and we may be at this for days".

Jenson snapped his Tanto into, its sheath, they then carried on walking to the wages office where they would be able to recuperate and rest and leave the formula in the safe where it would be safe and they could get on with saving the hostages. The ghost-faced killers were holding a number of lab technicians, seven in all. There were twelve Tongs in total and they wanted two things and those were Kirri Motto's head and the formula. And they meant business with a small arsenal and at least an aura of unnerving silence. Each of the Tongs held a grenade and they were prepared to break and run after pulling the pin on each one. But Jenson had an idea, and that was to pick them off it would take expert timing and no small chance of luck. They would need all the luck they could get. They hid in a corner and waited, watching the Tongs movements as they kept the vigil on the lab technicians. They were armed with Heckler Skorpions and Glocks. This made them a force to be reckoned with. The grenades were primed and ready. But Jenson and Darren and Kirri were unafraid of the situation. That was when Darren and Jenson showed true skill and courage.

They crept into the shadows that was all around the Tongs. They began to pick them off and were successful in eradicating the Tongs. Taking them from opposite ends of the long cafeteria hallways. And they started to pick them off. Darren used the commando dagger and Jenson used his ceremonial Tanto that was beyond razor sharp. They took out the majority of them quietly using the shadows to full advantage. Kirri waited until their numbers dwindled down to three or four. Then he made his move into the light, his tattoo catching the light that was shining onto him. He cricked his neck and again in Iron arm pose he smiled and entered into the battle. Two of the tongs saw him and cocked their weapons. The other two were dragged into the shadows and finished quickly and quietly. Then just as they were about to pull the triggers on their small automatic arms Darren fired off two rounds into their backs.

Kirri shook his head and said, "Bakai foolish Tongs".

Jenson and Darren began to deaden the grenades that they were holding. They unscrewed the explosive devices on each of them and deadened the charges by destroying the spark that lit up the gunpowder and set the grenade off. They deadened them all. Jenson smiled as this was a tricky job. And he began to sweat after the job was done. Delayed stress symptoms. This meant after the job was done, he had a small anxiety attack, the sweats and a spike of adrenaline that caused his hands to shake for like three to five minutes. He calmed himself down smiled and sat down.

Kirri walked up to the two of them smiling and said, "that is that".

Jenson looked at the man's bull-like frame and said, "Are we going for the head guy the Golden Tong?"

Kirri smiled a wry small smile and said, "Yes the hunt is on".

Jenson reloaded his .357 Magnum. "Good, I'm getting sick of these Tongs, I want satisfaction. I want their head man."

Kirri sighed and replied, "Yes Jenson San we all need to see this through to the end".

Carl smiled and shut the bullet wheel on the .357 Magnum. "We need to get to the next safe house then we will prime ourselves to infiltrate the Tong's den".

The said den was in the heart of Chinatown. The Snake Heads, as they were known, but seldom did anyone say out loud that name, as it was a forbidden to say out loud their name. It was like inviting the devil to tea and everybody knew this. And everyone understood what may happen if you uttered the name Snake Heads. Jenson wasn't superstitious but knew there had to be something in those rumours. But he kept the way clear and did what everybody else did and that was don't. He walked out to the car that they had arrived in and began to turn the engine on. The other two got in with Darren being shotgun. They then headed for the other side of the city where they could recuperate and start to plan their next offensive. It was a Mah Jong parlour where the Golden Tong spent most of his days. The old man knew something was up when he realised that his best men had vanished and had been left under the boots of the Bodyguards. He smiled and carried on playing. "They will come for me next" He said and carried on his winning streak. "Get me the best, get me my warrior Tongs".

The young silk wearing Chinaman bowed and walked out to the Tongs dens that were dotted about that part of the city. They were training in Wing Chun in one Den. The other it was Snake Gung Fu. And the last it was Crane and Iron Palm. They armed themselves with light pistols and various knives and half knives. Then they blended into the shadows around and adjacent to the Mah Jong parlour. They stealthily set up a watch on the exit and entrance, north and south of the Chinese populated district. There were thirty of them at each end of Chinatown. But it was a short distance from each end and they could make it In under two minutes and they were in contact with each other. Team one was set up and fully ready for anything. They had two cars at the entrance of Chinatown. They were poised with a full five ghost-face killers in each. The rest were housed up in flats above the entrance and at the other end of town it was the same set up.

Carl and Darren Put on their Kevlar vests and re-stocked their weapons with quick loads and magazines for both the Skorpion and the Browning automatic. Kirri produced a small Heckler and Koch sub-machine gun and he too donned a Kevlar vest that covered his large Dragon Tattoo. They got in the large luxury B.M.W. that was the safe house's stand by car. The Vauxhall was shot to shit, they had a choice of a couple vehicles but chose the B.M.W. as it was an automatic gearbox and could shift better than the rest of the motors in the garage. It was getting close to midday and they were in the know of the Golden Tong, Kim Lee, He was mean as anything and was the type who didn't take prisoners and those that he did were tortured and maimed beyond recognition. He revelled in the suffering and death of his enemies. But Kirri had been a major thorn in his side and at last he would have a final showdown with the Triad.

They headed towards Chinatown. Not a word was spoken between them, their faces cold and devoid of emotions. They had a job to do and this would be the end of it sine die. The Golden Tong would be eradicated and Kirri's honour would be satisfied. He would have revenge and the Tongs would be put finally to rest. Kirri held onto his Katana and Heckler and Koch. He hoped he would get close to see the eyes of the Golden Tong as he blew out his last breath. He patted the HK MP5 that was on his lap fully loaded and ready. He had seven 30-bullet banana mags. He hoped that he would not spend all the bullets he had as he would like to throw a load of them into the dying corpse of The Golden Tong. They neared the north point of Chinatown where the two cars sat looking out into the distance.

They saw each other and Jenson began to speed up, closing as much distance as he could. The Ghost-faced Tongs gunned their motors into motion. And both cars spun smoke as they eased off of the brakes then with screeching tyres they headed straight at Kirri and Jenson. Jenson flung the car into top gear.

"Chinese fucking chicken," said Jenson.

Just before they hit the two Tong cars Kirri screamed out ,"Banzai".

They hit each other and airbags went off in the three cars. They were smothered by the bags and Darren was first to respond. He cut the bag away and began to exit the car. He then let off a small burst of gunfire at one of the cars killing the driver of the car who was bleeding and bruised from the impact. Then Jenson came too with a sharp ringing in his ears. He got out and noticed that Darren had already exited the B.M.W. He was throwing bursts into the two cars killing the three passengers in the car. Jenson who was cupping the .357 in a downward trajectory. He was waiting to see if there was any more hiding in the street and it's housing.

Kirri was also concussed but had the energy to get out the motor. "God damn it Jenson, I know you are good, but god damn it, that hurts."

Jenson began to aim into the corners of the buildings knowing that they were not alone. He then heard the windows being opened on the opposite corner and two SIG SSG-3000 Swiss sniper rifles were set up and they were aiming at the three of them. Jenson growled and with nothing other than the naked eye, he positioned himself then counted to two before he pulled the trigger twice on his .357 Magnum. The Tong never stood a chance as both bullets smashed through his China white mask and blew a significant chunk of his face and skull off. But the second one squeezed off a round and hit Jenson in the chest. Jenson cursed under his breath and aimed at the second one, bang, bang went the revolver again this time catching the Tong in the throat and clavicle. Jenson then carried on searching the house windows across to the left then across the right. Suddenly the doors opened onto the street and seven Tongs began to back flip with their half knives sheathed and fastened onto their backs. Jenson waited until they made the next move. As they were moving targets and very near impossible to hit. Jenson went onto one knee and aimed. But they were too skilled and made it too difficult for Jenson to get an accurate shot at any of them. Then one of them stopped flipping and came to a stop, aimed his Glock 17, then he fired at Jenson again catching his Kevlar, but this gave Jenson the chance he needed to take out the Tong.

He aimed his revolver at the Tong and said, "nice and easy," Then fired the last two bullets out of the revolver. He then ditched the empty casings and reloaded with one of his quick loads. The bullets went into the cylinder chambers in no time at all. Darren smiled as he finished of the Tongs in the two cars. He made them into mincemeat. The blood and flesh covering the cars and soaking them in blood red viscose liquid. Kirri smiled and watched as the rest of the seven Tongs vanished into the street. But that was not an act of cowardice no it was prudent thinking on the Tongs part. They were just showing their skills. And that was not all they could do. Jenson levelled off his .357 Magnum and used the sightings as a good judgment on what he had just witnessed. His shoulders were hunched and he was side on to the area. Darren followed suit with his Browning high power with thirteen rounds per mag he had several magazines pouched up on his belt around his waist.

They were going to really need all their skills in the melee. Jenson was on sniper alert Darren kept an eye on the alleyways and Kirri brought up the rear. Crossing of all the variables. Silent and deadly attacks. Flying tongs going over the heads of Jenson and Darren. Eagle claws flying through the sky with the attention of skilled, serious blades-men. Jenson was first to hear the rustle of silk flying in the wind as they leapt over both him and Darren. Landing right in front of the Yakuza, Iiado blades-man, who was quick to unsheathe and take out one of the Eagle clawed Tongs who was slicing downward to the Yakuza boss. He sliced upwards and the bite of the razor-sharp Katana took off his leg. But this was down to the skill of Kirri who was unmatched and undefeated. In both east and western hemisphere. The second one managed to come down just as the mortally wounded Eagle was breathing his last breath. And Kirri, showing his optimum technique, cut the ghost-faced Tongs head clean off, leaving a geyser of blood hitting the skies. He shot all eight pints of blood leaving the body stiff and erect. Then the Chinese stars came flying at them.

Kevlar is pretty much knife proof, but the tongs being who they are didn't aim just for the chest. No, they aimed for the tops of their arms and the major veins in the legs. And you know they love their toxins, the more exotic the better. Black lotus poison, chrysanthemum numbing agents and your bog standard cyanide. They carried on forward, dodging throwing blades and various stars and other shaped blades. Jenson shouted out as the melee grew more and more unstable. "You get the feeling we aint wanted here." he said, then returned fire at two snipers who were just taking aim on Kirri. He got the two before they got settled in their sights. Darren was down on one knee squeezing off shots at the various ghost-faced killers that were gleaming in the dwindling light. It was crossing from a hard haze to a setting sun. Dusk was due and that could swing in either of their favours. But the Tongs were relentless they had nothing to lose, as Kirri was the one doing the whole honour routine. They came to a fork in the road, one way led into the Mah jong parlours, the back of Chinatowns gambling district, where often a bloody vow and honour killing had taken place. Where 'every once in a while' two masters faced each other and all you heard were screaming cat growls and deadly movements, when they were in full contact.

They came to the deadly steps off of the square, where the death of masters was watched, bet upon and savoured, as this only happened now and then. It was hidden deep into the back streets of Chinatown. Jenson arrived first, still hunched and pointing the .357 at a downward trajectory. He snarled as little had been done to hide the blood-soaked square. It must have been there since the Victorian days. As some of the stains had come from years of secret styles trying to be the only style that is best. This had been going on for centuries. But the various styles had grown, shaped into underground academies and secrets were only passed along to family. And being picked as a student of the arcane styles was an honour and they had to prove their worth in combat, fighting until one of you is dead. The victor getting the highest sash, often they were friends that had been brought up together. Jenson looked around seeing if anything was amiss. They were getting close to the Golden Tong and the air was stifling with ominous intent. The three of them could feel the energy rise, smell, taste and feel what was next. It was a certainty they had just walked into a Tong trap. But they were ready, and expected anything aerial, assaults, snipers and everything. They got there and went back-to-back.

Jenson smiled and said as he felt the energy rise, "Anytime now. Hold, hold, hold".

Just as the surge of adrenaline kicked into the three of them the Tongs numbers surged and they came unrelentingly at them. They emptied their handguns, hitting and doing the Tongs no favours. Once they unloaded all their shells, they each then knew what was next, blade on blade and martial arts. They got close enough to breath on the enemy. Slicing and stabbing in the most lethal of ways. Piercing major organs and slitting throats. The area that they were in was soaked with Tong blood. They had this under control and suddenly the fight ceased and the last of the tongs lost morale. They vanished back into the shadows. Kirri shook the blood off his blade with one quick flick of the wrist. He had done the most damage with his Katana. Whereas Jenson and Chord had struggled a little but grew more in confidence as they claimed Tong blood.

"Okay San?" said Kirri as he sheathed his Katana Iiado style, Jenson smiled and did a quick inventory on his shells and quick loads. He had two quick loads left on him. Darren did the same, he too had a couple left. Kirri on the other hand had used all his heckler and Koch banana mags. They all reloaded and headed further into the back-alley area, or as it was known Dragons Jaw. Kirri insisted on going on point. Whilst Jenson followed at the right-hand side. And Chord was on the left-hand side, both them bringing up the rear. Both with weapons ready to aim, mark, then fire. This was a speciality of both Chord and Jenson. But lack of bullets kept them from full optimum capability. They were in the thick of it again.

"No rest for the wicked," came the statement from Chord. He then drew his commando blade and drove into the Tongs. Jenson followed suit with his Tanto. Kirri was covered in blood as he sliced and struck with his weapon. He was at his most vulnerable in times like these, he had nothing to prove and everything to lose.

"They are getting sloppy." came a statement from Kirri.

Jenson whipped his Tanto in a clean slice on one of the Tongs that had gotten close to him. Opening a large gash across the man's chest. Chord stabbed and stabbed again at the Tongs aiming for their hearts. The Golden Tong on the other hand was steadily seeing his incoming doom. They then really got their chop going, both blocking and striking, with the use of their bladed weapons drenching the streets in viscose blood. Kirri was doing the most damage up front and being really accurate with the weapons that he had, but his small sub-machine gun had run dry in the bullet sense.

But Kirri had a major advantage as his blade bit and bit deep. His opponents were growing scarce and they too were running low on ammo. And the more that flew out the shadows the quicker they were taken down by the three of them. They tried aerial attacks again but the three of them had adjusted in the fight and were using high kicks and rapid punches at the Tongs as they flew at them in kicking positions.

But the fight was already won. Jenson looked around as they walked deeper into the Dragon. They were totally focused knowing only that they had to get close to the Golden Tong but he was guarded by some of the best Wing Chun artists in the world. All of them studied Yip Man's lessons. They circled the Golden Tong as he sat on what could only be called a throne. He had Fourteen expert martial artists. And God only knew they were in for one hell of a fight. Kirri growled and sliced down sending the rest of the blood on his sword onto the pavement.

The Tong made a stiff gesture with his right hand and three of them approached Jenson, Kirri and Darren. Kirri growled and began to tackle his enemy with a growl as he got closer. The Tong that was in front of him was armed with butterfly knives. And knew how to use them to their optimum.

Kirri and the Tong were circling looking for a break in each other. Kirri spat out the words "Come Chinaman. I'm only undefeated".

The Tong began to circle, the two blades knowing that this would wear out any sudden moves by the Oyabun. The clashed and again in Iron arm he pushed a buddha palm into the Tong. Sending him reeling and choking on his blood. They carried on their dance of death. But Kirri was gaining momentum and using his Katana well. He had succeeded in striking the Tong and caused him to think again. Kirri sliced with the four diamond cuts and his blade each time impacted on the short thick blades. Kirri knew this was no novice and he would try and use the sword breakers on the front of his blades to tangle and hopefully snap the Samurai's blade. But Kirri was one step ahead of him. He sliced a crane wing, severing the man's torso. This Ended the Tong in a bloodied and unnatural way. Jenson on the other was fighting fist for fist Budo style.

The Tong he faced relinquished his weapons. He too had a set of butterfly blades. But he rested them on the ground and showed a zen then began to circle the heavens with his Wing Chun set. Then he flew at Jenson who was ready to fight tooth and nail. The Tong came at him with kicks and punches that only a highly skilled martial artist would be able to defend himself against. And Jenson was no novice but the Tong was trained and trained well. He came again with the rapid-fire straight punches. Jenson smiled as he knew what was next and had tied many a knot in the Judo way. He was straight in there with a grappler's, favourite and that was a hip throw. He grappled and shortened the distance so that his punches were practically useless. But the Tong had learned a long time ago the half-inch punch and threw one at Jenson who took the force of the blow and flew back a number of feet, again into the grapplers grips and holds hopping that the Tong would run out of energy. But the struggled trying to get each other to bend the other in a throw or a lock.

Knowing only the deadliest of strikes and grips were on the menu and each of them was trying to out-manoeuvre the other. Then Jenson felt the slip of the Tongs balance and landed him next to the blades he picked them up, growled and began to swing them in a deadly web. Jenson unsheathed his Tanto and began to wield it deftly yet cautiously at the same time. Making sure his fist was pointed at the Tong. A straight Yaka Zaki to the Tongs chest a simple punch but effective. He then sliced with the tanto straight along the Tongs neck. He then finished him and finished him good straight into the man's solar plexus. It was clean wound and that was all a warrior could hope for. Quick and clean. Darren on the other hand was showing his opponent mercy and was toying with him. He was a boxer and that got him through his darkest of fights. He had been the local club's champion. And he didn't rate martial arts as combat effective But this was all thrown into the wind when he joined the army. He even studied a little Akido. This he had used in jungle creeps, using all kinds of manoeuvres. Especially when he had come across an enemy sniper that he had gotten close to. He had a number of close kills pinned onto him. And had never lost in the jungle, especially the Asian jungles.

He began to skip around the Tong and showed no quarter. The Tong would send out a side kick. But always just missed as the light footed sniper, was totally in tune with the fight. He too was showing his fist but in a Muay Thai way. Closing the distance just to land a quick jab, then a cross then another jab. He wasn't just pacing himself but also out pacing the Tong. This was going to take his skills to a higher level. He remained calm yet struck with stingers. And they were wearing the Tong down. The Tong thought he had an opportunity but it was a fake, a way to open up the Tong completely.

Darren smiled as he opened up a barrage of snap kicks into the man's Hari. Then they carried on their deadly dance. The Tong was thrown by these feints that Darren was showing. The Tong was taking a sound beating and began to growl in anger. The noise he hoped would throw the Sniper. But just as a child who was bored with his toy's he broke the Tong in two with a turning back kick, smashing the man's pelvis. Darren saw his time for the kill and shot forth with his dagger and struck the ghost-faced killer in the throat. These were all techniques that were used in special forces, training in them took years. And years of evaluating other systems. This meant getting down and gritty with most of his skills being trained and ingrained into his mind body and soul. Kirri looked at the other nine Tongs, knowing that they were in one hell of a fight with Wing Chun black sashes. They knew one thing they had to remain fluid and loose. No time for rigidity, no they were fluid as could be. And they would need all their martial prowess. Especially because there was three ghost-faced tongs on each of them.

Kirri growled and balanced himself in a tiger stance. With the Katana straight back resting his frame comfortably. The three that were on him were weaving in and out of each other. Throwing the Japanese Oyabun slightly off balance. But Kirri had skills beyond the patience and time that the Tongs had. No Kirri was quick and lightning fast with his Iiado swordsmanship. He cut one of their heads clean off and the other two both of them an arm each. Jenson started to move with the battle and gain an edge of confidence. He mentally counted off if he had any shells left and thought, 'Fuck it if it doesn't fire it will make for a good faint'. But his luck was in and he fired two shots blowing the first ones chest open then the second ones face turned to mush.

The third one shouted out "Gwai Lo you die." Then went straight into swinging at Jenson who had no more bullets left. So, he began to parry and block, the butterfly blades. Keeping himself at a distance of the Tong. They circled and the Tong grew more and more impatient. He started his deadly dance with the butterfly blades flowing and trying to keep Jenson in its deadly play. But Jenson had a working knowledge of Wing Chun and knew he would slip up eventually. They parried pushed used chin na and Jenson used Aikido and Jujitsu to its fullest. They were counter attacks, parry block then an offensive attack into each other's weaknesses. They were tied evenly each other and were showing each other a furious show of Martial Prowess, with neither of them getting anywhere. They were evenly matched and the Tong leader was growing anxious. Then all of a sudden, the ghost-faced killers head blew apart.

Jenson turned around and said, "Thanks Kirri".

Kirri holstered his Glock 17 after firing off the last bullets into the Tongs head. They headed for the Golden Tong who looked at the three of them with fear. The night suddenly turned much colder and Jenson smiled a small smile that stretched around his left cheek. "Gwai Lo, you know that they will just replace me with another Golden Tong".

Jenson's grin widened. And Kirri Walked forward and sheathed his Katana at the same time. Darren re-loaded his Skorpion, knowing in his guts that it wouldn't just end with the death of the Tong. No, he sensed that they were being watched by a whole clan of ghost-faced killers. Jenson loaded six fresh bullets from the recess of his pockets. They were the absolute last of his ammo. But Jenson was an expert Karateka. That and several years training in Gung Fu. Lau Guar, seven animal style. He wasn't a black sash but he only needed two more gradings and that problem would be solved. He was though a black belt. Shotokai style (way of the fist). Darren on the other hand was a boxer with a mixture of Akido and Muay Thai. Which was cause of some strange techniques. And Darren felt no fear when in the affray of a good fist fight. He had the advantage of boxing, but the skill as a trained hand to hand Akido expert. They made a great combination, and Darren was willing to try new things.

*

Kirri strode up to the Golden Tong. Then quick as a flash he severed the man's head from his body. The cadaver fell forward. And the blood pumped all over the square all eight pints of it. Oh, he was dead. The head rolled up to Jenson's feet. Jenson stepped away. They began to head out of the back alleys of Chinatown. And they knew that they were being watched by the rest of the Tongs. They covered their position well, even though they were at a slight disadvantage. But they carried on to the wreck of their motor. But in the boot was a Parker Hale 85 sniper rifle with three ten round magazines. There was, also shells for the rest of their arms. The Magnum .357 had a decent amount, of shells. As did the Glock !7. But the car was for shit. The engine in the thing had seized and burst into flames. The Tongs car was soaked in the dead Chinamen's blood. Its engine was also on fire. They planned on hiking back a good seven or eight-mile, to a safe house.

The streets were very spooky and quiet; there wasn't a trace of the Tongs. All they could hear was each other's gentle breathing. Jenson took point And Darren covered their rear. Using the cumbersome Parker rifle to cover their retreat. He was surprised how easy it was for them to get back to the Safe house. But something didn't sit right it was too easy. Kirri smiled and the three of them entered the terraced house. Darren climbed up onto the roof and set up his sniper rifle. And began a three four-hour vigil watching, making sure that they were all clear, Jenson rested as did Kirri. But neither of them slept completely no they were wired and psyched. And the two of them found the escape from Chinatown to be too easy. Then, dawn came and it began to rain, not a heavy rain, but enough to cause a slight fog Darren cursed his luck knowing that the Tongs were slippery enough without a mist no this just added to the pressure.

Darren smiled and carried on aiming through the Har. He growled as the rain kept up its relentless cascade. Darren flipped the collar on his old Naval jacket keeping the heat from his neck which kept him from chattering. But as he was a seasoned professional sniper it was just weather to him nothing more nothing less. He carried on his vigil. Just as he thought he was safe a shot snapped and popped by him. He looked at the battlefield and tried to figure out where they were concealed. It was very hard to get an aim at the sniper. "Snap" another bullet just missed him. And he still couldn't see the enemy. He waited then he saw a small flash from another sniper then the snap again. He aimed and waited for the target to become clear then he fired, then the recoil as one of the sharps went straight through the Tongs eye. He released the bolt and the empty shell spat out of the weapon. But he had a feeling that this had just begun.

Then he saw a car sidling to a stop. And four tongs got out he proceeded to take aim at each tong. And before they could get into cover three of them were dead and one was strategically wounded, He was lying on the ground gripping his knee, his left kneecap that was blown to pieces. Screaming out in Cantonese, "Help me". Darren waited for more. Then a white van opened its doors and seven Tongs exited the van. He began to pick them off. From his elevated position.

"Wicked thing gravity," he said as he fired off another round. That shot blew the Tongs chest to pieces. They were pinned down by sniper fire. Five of them left, below the van covering themselves the best they could. But having no other concern but remaining where they were. He kept them pinned down then went and spoke to Jenson. "Advance Jenson enemy pinned down".

Jenson smiled and advanced, cautiously slipping in and out the shadows, smiling the closer he got knowing they were keeping covered. He saw one and aimed at the ghost-faced killer. Drawing a decent angle he blew the man's head off. He then saw the other four and didn't hesitate, he killed with a quick aim at each letting the hand cannon blow away the four of them before he reached for some loose shells in his pocket of his camouflage jacket and reloaded the five shells in his six shooter. Then he saw about four or five cars speeding toward the bodyguard. He did a quick count on how many quick loads he had and realised he had enough, but this was going to take expert timing. He ducked at the front of the van and awaited their approach. Darren aimed at the lights of the cars and shot one out of each. This led him into a better position with the people in the cars, they were not too brave and those sharps that he was firing were making Swiss cheese out of the doors as they opened. They were the worst place you could crouch as the sharps were going right through the doors and right through the Tong.

"Nowhere to run and nowhere to hide," he shouted out in defiance of the Tongs reputation to be unkillable. Kirri put in an appearance in the street war which was classic urban warfare. They were in no way prepared for S.A.S. with a Japanese twist. The Oyabun made his way walking in true Samurai style showing his arm and Katana. No fear, and certainly no pain, he hadn't even been scratched, although he was a target of priority to the Tongs. But he had managed to walk without shadow, a skilled samurai trick that they used when confronting enemies that were slippy and could shadow walk. He carried on as bold as brass of a man who was tired of fighting and even more tired of losing family and friends. He growled and laughed, "Couldn't even match two Gaijin, Immortal Tongs you are a far cry from Samurai".

He then began to circle the van as did Jenson. Who came round the right hand side whilst Kirri came round the left. It wasn't a position of choice for the Oyabun, but it was necessary to keep up the left flank and shut down the enemies reserve. They were expecting him to tread tentatively and not leave anything to chance. But Kirri was none the less ready for an all-out assault.

He drove his Katana straight through the first guy and whipped up his Glock 17 and shot the man behind him. Then Jenson blew the men on his side of the car away with three steady sure-fire shots of his .357 Magnum. Three in total, he was beyond flesh wounds no he was sending bullets through bone on the chest and exiting and hitting the man behind him also in the chest. There was a slight splaying of a bullet and it ripped through the Tongs spine. Killing him painfully. He lay down jerking and contorting as the blood gushed through the wound. The large dome of a bullet smashed into the metal of the car. And sent bits of metal splintering into the fourth Tong's mask. Shredding his face.

Darren carried on aiming at the Tongs knowing they were only facing top S.A.S. and they weren't just in rank either, they were highly valued and highly skilled and totally covert. No, they were in a class of their own covert and highly sought after finding kidnapping rings, As well as various other things they were trained to bring about ends in actions that there was no end to. Conflicts in which they were stuck in a stalemate. They had completed most of their mission's and as always they had shown style, grace, and a true grit in the things that seemed impossible were worked out by Jenson and Darren Chord. They were, like I said, highly sought after, but this latest string of missions had been like a day at the races. Only they had held every winner to themselves and the smiles on their faces was priceless. They had saved oil barons and tycoons who thought that the jungles were a play area. Yeah, if you could survive more than two days. Fox holes, roaming patrols of Opium Merchants personal armies. Yeah, sounds like fun. In all seriousness you had to be twice the man the man next to you thought you were. In other words, survival and it weren't Kansas Totto. It was more like a maniac's idea of all you can eat. Saving churches, saving missionaries and taking the holy and the divine further into lawless jungle to save people from starvation and oppression. No, in the special forces game you have to have a delicate, yet forceful way with indecision if it came down to it and more often did than didn't.

The rest of the Tongs were picked off by the three of them, some of them seeing all hope was gone tried to run, ditching their faces, hoping to get off without getting hurt. They raised their arms and knelt at the front of their cars. Jenson rung it in to the local Bobby.

Darren came down from his elevated position, he smiled and said, "Who let the cat out the bag".

Jenson turned and said, "So much for the Emperors new duck".

They laughed and carried on tidying up themselves. Jenson smiled as he heard the police cars traversing their way towards them. They hadn't a thing to say but produced their special forces identification cards that had their name rank and serial number. They were then checked out by the Metropolitan and MI6 channels. They were cleared and headed off back to the safe house, where they would rest up knowing that they were safe as the bodies and Tongs that had surrendered were cuffed and sent straight for a black site where they would be questioned under rigorous environment's and severe hostile pressure. They slept fine until the middle of the next day. They then began to re load and sharpen their weapons. Jenson used the quick loads for his .357 Magnum. And put a bullet in each of them, then he loaded the weapon chamber by chamber. This was a habit that he had gotten into in the protection game and had a maximum of twelve quick loads. Each housed a .357 bullet, six per load. They then had something to eat; it was dry and salted meat and noodles. Or as they are sometimes referred to as iron rations, field meals. The said rations kept you filled with nutrients and vitamins, Especially B12 and vitamin D as they were doing a lot of night action. And would be depriving themselves with vitamin D and vitamin C. They carried on their meal that was as appetizing as a piece of cardboard. Kirri walked by chewing a nutrient bar. a Babe Ruth. Jenson just laughed and carried on with his meal. Darren smiled to himself, knowing that those Japs had it figured out. It got closer to night-time and they only had one thing left to do and that was take Kirri to the airport and say goodbye. It was a good hour and a half journey to Heathrow and they weren't safe yet. Even if they were, then they would have a whole heap of paperwork to get through. This was necessary and it was a strict policy for all MI6 to write down the whole scenario as it had happened and you needed to do detailing on weapons, yours and theirs. Everything was taken into account, including used shells and other weapons like blades and Shuken's. And no, it wasn't just Jenson and Darrens weapons but you had to note down the enemies, including sniper and bladed weapons. They were schooled enough to know what was being shot at them. Listening for muzzle velocity and suppressors. Yes, they could hear that whisper (Sniper training). It was ingrained in them they knew the value of silence. How important it was to listen to the area. They also trained themselves in deep embryonic breathing. A tip from the Japanese Pearl divers.

Mata Hari. This gave them an edge, a very real and skilful edge. They had both been patient in the studies of martial arts and they both excelled in its application. Darren being the better of the two. Kirri knew most of their training was down to prowess and subtlety. They were also both of them competent magicians. And Origami was how they learned control.

*

They sped away to the airport at the right time and they instantly picked up a follower, in fact it was three followers. Three Hyundai Jeeps all filled with Tong ghost-faced killers. They kept their distance and ran parallels with each other. But Jenson had seen this trick so many times whilst guarding delegates from British and American diplomatic embassies. He had saved a number of delegates when these methods were being used.

"Oh, we got trouble," said Jenson.

Darren smiled and produced his Commando dagger. "No guts no glory," he replied then produced his FN Browning High power pistol. He chambered a round just in case. Kirri produced his Glock seventeen. Jenson could feel them deliberately circling getting closer then he stamped on the brakes and the one that was chosen to get the closest stamped on his brakes also. One of the Tongs popped his head out of the back seat window and opened fire as the car stopped, stopped dead in its tracks. The small arms fire ripped into the Back Vauxhall. Smashing the rear window. Kirri ducked for as long as he could, then faced the Jeep and fired of four or five shots, but unlike his inept enemy he took that split second longer to tag and bag the little Chinaman. He also got the driver with another two shots from his Glock.

Jenson flung the car into gear and shot away from the Hyundai. Giving itself the advantage of disabling the first of the three Jeeps. That just left two more. Jenson sped closer to Heathrow. Knowing only by folly would they not survive. They knew every trick in the book. But then so did the ghost-faced killers. And they were just warming up. The passenger in the copilot side threw the body out the driver side and began to close the distance between him and Jenson. The other two were still not getting close to Jenson as he was pulling the best defensive driving that the world had seen. Short cuts down alleys jumping lights and sidling the pavement when the traffic became too heavy. Jenson smiled as he saw the underpass for Heathrow. This was going to go down in the car park in one of the world's busiest airports. Jenson growled as he spun the wheel and dropped himself at the front of the airport.

They vacated the Vauxhall and began to head for the departure lounge. Jenson growled as the semi naked Kirri walked tall and proud into the lounge and that was only a small moment away. The thirteen made haste and ran after the Bodyguards. As they advanced, they took out several Armed Police, shooting out the legs of the Officers. Jenson heard the shots of the Mini Uzi machine pistols and readied himself for what was going to be a major fire fight. Kirri walked into the lounge and pivoted around and took aim. Jenson and Darren snuck around a corner each, both them adjusting to the light and readying their pistols, looking down the muzzle of each weapon. They didn't as much hear them coming as they sensed their presence coming closer to the departure lounge.

They stood their ground and waited which was only seconds but to the three of them it seemed like hours. The sweat dripped of, Jenson's face and he waited not letting anything come between him and his business. They ghost-faced killers appeared and all of sudden the lights went out, someone must have gotten to the electrics and caused a blackout, this only unnerved Jenson and the other two slightly. They had true grit in their system and were not easily dissuaded from the task at hand. No, they took the pressure easily and calmly. They smiled into the shadows and light and knew that they only had one chance at this and it was a teeth grinding tour de force. The first Tong rolled into the open and took the focus away from the rest of the Tongs. Jenson shot him as he played them with his acrobatic skills. He blew one of his shoulders to pieces, nearly severing the arm at the socket. And mortally wounding him. The rest began to flip and beguile the three of them. Trying to get a bead on one of them. They came close, yet the three of them had great position and good cover. Darren ducked down and shot two of them in the belly, two bullets in each. He remained kneeling and began to draw their faces into his sights. And again, he drew breath and blew another one away, then he withdrew into the shadows and waited for Jenson to get a clean shot at a couple of the Tongs.

Jenson was smiling as the bullets from their Uzi ricochet past him with a snap and drilling sound, he took aim at the one who was partially out in the open. Again, the heavy calibre of the gun blew away a limb. This time at the hip, smashing the Tongs pelvis and severing a couple of arteries. This left the Tong mortally wounded. He lay jerking as the veins all emptied themselves. It was a blood bath. I mean, what do you expect with a hand cannon. He hadn't picked the weapon for its subtly, no it's stopping power. He smiled again through the shadows looking for an easy target. But none of the Tongs were stupid enough to go down their fallen brothers roads, no they were going to do what was the easy option and that was to retreat. But that left their backs open. And Jenson was not up to being courteous, no he began to blow their backs to pieces. The large calibre bullets smashing through their rib cages and blasting their lungs out if them. Kirri gave chase, slicing at them with his razor sharp Iiado katana. He was cutting into them and leaving huge gashes down their backs, these were so deep that the men fell bleeding and the pain, well they weren't accustomed to anything as sharp and severe as an liado quick draw katana, they fell and as they fell Kirri emptied a shell into them aiming for their hearts. The Glock hummed in his hand. This was sheer revenge, on Kirri's part.

Darren began to pick off the ones that had pushed themselves to the front. He aimed his Browning at them and the weapon cracked and echoed in the corridor. Like small bursts of thunder, deafening everybody. Jenson carried on blasting his revolver at the last of the Tongs, who thought as soon as they got to the main entrance that they could escape. Armed police suddenly surrounded them.

"On the ground now Chinks!"

They had no hope, And the armed police were annoyed at the loss of a couple of their officers, "Now chinks!"

The Tongs that had survived and it was only a couple, could see no way out of this dilemma.

Jenson smiled as the sergeant walked toward Kirri, Darren and Jenson. "Okay lads, we've been monitoring your pursuit since the Safe house". Jenson smirked a little.

"I'll need to see your credentials?"

Jenson smiled then holstered his hand cannon. And dipped into his pocket, "There you go sir".

The officer took the piece of plastic and spoke through his radio giving the credentials details to the operator on the other end. "Thats 1174 dispatch".

He stood and waited for a response. "Yep, it's clean". Came the reply.

Jenson smiled and returned the card back into his pocket. The officer ushered the three of them back to the departure lounge where Kirri put on his shirt then boarded his plane back to Japan. He smiled and bowed at both Jenson and Darren before boarding the next plane to Tokyo. Jenson bowed back as did Darren. They then left as the plane lifted off and headed into the rising sun.

Jenson Smiled and said to Darren, "Well that was an adventure".

Darren smiled a small sombre smile, growled slightly and the two of them left the airport. The carnage would be dealt with. I mean if you tallied it up it was close to sixty men they had gunned down. And the blood, well the blood was wall to wall. They vanished into the coming day and they went their separate ways. But it was a good move they had made, the chemical freezing agent revolutionised the medical world and was tested and used with great success. They had come a long way from the hotel and had managed to circumnavigate through the streets of London and Chinatown. They had done so cleanly and deftly. This had been an experience for the two of them and they would no doubt call each other to arms again.

The End

PARADOX

Kurt Lidel came out of hyperspace near the edge of Rygon Five. He smiled as he was about to make a rather large purchase of the drug Paradox. He was pleased with himself as now the parameters of how much he could sell were limitless. No, the Emperor's death had left everyone with a new hope. They could breathe easier. The war with the Trill had come to an end and things had settled. Kurt had settled into a smooth operation of affairs purchasing Paradox and selling the substance for a good profit, sometimes three or four times what he had put in. The Linsani worlds had ground down to a halt, having no business with the Empire and no need for it's, biological and chemical weapons. Kurt stayed away, as they had become primary users of various substances and they had a deep pipeline into the heart of the substances, especially Paradox. They were making noises as if they were the new tyranny in the Marches, with super enhanced soldiers who were physically at a level where they were impossible to kill with or without power armour. Kurt was not perturbed by the rumours of them being the deadliest and psychotic of soldiers. Kurt sighed as he entered the atmosphere of Rygon Five.

He lit up the console and switched the navigational computer into auto pilot so as he could put on his power armour. The reapers had done him justice and showed him the ins and outs of the weapons, ranging and targeting scopes which were AI and had primary selection where they were able to close all gaps of sudden error, you know, smoke and concussion factors, knowing the time of detonation from its vast catalogues of various explosives. It homed in and told the suit wearer what the best course of action was. Especially if on guard duty. Where they had to make the proximity ease to travel and what was the best way to shield the civilians that were being ushered to and froe. He smiled as the computer showed him a detailed schematic to the Paradox laboratories. He smiled as he set the ship to guard and protect itself from marauding junkies and various other types of slime that inhabited the Rygon System.

Kurt Walked back with the large plastic case filled with three million credits worth of the toxin. He smiled and put the drug into his small scout ship *The Wanderer*. The only thing that he held dear were his bootie and the small scout ship. He was indebted to the Reapers for not only the armour but for saving his life a number of times, which was climbing higher and higher. But to be fair, he had given back just as much as he took. And each time he had gained the ultimate power and that was the buzz, the who knows if your gonna wake from your sleep cycle. No, he was living by his testosterone. His ship was a bit, of a bucket but he and the ship were made for each other. He had no qualms about what he did and knew that the whole of the marches was only temporary. He was fixed with the fact that the whole existence thing was to self-serve and only one thing was clear and without a doubt, the absolute thing that kept him safe in his scavenging, which was the profit. Tiris had long since retired with the two squads of Reapers. The Titan reapers were hunted down and destroyed. That suited Tiris down to a tee, he knew that the rest of the Storm Troopers breathed a sigh of relief, knowing that whatever bonds held them to Imperium was smashed and they were free of the warring factions that had almost wiped them all out. Tiris had become a saviour, for the Universe and both mankind and Trill were indebted to him and his two squads of Reapers.

Kurt on the other hand took a back seat in the whole scheme of things. He was known as an ally of Tiris but wasn't going to make a big thing out of the circumstances. No, he liked to breathe without having to watch over his shoulder. And he didn't have to rely on his friends being there if anything sparked off. He could handle himself and had proved to be a great asset in the scheme of things. Tiris knew this of course but let the man lead his own way throughout the known universe. Kurt smiled and pushed the purge button on the console enabling it to clean and activate the nuclear-powered engine. He then headed into the Orion nebula. Where he would dispense the chronic substance. He would get a tidy sum of money for the substance and he was wondering who would make the most of a purchase. The Linsani, they usually purchased the most. And Kurt was always suspicious of the amount he sold to them. As it had doubled each time he had gotten their order. Rhey had told him this after every purchase. It sat as suspicious in Kurts mind. He knew those scientific boffins were into some-thing new and extremely harmful. He had heard rumours of shock killer soldier an interstellar commando. It was all very hush hush.

And everyone was afraid to ask them what they were up to. Kurts face was stoney and a cold glint was in his eyes.

He got to the Orion Nebula. And the first thing he saw was the Linsani cargo ship, docked onto the Orion space station. He growled and began to dock adjacent the Linsani Cargo ship. These rumours had weight and that's what really bugged Kurt. He thought of maybe sending a spy satellite, a dead man's pulse as they were known. He smiled and thought to himself, 'I must get in contact with Tiris to see if he could clean any of this mystery up. Kurt smiled as the space stations docking computer began to count down as *The Wanderer* made a clean docking manoeuvre and attached itself to the station.

Kurt stood with his skull under his arm and his suite was fully powered. He walked in and was almost immediately barraged with sellers and buyers. He smiled a small bitter militant smile and walked towards the Linsani entourage. Kurt approached. His face never changing.

The lead technician saw him approach. "Ahh Captain Lidel, with more substance I believe?"

Kurt didn't even flinch. "Yes, I am," he responded. Years in the military had made him immune to both flattery and abuse.

The Technician smiled and replied, "Usual price my friend?"

Kurt breathed a bored sigh then replied, "Double last amount, Double the price," then they exchanged product and money. Kurt sent the money to the docking doors and loaded the fifty million into his ship's cargo hold. He smiled as he was just about finished for the day. And he only had a couple of more buyers lined up.

And this was simply the only way for him to live. He would make the Paradox run in another day or two. The Linsani purchase, being the more rewarding of the sellers, Kurt smiled knowing that he was more addicted to the sale of the substance than the addicts themselves. No, he was on the right track to becoming a major seller of the narcotic. He figured that with three or four more purchases he would be halfway to being a major distributor of the highly addictive substance. The money just poured in and he couldn't argue with the fact that he liked money.

He had only one bug ups his arse, and that was why the Linsani were using the copious amounts of the drug, they were combining both human D.N.A. and various solutions at variant degrees of potency. He knew this because of the amount they purchased and how long it took them to need more. It was a puzzle to him, an itch that he needed scratched.

He smiled and said to himself as he flew into space to do another drug run, "Won't be long until they want triple the amount." He decided to put a small scanner come video unit onto the crate of Paradox. He would see what he could see. First though he would have to purchase more substance. He carried right on to Rygon Five. He wouldn't have anything to complain about if the Linsani tech heads were using the stuff in the enhancement of the human race. But this thought was, well it wasn't what he thought he knew they were up to sinister and deadly things.

"Some folks never learn," he said out loud and carried on into the Rygon area of the Marches.

*

The head Technician of the Linsani home world was busy with his fix of Paradox. He smiled as the rush was giving him a warm satisfying blood rush. And he smiled as the cargo was sent into the toxin advance human research labs where they were doing all sorts of human enhancements. Clones with abilities. Superhuman strength, advance vision as seeing into the dark. It was all going on. The ones they were testing on were used and when they had been exhausted of their strength they were burned after meticulous study and summoning up the qualities of each clone. No, they were closing in on the true power of the drug and it was all the Head Technician, a John James Sanderson, he had somehow managed to escape the Marches Imperial witch hunt.

The witch hunt had been ongoing for the last fifteen years. But whispers about the head technician were looming everywhere. He was some sort of sadist who performed evil and brutal operations, not just on clones, but also on troopers who were injured and had nobody to call family. They were hushed and sent for by the Linsani and they never saw the daylight of a sun again. Kurt decided it was a definite plan of action, a small recon bug to fly around and get as much information on what they were doing exactly. Kurt purchased himself more Paradox and slipped the recon bug into the crate that he labelled for Linsani. He then made the journey out to the Orion nebula. This took him three days at hyperspace, the first thing he thought about was getting in contact with Tiris.

He sent a beacon out to *The Defiant*. "This is Kurt calling a comeback call for Tiris and the Reaper squads". He sent the signal every two hours. Knowing that they could be anywhere. He waited it out whilst travelling to Orion. He just arrived at Orion and docked with the station when he received a follow up message, and this was because *The Defiant* was on the outer rim of the Marches.

"Okay Kurt I'll be coming your way soon, the next four or five weeks as we are helping a large number of Terrar colonists deal with a number of nasty bugs".

Kurt sent the standard 'message received' message back to Tiris. Kurt smiled knowing that he had one hell of a compadre on his side. He headed straight again to the Linsani Cargo ship. And again, got top price for it. He then sold the rest and then refuelled *The Wanderer* and powered up his suit. The rumours going around about the Linsani tech worlds was never spoken about in the open. This was because of what was called a Ghost Squad of Troopers who exacted out the executions of anyone who even appeared to be conspiring against the Linsani. They vanished and were used in the experimentation of Paradox and various biological weapons. None returned and they were never heard of again. Linsani were not easing the choke hold that it had on humanity. Some hailed them as heroes, others were suspicious of their ghostlike shadows and mirrors, smoke and silence. Nobody thought of trying to destroy them and their pets. And few were ready for them and this was a whole rebel network of Ex-Storm Troopers who had survived the faith wars and hadn't any way to see themselves fit in the execution of all the remains of the Empire.

They were living in confused times where they had hope for a new era coming into focus with hope and prosperity being in abundance. There were many ways of contacting the rebel Storm Troopers. And Kurt knew them all. But he stuck to the ones he knew and they were Tiris and the Reapers, Tooms and his crew of madmen. Kurt Liked them, especially seeing as they were notorious pirates. This was just two of them. There were more, some could be trusted others well, well you just stayed away from; too ugly. Kurt made it through the sale of the product and the small digital camera was hiding in a small invisibility cloak. He had five hours of feedback on the download with the thing, It was called a gentleman's butterfly. It was one of those pieces of technology that came in handy. Especially in the trade of information and Kurt had about five of the things. He liked to be in the know of certain things and this was one of them as he felt a sense of doom when it came to the Linsani and what it stood for, especially after the Dark Talon. It had apparently given up all the tech engineers who had spawned the Dark Talon, but said engineers were executed and their work was destroyed and the underlings were imprisoned. But that hadn't stopped the fascist dictatorship who were fleeing this way and that to cease all biological engineering. No, they just became more secretive, more silent, with only a handful of technicians being able to keep the sinister covert work operational.

No, times were just as suspicious as when Taxus was on the throne. Yeah, the wars had ended but still there was a shadow looming over the spinward Marches. Kurt stayed put in the station waiting for Tiris and the Reapers to come to the space station then he would activate the butterfly. They arrived two days later. And Kurt went to meet them at the docking bay five. This was reserved for military ships and regal convoys. He stood there waiting with his Skull Helmet clipped to his side. Tiris came down the ramp and walked over to

Kurt knowing that it was important, he knew that Kurt was not a man to be so needy and impatient.

"How you doin Kurt?" Was the first question out of Tiris' mouth.

Kurt was grim in the answer and his face showed it. "I think the Linsani are going to pull a major play for the Marches,"

Tiris smiled and gave a sarcastic laugh, "Aint that typical, we get over one tyrant and someone else is ready to step into his shoes".

Kurt Breathed out and explained, "They have been amassing a quite substantial amount of Paradox. Tiris they are up to something. I'm sure of it".

Tiris sneered and replied, "And how much we talking about?"

Kurt laughed and said, "About three metric tonne".

Tiris stopped dead in his tracks, "That is a lot".

They then carried on walking to the canteen and bar. They got there and sat at a table and ordered some food and ale.

"I've got a gentleman's butterfly ready to activate and show me exactly what they need with all that product"

Tiris smiled and carried on with his meal. They then went to *The Wanderer* and watched as the butterfly switched itself on in the laboratory. It then began to follow the tech heads who were wearing breathing apparatus whilst they started Paradox mixing in the oxygen tank. Tiris watched and noted the Paradox being taken into various labs where it was being cut and used as a stimulant on not only humans but various animals that were being intwined with Human D.N.A., Trill and various Xenomorph's. The paradox was being used to its full capacity and they watched as the substance was fed into various life forms and it was turning said life forms into super strength monsters. Some were easy to control others were sent insane. They were all muscle-bound and coloured the same colour as the Paradox, which was blue.

Certain hybrids were totally insane and ended up destroying themselves. But not before ripping into the tech's in the room. They were unstable to say the least. The Butterfly carried on its sweep of the Linsani laboratories. Some of the feed was ghoulish to say the least. They were also implanting various steroid enhancers into some of the troopers, this would boost their metabolism and give an unfair advantage in the killing fields. They would go into a deathly state, then just as you thought it was safe, the enhancements would kick in and the zombie like creature would spring to life and begin with total vigour as if it had been resurrected by the Gods themselves. They both sat and watched the sweep with interest. As it gathered information and was never seen, they had the best of the technology. And intended to use it. Kurt smiled as the little butterfly flew into a corner and set itself to self-destruct. The thing had come through and did what it was built to do and that was spy and send back the images to Kurt and Tiris.

"looks, like we got problems Tiris". Kurt said and shook his head.

"No, I think the Marches has a need to know about this," Tiris nodded and puffed away.

"It's the ghost like paramilitary we should be wary of. They know everything." Kurt smiled and drank some more ale. He smiled as the rich amber refreshment satisfied his palate and eased the dry recess of his throat. "Well, I'm sure they won't want to mess with either reaper team one or reaper team two".

Tiris smiled at this statement, he was not one to mince his words, this was one of the reasons that Tiris liked the guy. They carried on their meal and discussed tactics mainly about the ways in which to deal with the Linsani and its deep, dark secrets. Tiris wasn't worried about the ghost like paramilitary. Him and his squad had handled worse and more dangerous opponents. No, he was worried about the new complex studies that they were diversifying. These things weren't bred for a school picnic; no, they were enhanced troopers with bio-mechanical implants and strong addictions to Paradox. That in turn made them super-human and extremely dangerous

Tiris sat back and puffed on his stogie. "Well Kurt," came the question as he carried on puffing. "We know now what we are facing".

Kurt nodded and continued to look grim, "And forewarned is forearmed".

Kurt took another sip then asked, "Yeah I know this but what are going to do about it?".

Tirris carried on puffing and said, "Well we aint going to do nothing, let them know we know but keep our identity a secret".

Kurt saw the sense in it, smiled and replied. "Whatever you say Tiris, whatever you say".

They then finished their meals and shook hands. Tiris asked, "Can I get a copy of the video that you just downloaded?"

Kurt smiled and said, "Sure Buddy, sure." Kurt smiled knowing that he was going to study the experiments with a keen eye and leave no stone unturned. "I'll send via the alpha niner channel," said Kurt.

They then parted company and headed back to their ships. Kurt headed off onto the Rygon Five system to pick up more Paradox, some for the Linsani and some for other parties. He smiled as he sent the engines into another purge sending the scout ship *The Wanderer* into hyper drive. He would rocket through the galaxies and space time continuum. This he had done lots of times and had procured a safe amount of credits that summed into the billions. He sat back in his chair and sent the video surveillance data to *The Defiant*. He felt he was doing the right thing in showing the data to Tiris. He just hoped that the Linsani were not expecting anyone snooping around their laboratories. And the butterfly had served its purpose. He smiled as he punched in the send button to the Alpha Niner channel *Defiant*.

*

John James Sanderson was the head technician of four different tech stations each orbiting the Linsani worlds. He was head scientist and head commander. He was as usual working on various Paradox compounds, heightening its effects on various muscle-bound cybernetic organisms. They were completely insane and John was glad to watch as said subjects were tested. Each organism was being tested in various ways to be more combat effective, in things like zero gravity, heightened light and also under water. They were also tested to withstand wounds of the maximum kind. They were then given a sudden shot of Paradox that would revive the trooper and send him on a killing frenzy. This was all done very methodical and meticulous. They were achieving results, results that were beyond expectation. The Paradox was just another thing that helped these monsters to becoming killing machines.

He carried on with subject Sv 118. Insertion of Paradox to the upper left lobe of subject. He smiled as the subject woke from his death-like slumber and turned instantly into an optimum killing machine. He then left as the thing battled with his restraints. He sniffed as the lab door slid shut and the restraints were taken off the thing that was part metal and part human. Then they sent in two ordinary troopers with full K78 armour and a sub-machine carbine each. The shots fired by the trooper only angered the monster who was a good foot taller than the two of them. The monster began to advance on the two troopers as they emptied a clip each into the subject. And it didn't make a sound. It wasn't breathing but animate oh so animate. He grabbed one of the Troopers and began to separate the troopers head from his neck, the enhancements that were keeping the thing moving began to fire off and the head of the trooper ripped off of his neck and blood, well the blood gushed everywhere. The second trooper looked on and decided to take the easy way out he put the barrel of his small carbine under his chin and ended his life. The monstrous thing began to devour the two troopers.

John James Sanderson stood and watched through the reinforced blast shielding, he smiled, "Well I am satisfied with that result".

The rest of the technicians who were privy to the results all nodded and said how grateful they were to watch a master technician at work. Most stood in awe as the inhuman atrocities were on display. Most technicians were highly immune to the shocking show of carnage. But some, the new ones, well vomiting and gaging was more than frowned upon, it was treated with the option kill yourself or be fed to the Monsters that they were making and more often than not they killed themselves. This was done by cyanide or bullet. Preferring the first as it was easier to ingest a poison than it was to shoot yourself. John smiled at his technicians, knowing that they had all been schooled in the ravages of war and science. This had brought the majority of the sadistic killers who had started with poisons and toxicity. The ghost paramilitary was on constant watch of all the technicians, especially the Biological Division. They were known to witch hunt through the technicians. Especially when they were finished with a new life form. No, they were often killed in a fascist way that meant they had too many secretive ways. And were a liability to the Linsani cooperation and had been deemed unfit for any more duties. Very few had seen the end product of what they were nurturing and making. No, they were seen as a liability and vanished.

It wasn't a question of loyalty; no, it was a question of dog eat dog. And after the war had ended, they showed no progress in the fields of Xenomorphic research since the Dark Talon. Now they were working on enhanced soldiers and they were confident of achieving a greater soldier with biomechanics and super enhancements on biological advanced humans. Humans who were picked mainly on their physical attributes, you know, height muscle mass, high constitution. If they had all three, they were sent straight to John. He relished in the biomechanic world like Frankenstein. Only Frankenstein had emotion.

These subjects were devoid of anything other than killing and feeding on fresh flesh and blood. This had surpassed the whole id thing that all humans had, no it was ten times most savage. There were break throughs every other day. But whispers were floating around that John James was nearly on a mass scale production of a cybernetic, cannibalistic superhuman life form. There studies were through the roof and completion was almost in hand.

He smiled as he carried on the work of making the Paradox powder a hundred times stronger. And it was being used to its full potential. They were highly adaptable soldier's needing nothing other than the flesh of the enemy and a constant source of Paradox. He had tonnes and tonnes of the chemical and was wise in the ways to make it purer and make it stronger. This was a fine thing that they had endured. The number of Failures and the number of deaths at the start was quite astonishing. But John James Sanderson had finally come up with the right answers to the fact he was malevolent in his way and more or less inherently evil. He liked to watch as the drug took hold and its strength surpassed anything that had been done before. It was breakthrough after breakthrough. He smiled and walked away whistling. They were close and still he had more things to try, more things to satiate his taste and give him more chaos. More, more, more. "But the final result," He said and carried on whistling as he walked.

*

Kurt smiled as he again entered the Orgis quadrant of the Spinward Marches. And again saw the Linsani ship docked in its usual docking bay. It switched off his ships engine and again donned his K 11 armour. He then put the skull over his head and listened to his A.I.

"Nothing hostile," she said in her electronic voice. Kurt smiled and left the docking port and headed straight for the Linsani cargo ship. He got there and noticed something was wrong with the head technician. He was jumpy, nervously looking all around with wild scared eyes.

Kurt smiled under his helmet and said, "Okay sir, double the last shipment double the pay" He then held out his hand.

The technician seemed to be preoccupied. "Sorry s-s-sir," said the technician.

Kurt looked at the man and heard his A.I. go mental, "This man is dangerous Kurt, this man is dangerous".

He drew his Laser pistol and the technician tried to stab his way onto the chest of Kurt but Kurt had enough warning and fired off three laser energy blasts. This, blew straight through the man's sinister gothic looking clothes and hit the Linsani ship. Tearing a great big hole through both the tech and the ship. Kurt headed back to *The Wanderer* and got straight on the Apha niner channel to Tiris. Nobody bothered about what had just happened, it was just another drug deal gone bad. And Kurt had just defended himself. Th alpha niner channel opened and Kurt spoke in a small panicky way.

"Tiris I've just dusted a Linsani tech and fucked up his ship"

Tiris sighed and said, "The joys huh?"

Kurt laughed at the off the cuff remark.

Tiris smiled and replied, "I take it you didn't go through with the deal, and now you are stuck with a whole tonne of product?"

Kurt laughed and replied, "Yeah, you interested in taking it off my hands?"

"I might be," came the reply from Tiris.

Kurt smiled and said, "Okay, I take it you want a discount?"

Tiris smiled through his teeth. "Yeah man I would be receptive to a discount".

Kurt sighed, "how much you willing to pay for it?"

Tiris smiled some more, there was a small pause by the two of them and Kurt responded after a moment or two. "I'll give you it just over cost".

Tiris sighed a bored nonchalant sigh. "okay," he replied.

They then made arrangements for a rendezvous on the outskirts of the Orion system.

"I'll be there two cycles tops," said Tiris.

Somebody must have cottoned on to the butterfly. Then he relaxed lay back in his rocker chair. And slept. 'It's of no matter' he thought then fell into a comfortable slumber. Kurt carried on the journey to the outer rim of the Orion system. Where ,when he got there, he shut down the nuclear engines and left the ship ticking over on manual. This was what the ship did when it was set that way. Kurt ate some dinner and lounged about waiting on *The Defiant*. Halfway through the second cycle *The Defiant* arrived. And Kurt readied himself for docking procedure. The A.I. came on as the procedure went through the stages of locking and docking. The ships A.I. counted down the last ten seconds of the procedure. 5,4,3,2,1, docking initiated and the doors opened.

Tiris was in civilian attire and the other members of the squad were resting down in the cargo hold. Tiris gripped Kurts wrists smiled and said, "You think the Linsani have cottoned to your butterfly?"

Kurt replied "Yeah maybe if it didn't completely evaporate" Kurt and Tiris walked to the main deck on the small scout ship. Then Kurt gave him a blow-by-blow description of what happened with the tech head. Tiris listened nodding every now and then.

He smiled and said, "Thank, fuck you were in armour".

Kurt smiled, looked at the Colonel and replied. "It was the helmets A.I. that rang alarm bells".

Tiris smiled, "the things a marvel to military warfare," he said, then they sat down and had a meal. Tiris then began to barter for the excess Paradox. They shook hands at just under a billion. Kurt then went and remotely pushed the large crate that was on a gravity cushion holding the large amount of Paradox. Floating a good two feet of the ground, it was easily manoeuvred into *The Defiant*. The money was then exchanged and they parted company, Kurt asked the million credit question, "Who you gonna sell that to?"

Tiris laughed and said, "Linsani of course".

Kurt smiled at this statement and said, "Figures"

They then went their separate ways and knew that it was the best way for the two of them. As only the two of them had their sort of relationship. Kurt unhinged the docking couplings and smiled, you know the smile, one that said, should have seen that one coming. Kurt flew away into the cosmos, heading towards Rygon Five. Where he would acquire more Paradox. But this lot would be used as strictly small change.

Just as he was about to enter the atmosphere of Rygon Five, he was suddenly surrounded by three ships out of Linsani, it was the ghost-like paramilitary. They sent a message, "You Sir are wanted for treason and the sale of illegal secrets with intent to usurp the Linsani biological research and development."

Kurt strapped on his armour and set the main weapons system onto fire at will. The ships A.I. took over and made sure that they didn't have to put up much of a fight. The ghosts that were there began to board *The Wanderer*. But Kurt was ready for them. He had a Plasma cannon on one hand and a small arms carbine, loaded with splitters. He smiled and watched as the shadowy men with Paradox inhalers began their assault. They were surprised to see Kurt with the power armour on. Standing his ground, He began by sending forth a plasma beam right into the first two. This had an immediate effect on the dark ones. Two of them, one in front of the other were blasted by the ion wave plasma gun. A big hole appeared in the two of them, right through their chests. Then, with his other weapon he fired off a full clip at the remaining ghosts. The splitters did their work and did it well. Ripping through four more of them. He smiled as the A.I. in his helmet told him the best trajectory for firing at the dark ones. They tossed a couple of frag grenades at him, he smiled as the A.I. told him the type and how long to detonation. And whether he should move or if the suits integrity was at full power. And he knew that they were like hitting a vehicle with thin sticks.

"No sir, the suits integrity is at maximum," said the feminine electronic voice.

"Thanks, sweet cheeks," said Kurt to the A.I. Meanwhile the ship was holding its ground and holding well. He smashed two of the ships with sidewinder tactical nuclear weapons. This led to the knock-on effect of one of the ships smashed into another. Then went spinning into the atmosphere then crashed and burned. Again, the A.I. saved the day. He was encouraged by the sheer viciousness of his assault, he made killing easy and these freaks were, well, they were just the ticket to give him a good workout. There were two ships left and they were high tailing it out of there. Making sure no one was following they did this with space mines fired out their tails.

"Run chickens run," shouted out Kurt then he let out a gut rushing, "Yahooo". Tiris who was four quadrants away had a feeling that Kurt was getting fattened up for the Kill. He opened the Alpha Niner channel and sent a message ,"You alright kid?"

He waited then just as he was about to repeat himself a small subspace message appeared on his com link. It was Kurt and he was celebrating the defeat of the ghost's. "Yeah, I'm fine man, they didn't know what hit them".

Tiris smiled and said, "They never do kid they never do".

Kurt smiled some more and poured himself a glass of beer.

Tiris asked, "I take it you needed the armour?"

Kurt humphed and replied, "Best thing you ever gave me".

Tiris smiled and carried on his journey to the Linsani laboratories. Kurt smiled then signed off. They were never far from each other, just over the comm link. But, if ever they needed each other, they would do their best to get to them. Like I said, Tiris had saved Kurt's life and Kurt had saved Tiris's life. They were bonded in war and blood. They had both been troopers in the Faith Wars and knew exactly and to a tee what each other's capabilities were. They had a strange psionic ability, an uncanny brother like state. It was borderline psionic. And that and the A.I,'s in the suit it made a healthy and dangerous mix. They were very, very seasoned troopers. And that was enough for the pair of them to contend with. Kurt carried on his trade of Paradox and went and bought more for his more affluent of people. You know upper class and highly educated, 'God knows what they want with this shit?' was the thought that was on Kurts mind. He dropped off several major purchases on worlds that were known for their Intelligent and upper class. Where things were more relaxed. They had their own vices. Xenomorphic battles to the death. Enemies of the state were executed in full front of their whole world. This all felt familiar up until one or more governors then there would be a play for power. Then well, they were supposed to be intelligent and nobody cared for anything they had to offer just another throne and mantle to claim. It was butchery after butchery, men who made it to the throne were quickly cut down. And no one could see sense only murder and mayhem.

"Fucking politics," Kurt said out loud. And all the while the Linsani were still messing with bioengineering, trying to create a super soldier. Something that was only a thing of nightmares. And they were getting closer every day. People were still vanishing. As the enhancements were growing into new and sinister ways.

Kurt cursed again, "Fucking technicians". He knew he was on their wanted list, as the trade he had bartered for was, well it was over, Kurt smiled and headed to the Orgis nebula next. That sat right next to the Linsani planetary system. That comprised of seven home worlds all of them were a massive collection of laboratories. Varying on different studies. Chemical warfare, xenomorph growth, And Paradox super enhanced soldiers with state of the art, cybernetics implanted on each. They were deep and dark motherfuckers. And their ghost militia was always something to fear. Seeing as only the few who had survived a raid by them were quivering wrecks. Kurt smiled some a wry corner of the mouth smile, that only made his point of charm all the more glowing. They were a force to be reckoned with and he had this strange feeling he would be going head to head with them again.

*

Tooms woke as the ship that they had acquired was coming out of Hyper space. Him and the twelve men he had were smuggling some slaves from the Terra home world to the Orion space station. This was getting to be a regular thing. The amount of people who had jumped ship and left the last of the old Empire to flounder in its waste and ruin, well the number was in the hundreds. Tooms smiled as he noticed that several of them were officials of the old Imperium and they needed to be anywhere but there, in the fact that rumblings of rumours that the Linsani Tech heads were in the lead positions at starting up the old ways and there were whispers of monstrous soldiers that were indestructible.

Tooms smiled and kept his shit wired tight. Him and the other twelve pirates were making a huge number of Credits and well they hadn't come across anything they couldn't handle. A couple of units of space guards who were just making sure everything was above board with the ship that had smuggling space in the craft right under the engine room, they had bartered their way out of most troubles. But they knew they were going to end up in a fight with the Linsani's ghost squads. They carried on their journey.

Tooms decided to send a message to Tiris, he opened the alpha niner channel and said, "Alpha niner this is a message to *The Defiant*"

Tiris woke instantly and replied, "Tooms is that you?"

Tooms smiled. "You must be close?" he said, then flicked the engine over to automatic. And started a conversation with Tiris.

Tiris told Tooms about the Butterfly and how it had captured the whole of the Linsani's experiments with soldiers and enhancements, they had also caught them injecting and making the soldiers super beings, who were practically impossible to kill.

"Fun and Games huh?" said Tooms after Tiris had finished speaking.

Tiris smiled and said, "Do you want a copy of the butterflies data?"

Tooms smiled, "Yeah man, that would be helpful".

Tiris punched up the data and sent it straight to Tooms. He then finished the conversation and Tooms went back to smuggling. The images caught Tooms with a wicked glint, he had heard but wasn't prepared for what he saw, the images were disturbing to say the least. They were soldiers, only they weren't soldiers anymore, he looked at the images as they drew to a final standstill. He was angry and not one to leave anything to doubt as he watched them being dosed with Paradox, then watched as they tested the Mutants with weapons and saw how much damage one of the greyish creatures could take. He sat and watched as the things began to fight various captured troopers and other civilians. They made short work of their victims. Enjoying the frenzy as they revelled in their baser instincts.

Tooms sat watching with a stoney glare in his eyes. He stopped the data for a quick drink and also to ponder on the images that were spilling out the proof that the Linsani were not messing around, this wasn't a couple of techs with a chemistry set, no this was a full on genetic, and biological work. With abominations being produced. They were close to sealing the fate of any who went up against them. These things were violent and wild. And had enough strength to tear a human being in half. As that was done on one of the more joyful images. No, they had problems and that was registering with Tooms. These things were totally insane and had only one purpose and that was to kill. Mainly with their bare hands but sometimes they would use a knife or a gun. But mainly they used brute strength.

With the mechanised enhancements proving to be invaluable and giving them a strength of at least ten men. They had problems and Tooms could see where this was going. He watched as the super enhanced (but repulsive to look at) soldiers made short work of their victims. And all Tooms could think was fuck that, fuck that. He gathered around his twelve men and said that they all had to watch the film capturing the bio engineered weapons that were looking at the final stages of their ultimate weapon. They all settled down at a terminal and watched as these things ripped, gorged and attacked with complete insanity. The squad of pirates watched until they had the images burned into their minds.

Tooms smiled and went and checked on their cargo a dozen officials from the Terra sector, they had worn out their welcome and were facing the death penalty. They had made contact with Tooms as it was their only option. They had been at the forefront of a political shakedown. A shakedown that had left a lot of their friends dead and not much hope for them. Fortunately, Tooms had offered an escape plan. They glided past an old Imperium military station. One that had housed a garrison of Troopers and also had been a stepping stone for Tooms. He was thinking back to then and wondered what it housed now. Some stations were desolate other housed Paradox hungry mad men, He continued to think never knowing if he would have the time to ever investigate the ghostlike station. He knew that certain cyborgs had stripped most of it. And they were glad of the parts some of them taking the A.I. and restarting it into their memory chips. Re-booting it and using it to focus on enemies. But apart from that they were dishevelled and had little concern for anything that couldn't be used to enhance them. No, they were scavengers and all the parts they compounded were used to help them either fight or eat.

Tooms had been attacked by the meat pirates once or twice. Both times they were able to destroy enough of them into fear and running away from the squad of well, the squad miscreants. They didn't hold any allegiances to anyone, and they had felt the hangman's noose slipped off each of them. They were grateful for the last of the Faith wars closing the way it did with both sides annihilating each other. They then knew, as did all the deserters, that they were home free. And Tooms kept up the smile on his face. He knew that the station had maintained its axis on the rim of the Trills home-world, where the Trill had the most difficulty in breaking through the barricade. They were succumbing to The Empires deadly chemical war fare. The Medusa Seed. After the reapers had sold the Medusa seeds compound the station was over-run with Trill who now knew nothing could stop them. Boy were they wrong. The Dark Talon was a sure fire way to wipe out an entire planet of Trill. Again, the reapers had fathomed a way to destroy them. They were already a legend for deserting with the K11 armour the most powerful armour that was in effect in the Marches. They were undefeated in the known universe.

Tooms smiled as he saw how content Tiris was with his two squads of Reapers, And no casualties , except Alex Cauldwell. Tiris had seen to his death by figuring out a chink in the armours system. The pulse regulator and systems bypass had been a small glitch in the armour, and Tiris had acted on it and had figured out a way to stop the suit of armours power diverter. Thus, leaving it inert. But he knew that this could be used against him as well. The picture in Tooms's head was Tiris blowing out a match after lighting one of his cigars, his face was passive and held a smile through it. Tooms smiled, he really respected Tiris. And was glad he was on his side.

*

Tiris dropped off the Paradox at a Linsani station where they were treated coldly and with great disdain.

They shook hands the technician and Bucker who was fronting this deal. This was so they didn't get any Ideas about turning on the reapers. It was a foolish thought as Tiris had just about had enough of the death-dealing, soul-stealing Linsani worlds. He had a good mind to throw a couple of thermite grenades into the Linsani station, especially after he had seen what they were doing, it was against the very laws of nature. They were creating a species of soldier and they were way too bloodthirsty. And the way they treated people who got too close, well it was tyranny and it didn't sit well with Tiris. But he knew that a full-frontal assault would only leave him with the choice to destroy all of the Linsani worlds. He was hoping for some sort of silent way, a covert way that could settle the score silently and well finally.

It was just a thought to deal with it quietly, showing no mercy and sabotaging the whole lot of them, he left the Linsani station and headed to have a meet with both Kurt and Tooms. He had a bad feeling about the Linsani but didn't want to take it too far as he had a feeling that what they had seen was just the surface of a deep ass conspiracy and he would need to be patient as the things that he had seen were, well, they were just the beginnings of something more deadly. He wasn't afraid, just wary of the whole thing, he didn't want to step in anything that could blow up in his face. They met in the Rygon system. They had been able to keep in contact through the Alpha Niner channel. But he needed to catch up with Tooms and Kurt. Kurt was saddened that he couldn't get more information on the Linsani Psyche Soldiers. No, he wanted to see more about these things. And whatever they were, splicing. Genes and various toxins that they had made themselves for theses super soldiers. They had gone through tonnes of Paradox and that was just what Kurt had gained for them. They paid and paid well. But they had grown suspicious of Kurt so he was no longer in the know of the things that he suspected. And there was so much more going on.

They met in a weighing station just off of Rygon Five, the main station that ran the substance out into the Marches. They sat in the canteen having a meal and discussing the things that they had seen. All of them put in their point of view and it was a varied discussion, with as many points of view that they could muster. Tiris was taking notes in his A.I. system and making sure no stone was unturned. And it surprised Kurt that they all had a good point of view. They watched as certain soldiers were dosed with Paradox to the point of an overdose. Then they were surgically enhanced with top of the range bio-mechanics. This had killed a few of the troopers, but not them all and that really scared Tiris, Kurt and Tooms. They carried on watching whilst they ate and came up with various ways to deal with them. The soldiers that survived were taken away deep into the laboratory and never heard from again. They were always fixing troopers who had signed on, not knowing what was being done to them. They were in it as soon as they walked through the lab doors.

They finished their meals, then they headed back to their ships for a sleep cycle, then in the morning they were gathered again to discuss the best ways to deal with the front of the laboratory. Because, as sure as anything they were in deep with this mission.

The Dayton pipped in, "what are we expecting sir?" Tiris looked grim as he chewed over the question.

"Well, we aint all going to survive".

Dayton smiled, "Wouldn't have it any other way".

Tiris nodded at the statement and replied, "Well we wouldn't want it too easy".

Dayton smiled again. "I take it they are planning on taking over the Empire?"

Tiris' stoney, wide stare was gazing at them. "Well, we can assume some sort of military action with what they have and they are well pretty much ready in the experimentation ways".

Kurt smiled and spoke next, "We only have a short number of details on the insane way they are making soldiers."

Dayton smiled and circled one question that he had been pondering. "Ahuh," He replied as he moved on to another question. "How many do you reckon they have of theses cybernetic soldiers?"

Tiris stared grimly at the troopers and the reapers. "Thousands by estimate".

Cauldwell went, "Woo-hoo. We're going to go up against an army?"

Tiris replied, "Yes soldier".

They carried on the meeting with various tactics being sent to the reapers A.I. But just as a certainty he went over some of the tactics for Toom's and his pirates. They were best to consider all angles and did so with a perfection.

"Like I said I don't expect us all to make out of this conflict, but we have a better chance by knowing what we are going up against so any ideas that you may have will be received with all ears". Tooms was smiling as he noted down what would be the best way to deal with the Super soldiers. They were known to fall, then the mechanics that they were enhanced with would come into play and they would be right back in the fight. This was just one of the attributes that these soldiers had. No, they were known to have the strength of ten men. And were completely muscle-bound, with the bio-mechanics that they were enhanced with giving them sure-fire sniper tactics that was part of the bio-mechanics. Night-vision and other things that would enhance them like superb running. They also didn't breathe oxygen as they were completely dependent on the Paradox that they breathed all the time.

"What about weaknesses?" Asked Cauldwell.

"We haven't found any so far." came the reply from Tiris.

"So, it's a suicide mission?" came the question come statement from Cauldwell.

Tiris harrumphed and replied, "Yes it's a one-way mission."

"Woo-hoo," Again Cauldwell. "You can all relax we aint in it for the money or the Glory, no we are all in it to save the Marches. Are we clear?"

They all murmured and Tiris said, "I wouldn't ask if it wasn't a grave undertaking. The soldiers we are fighting are bred to wipe out entire planets".

Tiris stopped himself from losing his rag with the rest of the reapers who were obviously just as cold as the other pirates. No, this wasn't a thing that you could finish with nuclear strikes, no they were ready for the thing to be really ugly. And these soldiers were just the beginning of things, as the Linsani were proving themselves to be a force to be reckoned with. No, Tiris was hoping that they had the right attitude and that they were prepared for an unholy fight to the death.

They all smiled. "I take it we aren't tied to this; this is truly optional, we don't sign on you let us go?" Asked Cauldwell.

"Yes, but I can't overestimate how much you will be needed, as this is the end of the oppression, They are holding out for a new empire, a new leader who will carry on the war with the Trill." And still they were arguing over who was the best option, who was best to rule the Empire but each of them who had tried had been rubbed out by the silent ghostlike militia, they were all ex-storm troopers and had advanced armour, not as advanced as the Reapers but advanced enough to enter silently and take whoever it was sitting at the throne. They were sinister and slick. They had proved themselves to be highly invaluable to the Linsani Laboratories. They had only lost out to a selection of crack special forces, a number of twenty against nearly four hundred of them. They weren't invincible but they had a cracking way about them, shadowy and sinister. But they hadn't fought the reapers. And they knew it and the fact at how tough the reapers are. They knew that it was inevitable, at some point they would have to face the Reapers, It was something that they were looking forward to. They had to be prepared and ready for, them. The Captain of the ghost squad was counting his blessings whilst blasting himself with Paradox. He knew one thing and that it was either him or the Colonel Tiris.

*

Tiris smiled as he went over the floor plans of the main laboratory with Kurt, Tooms and Bucker. There were four ways in and only three squads. So, someone was going to have to destroy the main entrance and exit, then the rest of the squads were going to have enter with extreme prejudice. This was fine by the Reapers. There armour was full on, take any blow, power armour. They powered up the armour and Tooms and his band of rag tag mercenaries, this sat just fine with Tiris, he knew that they were crack elite fighters and fast on their feet. They would do the maximum damage and that was all Tiris and Bucker could ask for. They carried on with the plans, Kurt would be the one that set the thermite charges at the main entrance and exit. They were advanced titanium doors and it would take five thermite charges to destroy the heavy blast doors, that would stop most of the lab technicians from escaping. The other three ways were then to be assaulted by two squads of Reapers and one squad of mercenaries. They would then made their way to the main labs in the centre of the complex.

They were scheduled to strike in two days-time. Kurt would lead up the rear into the complex taking out the ghosts, as they were trying to bring up the rear Bucker would take up the rear of the other squad and he was promised with plenty action and knew that he had to make sure no one would come up from behind them. They had it timed to a tee, they would enter and hopefully they would be in and out in under twelve minutes. Tooms and his mercenaries were standing fast at the third entrance they would get the orders to carry on into the complex after Tiris and the other squad of Reapers met in the middle, where most of the soldiers were being produced. They would close it down in the most severe sense. Thermite Nuclear charges.

*

John James Sanderson had a feeling that he was about to be assaulted and was taking nothing for granted, he knew of the Reapers and knew what they were capable of, mostly he thought he was in a prime position. It would be a wakeup call to all mercenaries in the Marches. He smiled as he thought about the Butterfly he had sent with Kurt. He had a fully operational and state of art butterfly and it had managed to be concealed for the whole meeting and operations, John James Sanderson knew all their plans. He smiled and watched the meeting as it continued with nothing being left to chance. No, he was cooking up a plan of his own, one that would show the whole of the Spinward Marches who was the strongest and most powerful Planetary system in the known Universe. Then after he sealed their fate, he would waltz in and take the throne with no objections from anyone. He would then destroy the last of the Trill in a bloody and massive assault, with his new and improved troopers.

They also had several stations with Dark Talon that they were going to use on the Trill. But first he would see to the end of the Reapers. It would be a bloody and fierce fight to the bitter end and he would have front row seats in his skiff just a couple of hundred miles off of the main Linsani base planet. He got the details of the Reapers and Tooms and Kurt, he knew he was going have to seal them in that station and had planted a couple of sergeants of the ghost militia who would render Kurt immobile and they would have a way into which they could seal their fate. This was going to be done by sealing the doors, all of them, then let them have their fight and that would leave only him in charge. He had the perfect information but this was not foolproof, in the centre of the labs were sat fully functional psychopathic super troopers with enhancements. At least a hundred all ready for the Reapers. They would be in a fight for their lives and they had no Idea, they thought in, out and cripple their base of operations. But John James Sanderson was well, he was ready as ever. And the Reapers were in for the most destructive fight that they ever had known.

*

The Defiant sat waiting at the orbit of the Linsani main home-world. They got in their drop ship and waited, Tooms on the other hand was landing with Kurt. And his band of mercenaries who swore absolute allegiance to Tooms and Tiris. They landed about five miles from the main entrance and Kurt slid into the shadows of the highly technical world and headed towards the main laboratory. He got to the main entrance, began to set the charges and ready himself for the full on assault on The Linsani main station. The other three doors opened and there was surprisingly only a small amount of resistance they were just low level lab techs that were expendable. Kurt began to set the charges at the main entrance and blew away a couple of the dark lab coated technicians. This was only a minor inconvenience to Kurt He had been fully aware that they would put up some resistance but Kurt was way ahead of them with the Reaper helmet calling the shots, he was well ahead of them in the game and was not noticing the ghost squad that was moving out to the rear of him.

He set the detonator and headed back out into the urban jungle and just as he got back to *The Wanderer* he realised he was being stalked by the ghost squad. Then he went to push the button on the detonator. Nothing; he was sat there with nothing happening and the ghost squad had come up and had disengaged the coupling on the scout class ship. He couldn't take off and realised that he was a sitting duck there. No hope, his best plan was to fight it out with the ghosts. He slapped in a large 100 round clip of splitters and in his other hand he held a laser pistol with twelve shots before the pack ran out of juice. He started with a quick napalm grenade to the front of the ghosts who opened fire as soon as they saw Kurt, but the Reaper Armour was strong and powerful and practically impervious to most weapons.

The napalm grenade exploded right in the middle of the ghosts. Destroying three of them in the powerful flames. The flames stuck to the three of them and burned through their Kevlar armour and as this happened, he let off a barrage of splitters at the rest of them there were four left and more running up on Kurt. His helmet A.I. made the targets easier to track and fire. He was spot on with his aiming and firing, he didn't need to go over the separate ghosts. No, he was spot with the A.I. telling him what kind of weapon was being fired at him and how much power he had. He was generating a good proportion of energy that was just one layer of the heavy armour. But the gravity field was good and was holding as they shot at him.

He tossed a high explosive frag grenade into another group of the ghost-like militia. It blew one arm and two legs off of three of them. The Artificial Intelligence showed him some sort of blind spot that the ghosts had figured out. And they were trying to use the blind spot against Him. But he had it sussed and fired two blasts off of the high energy Laser pistols. The beam went through one and again through another. The second high energy blast went through another two of them. Leving them with a laser burn hole through four of them. This had killed four with two laser beams. He then turned as the bullets ricocheted of his power armour and started to lay down a blanket of automatic fire at the rest of them, being as there were twelve left and they were running for cover with three or four of them succumbing to the Carbine that was loaded with at least sixty splitters left. He had it under control, they were running for cover. He threw another couple of Napalm grenades at the main amount of their forces. He stood at the rear of his ship and kept himself covered.

He didn't like the Idea of sitting there but he decided that his best solution was to call for backup being as he was being swarmed over by the ghosts. He needed back up and needed it sooner rather than later. He put in the message to Tooms knowing that he would have a better chance at protecting himself from the ghost militia. Knowing the time frame and the parameters he knew Tooms was the closest to him.

"Tooms, this is Kurt need backup now as being surrounded by enemies. I repeat need back up as soon as possible".

The airwaves parted and he still laid down the cover fire that was saving him from being swarmed over. No, he was in deep.

"Kurt this is Tooms we will be with you in three minutes".

The small scout ship was taking a lot of fire and Kurt was worried. He tossed another couple of frag grenades and a couple of napalm grenades. He wasn't giving up hope as he blasted through a couple more ghosts with his laser pistol. He was a crack shot and made sure he hit at least two with on charge. Then after a couple of minutes he heard the ship that Tooms was in hovering like a bird of prey. They began with high energy blasters and took out seven or eight of the Ghosts, they then began to pick off the leaders who had made it their mission to not get wasted by frag and napalm. They were cursing their luck as they were picked off by one of Tooms's mercenaries. It was Chino, a crack shot of a trooper, who was always trying to get better at his sniper tactics. He revelled in the power that he had accumulated and was never a let-down. Tooms carried on barraging the area with high energy pulse weapons. The ghosts had lost and they never even winged Kurt. Kurt signalled and sent another message to Tooms just as the dying embers of that conflict were flaming and flaming well. Kurt headed back to the main entrance in the Linsani lab. He knew he had to destroy those doors and stop any further assistance arriving and creeping up on the Reapers and Tooms. He reset the timers this time for just under a minute. He got back to *The Wanderer* and began to circle the complex making sure that they had enough time for the rest of the assault.

*

Tiris dropped of Bucker and Reaper team two outside the right flanking lab door. Then headed over to the left door where they began to start their assault. The doors opened and they started their sweep and clear. Taking out various ghosts and technicians as they pushed forward into the complex. They could smell the Paradox as they entered so they all switched on their oxygen pumps and kept themselves clear of the toxins. They carried on further into the laboratory firing off as many splitters as they could, they moved deeper into the complex Bucker was coming up aces with his squad whereas Tooms and Kurt got torn into the front entrance where they set the thermonuclear device with the right amount of explosives to render all exiting from the laboratory near impossible. They then carried on into the main complex and started to head towards where they hoped they would get the drop on them. But knowing their luck they would probably encounter a full army of the mad crazed paradox addicted with implants all over them.

They got to the centre and the three of the teams encountered only a miniscule of resistance, and that made Tiris uneasy. He knew they were hoping for a stand up fight but they were not going to get one. The paradox crazed soldiers had just come out of the carbon freeze and were hungry. Tiris was first to notice their movements. They were sliding in and out of the shadows. They had no heat signature so the A.I.'s in the Reaper suits was useless at spotting them. They got their first taste of fear, something that none of the Reapers had really experienced. And they knew that this was going to be a close one. Then all of a sudden fourteen heavy built monstrous mountains of soldiers ascended on them. And they had just managed to meet each other in what had to be the centre of the labs. It was a wide open area and it had several exits leading into various parts of the labs where it housed several

Paradox crazed super-skilled and super strength killers, it wasn't what they had been expecting.

They formed a circle and wave after wave of the blue tinged muscle-bound freaks attacked. Bucker was having an all you can shoot time. And was doing remarkably well. They all began to gun down the Monsters. Tiris shouted through his comm, "Aim for the tube that's directly into the lung.

Bucker sniffed and said "Check".

Then they began to show these fearless troopers how tuned in they were in the fire of combat. They all began to check. As they signed off showing these fearless freaks what it's like to be the top of the most wanted list. Tooms and his squad started to roll Napalm grenades into the halls that the creeping troopers were coming from. This was a wise move as it jammed them up and gave the lot of them more time to manoeuvre, and more time to re-load. They saw hope in this hopeless situation. Tiris re-loaded his carbine with another hundred round mag of splitters. He then signalled for them to retreat and they would finish of the whole station from orbit. They began to exit leaving behind quite a mountain of bodies. They got into their ships and headed back to *The Defiant*. The hissing as the gas mixed with Paradox then was lit by Tiris who was the last to leave. He dropped the match and it was instantaneous, the burst of flame then the whoosh as the fire drove deeper into the station. He stood and laughed as the flames engulfed him. But he was secure and walked into *The Defiant's* skiff and shot straight back into *The Defiant*. As did Bucker and Kurt who was heading straight back to the Orion system. *The Wanderer* was ready to speed off into the cosmos. Tiris got to the helm of *The Defiant* and aimed a whole barrage of missiles into the lab. They never knew what hit them. Tiris who was smiling as the rest of the troopers settled down. He opened up the Reaper comm link and asked, "Any wounded?".

"None sir," came the reply. But he never knew that the majority of those creeping troopers were already invading a Trill home world. Tiris uncoupled his armour and set it on charge. He then had the most crawling of sensations that the attack they had just made was easy. Too easy, It was right on time the Trill High King contacted Tiris

"Rip cord ,this is cat, can you give me the skinny on these Creeping troopers?"

Tiris heard the urgency in the Warlords voice and replied, "Is there a problem Cat man?" the airwaves went quiet, and he thought he could hear laser repeaters firing of in the background, heavy duty laser repeaters.

Then the warlord spoke again "These fucking things won't stay down." Tiris grimaced and replied, "I'll give you all the information we have on these Creeping Troopers". He then sent the video data he had from the Butterfly straight to the Warlord. He added just as they began to wind things up, "I would take precautions against another onslaught of Dark Talon, just in case".

The comm link was then turned off. This had sent The Trill warlord state to the defence. He smiled knowing that he was well indebted to Tiris. There were few Troopers who, after the Faith wars, would never trust the Trill. They were, shall we say cautious, but Tiris, he had forgot the wars completely. He had no grudge to hold if anything he hated troopers. He hadn't enough time to go over all the reasons. No, just after seeing the weapons of the Imperium and how destructive they were, the Trill were and always use to be Allies of the imperium. But their high King and his mighty Emperor were at each-other's throats over the Paradox laws and how they could be used to full effect. But the Trill wanted too big of a piece. This had caused great friction with the two sides never budging an inch. It soon escalated and the two races were at war with each other. It was a long painful campaign for both sides and it looked from the start as an unwinnable war. Them both tossing everything they had at each other. But two Emperors down and no sign of a new one.

Tiris took his time when thinking who would be next as there were several candidates. Each had both plus and minus attributes. And he was glad he wasn't in the Troopers ranks any more. No, he felt a casual attitude, glad and non-conforming. He only held onto his two squads of Reapers as he knew that they would be needed. But life goes on. And the two major candidates for the throne were, well let's just say, fanatical. They made great speeches, promising that whilst they were on the throne they would do away with the bullshit and start a new peace treaty with the Trill. But Tiris had heard it all before and the smell of corruption was coming from the Throne room. Tiris had another reason to charge up his power armour and that the power-hungry sociopaths were always willing to cut each, other's throats. Tiris kept his finger on the policies of all the candidates. Not liking any of them, they all had a mad despairing look about them, a way in which sinister registered in a malevolent way. There were seven of them, the first was James Sanderson, head of Linsani Tech. He was a cold calculating fox who had the right amount of support. And also had an army of Militia, ghost militia and he was well in front with most people knowing him as a man not to be crossed.

After they rippled through the known universe arresting and executing a number of trooper deserters. People held him in awe. Tiris was keeping an eye on that one. The others all had small armies around them, but this mattered not as John James Sanderson was cleaning up and promising that when he was on the throne he would disassemble the Old Troopers and put into force his killer Elite, but few knew this and the ones that did were silenced and taken away. The Universal Secrets Act was a power play that was leading the new Imperial candidates.

The next was Janus Regan, he was strictly old guard and a major thorn in James Sanderson's side. He had a killer elite himself ,one that he headed. Tiris kind of liked the guy as he got his own hands dirty and never depended on anyone to heavily. But he too was insane with drug addiction and alcohol consumption. Most of his squad were either dependent on Paradox or they were just out and out psychotic. He blow you a kiss one second then shoot you in the back the next, but only if it was in his best interest and that was most of the time. He held no one in regard, or respected anyone. He was insane to the point of never being sane ever again.

The third was a small, shaven headed man called Tarius Jacks, he was completely wacked out of his mind. Raping and torturing was how he got to number three. Him and his death wing troopers were unstoppable. They took prisoners, but nobody wanted that as they were sadists of the worst kind and were known to take over space stations and interrogate the head techs and soldiers, leaving nothing but blood to be measured. Tiris liked him the least. But he had nothing to worry about as he and his Reapers were too much for him to handle. And Tarius knew this, but he also knew that someday he would go head to head with the Reaper squads.

The next four were warlords with a scattering of old navy warships. The fourth one was Wade Summit. A huge mountain of a man who could easily squash a Troopers helmet in one hand and that was his left hand. He had three warcrafts and each housed a battalion of mean as snakes troopers who were loyal to any command he gave. And they sure as hell weren't going to desert. The fifth was another trooper from hell, Jarson Reddit. He was a known demolition man and had rigged up at least seventy Trill warcrafts, scuttled them to junk. Then there was Terry Reprose, who had a squad of seventy come out the shadows blade experts. They never missed and they were known to handle even the biggest of weapons aimed at them. Their shadow play was extraordinary. And rumour was they had killed over several hundred in the climax of the Faith wars. Last but not least, the female renegade Karin Nova. She too was stuck in the shadows but all her Troopers were female and they too hadn't lost a fight. Tiris admired her, with great longing to do either one of two things with her, make love or fight the woman.

That was the list of candidates for the Empires Throne. He felt a huge surge of promise when he thought of himself and the two reaper squads. And knowing that he would have to make plans at confronting one of them at a time. This would take expert precision and great tactics. Tiris smiled as he thought on about just where they sat at that point in time and who was most likely to come at them first. That would be James Sanderson and the other heads of Linsani Tech. They were competent enough to track and trace the Reapers but as for finishing them off, He doubted it. They were prepared for all sorts of action and Tiris was still number one, most wanted. He smiled and puffed away on his stogie. They were out bidding each other in the Paradox game. And none of them claimed the throne as of yet. No, they were trying to get a foothold on the terra firma and other civilian outposts. They had problems, especially with trust, after what happened with the Trill, they were not popular, especially the Linsani tech labs.

James Sanderson who was never one for kissing babies and shaking hands was trying to keep the Linsani tech weapons, as all its aces, the Dark Talon, the creeping soldiers. Various chemical weapons that worked on both the human and the Trill. But he was only in front marginally. But if anything else happened, that wasn't expected he would have one hell of a fight on his hands. So, he sent the first Battalion of Creeping Troopers to the second largest home world of the Trill.

*

Tooms headed back to the Orgis system as did Kurt. *The Defiant* sped off into the cosmos towards the Trill main worlds. He had to take a look at the carnage they were causing. He knew that all help would be appreciated and that the Trill were seeing a mass assault. By the time *The Defiant* arrived most of the damage had been done but still the Trill kept vanquishing the enemy to the best of their abilities. But like they said, they took hits and just got back up. The cybernetic implants powering up and make their strength ten times as did the Paradox that they were constantly breathing.

"Aim for their main inhaling tube, on the left side of their bodies," said Tiris to the Trill warlord.

"Check," came the reply and the news of a possible flaw had given the Trill the urge to fight.

Tiris smiled. "That shows them," said Tiris. Then he noticed another problem darken the sky and they dropped large pods onto the ground and they opened and screaming and running came the thing that Tiris thought would be able to be quashed, the Dark Talon. He was right, as the Trill command station sent several planetary skiffs on a bombing mission using the foam in all its glory. The things melted and the ones that managed to join the creeping troopers were half dead and burning. The fight was won by the Trill. And *The Defiant* headed away back to the Orgis system where they would celebrate the victory. They spent the next three to four days relaxing. And they then knew that they had done the right thing in the destruction of the Linsani labs. But the war was not over, just one of the many battles they would face. They had stiff competition in the form of not only cyborg mutations but ghost-like militia and shadow assassins. They also had fanatical troopers who had no other loyalty than Janus Regan. He was the first one that Tiris was going to bump heads with. He just had to carry on the Paradox trade as if nothing had changed. No, he was non-plussed about when he had to meet Janus. He knew one thing, it would be one hell of a fight.

He gathered his two squads together and told them what was in store, "You men are the best of the best, anything else is reticent to the point of useless. WE are Storm Troopers; we do not fail in our task; no we do not come away saying that was simple. No, we use our hands, we use our strength and every motherfucker knows we are the best".

They all roared as Tiris carried on checking the product and making sure they were well armed. He summoned Bucker and Dayton to the helm of the ship. "You two okay?" He asked then lit another match for an old stogie.

"Yes sir," came the reply from Both Dayton and Bucker.

"I think I'll go and try to find a ship equal as the E.S.P."

Bucker cackled a loud laugh, "Thank you sir". He said and then smiled.

"You, on other hand Dayton, are getting the second squad command".

Dayton smiled, "Thank you sir".

Tiris smiled and said as he puffed away, "I know just the place for a new skirmisher".

They both felt pleased with the results from the attack on Linsani lab world.

"Where?" came the question from Bucker.

"Sigmus twelve," said Tiris.

Bucker smiled and said, "Tech twenty world fantastic machines".

"Yes, after this next drop of Paradox we will be comfortable enough to make a decent purchase of a state of the art small skirmisher. We'll get the works; cloaking device, cold shielding to stop emp from rendering her inert. Also, enough fire power and sand throwers to make her invincible".

They off loaded the Paradox and started to head for Sigmus twelve. With a cool six billion (more if they needed it). They then began wander the starports looking for a nice craft. They came across a craft that was a little bit like the E.S.P. Her name was psyche. Bucker fell in love with her as soon as he saw her. They decided to get the ship reinforced, to the best of its abilities. The cold shielding, the cloaking device that kept it from sight and radar. They got the Missiles, nuclear sidewinders. Laser cannons and heavy-duty laser repeaters. The ship was also armed with heavy duty nuclear mines.

Bucker looked around her getting the feel of her. Smiled as he settled into her helm. "Yep, she's a beauty," he said as he looked over the firing mechanisms. Made sure she was laser targeted and ready to rock, He opened his suits private channel and said, "She's the one".

Tiris nodded his head and smiled, "You sure?"

Bucker flicked auto engage on and replied, "Yep definitely the one".

They paid the tech seller and went and headed to load the thing with everything. They then flew *The Defiant* into orbit and Bucker flew *Psyche* onto piggyback position. They then flew out into space and headed towards the Linsani lab worlds. They were sure of one thing, that they had to finish off the new creeping troopers that were apparently invincible. They also had a large quantity of Dark Talons. These were bred solely to help the Creeping Troopers as they were flawed but not as flawed as the Talon. No, they were just giving the Linsani Tech officers more of an advantage. They were smiling as the wave of Talon began to encroach the

Trill. But as ever the Trill were waiting to place their ace. They waited until the last of the Dark Talon had been expended, then the silent code as the ships threw the foam at them. Melting as many as it could, then the Creeping Troopers began their assault.

The Trill steadying their nerves as the wave of Creeping Troopers surpassed anything that could be avoided, the Trill began to aim their laser repeaters at the tubes on the chest as it fed the Creepers Paradox, enough to make it invincible. So, their Laser repeaters were aimed at the cybernetic tubes that were pumping the steroid type narcotic and giving the creepers their superhuman strength. The lasers were tearing through the tubes and causing an incredible combustion on the Creeper. They then exploded and took away half of its Torso and half of its head and shoulders. They saw the end result a dead monstrous machine of flesh and cybernetics. They smiled as row after row of these Creepers were taken down with the explosion taking out two Creepers at a time. But it seemed as though it was an endless assault with them getting closer to the front ranks of the Trill, who were competent enough to back away as the laser rifles made short work of them. But the Linsani had another card up their, sleeve, an amalgamation of Creeper and Talon. They came bursting out of their carbon frozen pods that housed seven of the Creeping Talons. Tiris was watching as the organic blue and black pods were dropped into the battle fields.

"Uh oh," he said then smiled as he took a pot shot at one of the pods. He aimed his plasma cannon at one and fired after a quick guiding lock. The energy weapon rushed out and the thing was fried in mid-air only to hit the ground with a sickly splat, No survivors. He then aimed again and began to watch as the Pods released their deadly organic cargo. They were innumerable and also invulnerable. Part Trooper part Talon. And on the whole completely without fear. They were bred to kill and kill is what they did. Human torsos and legs of a xenomorph. No, they were the super killers that the Linsani had been working on a mish mash of Creepers and Talons. They were unstoppable and were unafraid. No fear, no matter if they were winning or losing, they were animalistic pure savage and on the whole the only thing that the Linsani were sure about.

Tiris aiming still at the pods as they came bursting through the atmosphere. But there were too many of them and the foam was only working on half of them. The rest were killing as they gathered momentum. The Trill felt the fear as the enemy encroached on them again, rushing full on and savaging and eating the Trill. Tiris sent the all clear to finish off these biological bugs, they would have to nuke the planet. Not a thing that you entertained regularly. He hit the purge button and cleared the Trill quadrant as their warcraft ladened with planet destroying nuclear warheads approached Yep, they pushed the button. And everyone who could be saved, well that was luck on their part. They got safely away and headed back to Orgis two. That was two planets the Trill had lost to mass destruction. And Linsani were only showing a momentary weakness.

Tiris spat a small piece of tobacco out of his mouth, the stogie was sopping wet and it was inflammable. He threw the thing away and said through the suits intercom, "We are needing a serious meeting with all our allies. That was close; too close."

The rest of the squads and mechanical teams all murmured a small curse. They all carried on maintaining the ship and squad training. Tiris was pushed for ideas in the way to annihilate the enemy. Linsani was winning, and Tiris didn't like that. I mean the faith wars were the faith wars but this this just sent a message of terror throughout the Marches throughout the known Universe. James Sanderson was going have to come to a silent and deadly end. But the more people tried more he gained recognition as a deadly adversary. And that he was a force to be reckoned with. Tiris settled down as the ship took them to Orgis. On the rim of the Marches. He would get in contact with all the Allies of Trill and various other militant forces. They would need to have a war meeting because as they were preparing, the Linsani were gathering up another army of Creeper's, Talons and mixture of both.

Tiris settled back in his chair and let the momentum drift him to sleep. They were there in two days and Tiris passed out the secret word for pow wow. That word being taint. Two days later several small Paradox sellers and a whole host of bedraggled Troopers gathered together knowing that in truth they didn't have much chance but this was the best they had got, they smiled as their ships flashed the word taint to each other. Knowing that this was the only time they got together. Tiris smiled as they docked with each other making their ships one massive collection. They then went to the centre ship and all met up. This was where Tiris showed the footage of the end of another Trill world. They all grimaced at the vision and spectacle of death. Tiris smiled as he met with a few of the other delegates from various Deserters and criminal minds that were all involved in the destroying the oppression of the New Empire.

They all gathered in the centre of the ships collective. Where they spoke freely about the state of affairs. Nobody had much information about the scourge of the Marches. They were all hoping to gain some information about the various runners in the politics of the new Empire. Particularly James Sanderson. He was leading the deadliest of campaigns, as he held the most diabolical of weapons and was gaining more support in the fear and destruction of the Trill. But now things were getting bloodier and bloodier. And Tiris was getting more impatient he had only destroyed one lab complex and was thirsty for more. They all began to talk about the various leaders and their armies. Janus Regan and Karin Nova were hot on everybody's lips as they had been the scouting mission for the Linsani. They had entered the Trill world and exploited it's weaknesses then gathered all its information and set the campaign in motion. But this had only made the superior forces of James Sanderson more powerful and destructive. His Creeping Troopers were, well, they were doing the optimal damage. And all the other creatures that the Linsani had been producing were getting used up, but the more they seemed to use the more in strength that the Linsani leaders were getting. No, a power move that was what they had just used on the Trill. They all started to talk about tactics and the best ways they could be used covertly. Skirmishing here and there against the various Warlords who were as it seemed were gathered together and being on good terms with each other.

They were complacent with James Sanderson being their natural leader. The various pirates and deserters began to discuss plans to how they could get at the various leaders with minimum casualties. They were going to have to destroy the various space stations that housed the Creepers and the Talon.

Tiris smiled as he went through the details of what he could use and said, "They won't expect to be attacked so repeatedly and so hard, we must make destroying all the Biological weapons and destroying all new weapons utmost priority."

They all nodded in agreement.

"There is no doubt here gentlemen we are down the rabbit hole and wonderland aint so fucking wonderful".

They murmured in unison. Knowing they had to take on a new and sinister enemy. But they had all teamed up and there was loyalty like a band of brothers. They relied on each other and kept in contact with each other; this war was going to get ugly. They had no illusions, no, a lot of their blood would be shed and destroyed, they would be faced with the most unnatural of enemies. The cybernetic Paradox-induced Creepers and the deadly Talon who were more than just a xenomorph, no they were a bug with a huge appetite for destruction. They were also spliced into the Creepers which was proving to be the trickiest of enemies. They began to look at not only the space stations but the lab worlds that were tucked away secretly in the Marches. They all gathered the information that they could and would use to its fullest. Potential.

The Trill were present at the meeting as it seemed as though they were dying for some pay back. They headed to their standpoint and waited for the code to start their covert action and scrutinised to the finest detail. They smiled as *The Defiant* was first to leave the congregation, it had its silent and deadly mission to finish. It was to try and get as close to the leader of the Linsani. Hopefully, they would destroy the tyrant who held all the aces. But this was very near impossible as both him and his lab techs never stayed in the one place longer than a day. They were constantly moving and producing more and more abominations. Always they were ready to use the biological weapons. But James Sanderson was a shrewd thinker, he kept sweeping all his lab decks with energy sensors, they caught a couple of Butterflies and a couple of ears. They did this religiously. Nobody had been close enough to put a dead man's pulse on the ship that was a gargantuan three miles long and eight miles wide. It was virtually invulnerable and had never been breached. I mean people had tried to board her but had subsequently disappeared. It was a labyrinth of labs and various housings where the techs lived and studied.

They had made sinister breakthroughs and new ways of improving the Xenomorph's and Creepers. The Paradox that they had accrued and were constantly improving turning more potent and more deadly, they had come a long way from the medusa seed and the organic chip that was implanted on the Troopers to stop the Trills main weapon, which was used decisively and to great effect. They began to win. this had been a great lever in the winning of the Faith war. Tiris had stopped the Linsani in its tracks by getting the Medusa seed destroyed but then the Dark Talon came along and proved to everyone that Linsani were a force to be reckoned with. Tiris smiled and lit up again, puffed his stogie into life. He got the coordinates of where the Linsani power ship was and he smiled and set The

Defiant to automatic pilot. He switched the comm link and pushed the button for Bucker.

Bucker smiled and said, "I had a feeling you would want me".

Tiris smiled and blew some smoke, "You need to test that nice little skirmisher".

Bucker started to flick the switches and power up the cloaking device and armed his weapons. Tiris smiled and said, "Adios Cochise".

*

Bucker disabled the couplers that were holding the craft onto the top of The Defiant. He slipped away until he couldn't see *The Defiant*. And he headed straight towards the Gargantuan ship. Turning on the cloaking device as he grew closer to the huge ship. He began to run a laser scan seeing just where he could dock and sneak on board of the ship. He smiled as he saw several docking ports but the problem was docking without setting of an all parameters alert. He smiled and set his suit to on with the skull lighting up and scanning ahead of him for any hostiles. He was clear and sent two butterflies ahead of him using their vast knowledge of what could be avoided and sending the intel of various possible weak points in the massive ship. He slipped into the shadows and began to assimilate and look for life forms, anything that could be used as a weakness.

He was lucky enough to realise that the ships inhabitants were busy elsewhere. So, he sent the ships stats back to *The Defiant*. Bucker was just finishing of his sweep gathering enough information to show any possible weaknesses, he found a few that were clear cut demolition missions and several technical assassinations on key techs that were handling the ships trajectory and also the loading and off-loading of various weapons like the Creepers and the new Talon. The ones that were spliced into Creepers. They seemed to be in the process of a new Medusa seed. But this one was used on all genetic breeds humans, cat and all other life forms. He slipped back on board of *The Psyche* and fell quietly away from the massive gargantuan ship. The two Butterflies were set to self-destruct after they gathered any and all information that they possibly could. Bucker flew back to *The Defiant*. Settled back into piggy-back position and Bucker rejoined *The Defiant's* crew. Tiris was going over the information that the two Butterflies had sent back to him and *The Defiant's* crew. He studied all the intel and began to calculate the weak points of the massive ship and all the malign inhabitants that it housed. Of course, it wasn't a full sweep of the ship but enough to outline any and all weaknesses that there were. He smiled as he saw the Oxygen tanks and Paradox tanks mixing the two highly explosive substances. They made a note of where each of the gasses were housed and the strange thing was, they were housed in close proximity to each other. A major flaw, one which they would exploit.

Already, as Bucker came back on board he was greeted like the wandering hero Knight who had vanquished the evil dragon. His intel was completely necessary and he was onto a winner. He smiled and sat down next to Tiris who smiled as he looked over the video's and images.

"They are working on a new Medusa seed," said Bucker as he watched the images of the different labs with the technicians who were busy producing new and completely diabolical creatures and chemical weapons. Weapons that had a 100 percent kill rate. Tiris carried on studying. The images were a god send and they were lucky that they had them. Bucker smiled as he pointed out the weakness with the Oxygen tanks and the Paradox Tanks. They were right in the blast radius of each other. And would cause a small nuclear like explosion. Enough to send a string of explosions right through the giant ship. Tiris patted Bucker on the back as he made notes of the way and when the best time to strike was at the Linsani. The ship flipped into high alert and Bucker boarded *The Psyche*.

It was now or never; the ship was ready for any and all firing upon them. Bucker again took off from *The Defiant* and headed for the same point he had docked with before knowing that any and all weaknesses would be utilised and used. They had waited two days for this pre-emptive strike to be used. He smiled in his skull helmet and laughed this being the way with a Reaper as they knew that death was nothing and that a competent death was all each of the Reapers could hope for. That's why they laughed as they executed their tactics. They were willing to give their lives in combat but nothing had come close to scare any of them yet. He slipped again into the shadows using all his abilities in covert Guerrilla action. Being careful and alert in the executing of his orders. He smiled as he left a remote sensor with a timer on it counting down five minutes. He then laid a few motion detecting explosives as he went back to *The Psyche*. These would either trip on proximity or explode as a knock on effect of the Thermite timers. Either way they would destroy a huge chunk of the thing. This was all going to plan. And Bucker let the couplings retract from the docking position, again he put on the cloaking device and again headed back to *The Defiant*. He settled in and went again to the helm where Tiris was sat smiling and said to Bucker, "You have a good trip?"

Bucker smiled and replied, "Yes sir".

Tiris smiled back and looked at the sergeant.

"Yes sir everything went as planned," said Bucker. Tiris smiled 5,4,3,2,1. Then there was an almighty bang enough to put a black hole to shame. The ship was torn in two then the smaller part had a huge section of explosions as the ship fell apart. The bigger piece was all of a sudden made into a self-sustaining ship whilst the other part blew itself to pieces. Bucker Laughed as the ship really fell apart. They then headed back to the Orgis system. Shielded, safe and in the best shape that it ever was. They headed out to the outpost of the Orgis system where they would be able to celebrate their newfound win. They spent the next four five days in the lap of luxury. They knew that the last action was a crucial one. And they celebrated and celebrated well. But things were far from over. James had managed to save a lot of tech heads and their experiments. He then headed in the direction of the Linsani worlds where he would divide up what was left and secure enough to keep the whole new war together. He looked over the wreckage of the ship and saw that it wasn't as bad as he thought. They lost about twenty percent of the Creepers and fifteen percent of the Talon. James sent out a S.O.S. transmission asking for any and all help to come to him at the Linsani world.

Janus was first to respond. Wade was next then Jarson, and the rest followed suit. Janus took a look at the leftovers from the Reaper strike and got in contact with James straight away. "James this is Janus. You look like you're just out the tail end of a nuke fight"

James smiled and replied, "Yep you got that right Reapers are proving to be highly important and so much more deadly than we thought."

Janus smirked, "yeah well, we are ready for them".

James smiled. "It's a minor matter," He said. "We'll decide on tactics when the rest of you appear".

Janus nodded his head and replied. "Well, that's a mute-point as I knew they would start with you, being as the best way to start is to cut off the head of the snake".

James laughed a little at this. "Well, they very nearly did".

Janus laughed back, "I take it you have got provisional plans for situations like this?"

The question was warmly received and James replied, "Yeah well. I wouldn't be much of a leader if I hadn't contingency plans".

They carried on talking for a good ten minutes more than Janus appeared at the Linsani home world. And entered the atmosphere of the main home-world. The rest of the political warlords landed soon after. They all meet and they were all up in arms, as the subject of the Reapers was touchy. They knew they could handle them in a straight up fight but the Reapers were masters at sabotage and silent fighting, Special forces that they were, was an understatement. They had grown more confident, and more lethal practicing covert strike missions and other specialist ways. They came quietly and reduced the enemy to rubble. They were growing more popular with those who wished the Faith wars to be over once and for all.

They all gathered together and watched from a distance the collective of the Linsani and other various malevolent forces gather together and plot. Tiris smiled as he sent an electronic ear through a satellite that they had gained access to. They watched and listened to the gathering of Generals. They got the gist of the meeting as they plotted and planned a strike on the Reapers. They would use bait, they had captured a flagship of troopers as it had begun it's desertion, on board the ship was a friend of Tiris. A Trooper who Tiris had much respect for, his name was Carl Stone. And him and his small battalion had been getting sick of the Faith wars since almost the beginning. They had a high kill ratio and never lost their cool amidst the battles. They were like a death squad, and they knew they were highly decorated and exemplified. Tiris heard the S.O.S. beacon as it headed away from the Linsani meetings having gathered all it could on the evil and malignant Generals.

"This is a code three one zero, we are in trouble one of our engines is leaking cold fusion, and it looks like we could blow." The ship was called *The Haunt*. It repeated the signal and Tiris responded.

"Haunt this is *The Defiant*. Carl is that you?"

Carl smiled and said, "Yes Tiris, it's me we're about to blow, can you help?"

Tiris smiled and replied, "We'll be there in a Jiffy. *The Defiant* purged and threw the ship into full throttle. Bucker manned *The Psyche*. Just as *The Defiant* drew close it came under attack by troopers manning a small, but fully armed warcraft, with a cloaking device. The Troopers were soldiers Of Karin Nova's elite entourage. *The Defiant* didn't have a chance until they were in the thick of the action.

Tiris smiled and shouted, "Good a fight". Then switched his engine on to battle stations and they began to fire Laser Repeaters and Plasma cannons at the warcraft. Meanwhile Bucker was circling *The Haunt* and getting no readings of a nuclear surge.

"Tell Tiris. Tell Tiris I had no choice they have my family and they were talking about feeding them to the Paradox zombies".

Bucker looked over the ship then he saw it the ship was rigged from the outside of the engines it would take large explosions but they had rigged it good. Bucker turned the skirmisher around and headed back just as *The Haunt* began to explode. He got to *The Defiant* as it was fending off the enemies. There were several warcraft and they were beginning to make mincemeat out of *The Defiant*. But Bucker knew how to handle this situation, he smiled and thought they know our armaments. But they didn't know about *The Psyche* and how well prepared she was. He began to slip through the firing of Laser repeaters by *The Defiant* then he got a laser lock on one of the warcraft. And sent a tactical nuclear sidewinder at the craft. Blew it to pieces, Tiris smiled as it fended of the rest whilst Bucker came round to the rear of the warcraft. He burned a huge hole in one of them then blew another one to pieces.

By this time *The Defiant* had made enough of a mess leaving only two ships left. Both of them began to retreat. They sped as far as they could. And Tiris told Bucker to come back and they would head away to get re-armed and repaired. Bucker smiled as he began the docking procedure with *The Psyche*. He headed straight away to the helm of *The Defiant*. The ships began their journey to the Orgis system where they would re-arm and re-fuel, they had lots of time to gather their shit together, pay who needed paying then head back out into the cosmos. They had one thing to do and that was purchase more Paradox.

They headed away to Rygon Five and began to settle into the sleep cycle. As they neared the end of their journey, they slipped into the atmosphere of Rygon Five and made the descent into the world that was part Zombie and part militant. I mean the planet was policed and policed well, but still there was areas in the populace where even the Reapers wouldn't go. Tiris loaded up another massive weight of Paradox. They started to ascend back through the Planet's atmosphere. Then it was a straight shot to the various systems where they would sell the product and keep on gaining Gold Credits. They were well into sixteen billion credits after they sold the product. This money would only carry on growing and growing until they could live off the profits without having to touch the proceeds. This gave most of the Reapers a big satisfactory smile. Something that they could all keep to themselves. All this was well and fine but they were still wanted by most of the run ins for the Emperor's Throne. They had a huge bounty on their heads but most troopers stayed away from them knowing how lethal that the Reapers were. I mean two Emperors had tried to catch them but had failed with contempt.

This had only showed the Reapers were made of stuff harder than most metals. They were steel in spirit and never missed a beat they had very little in the way of scars but had training that set them years against the opponents. They had never been caught in an ambush. Or when they thought they were safe from fire, their armour ricocheted the various weapons and lasers glancing of the Power force, that was the major asset for the K eleven Armour. And the cooled heads of the troopers that showed on the field of battle was well, legendary. Nothing had come close to taking down the Reapers. They were cool calm and collected. And had nerves of steel.

Bucker was primarily in charge keeping the troopers on their toes. Showing his major skills that were, advanced hand to hand and advanced marksmanship, He had been known to get really close to his enemy and I mean really close. His hand to hand was legendary. And his skill in a chameleon suit that blurred and reflected the light; well, he was known throughout the Imperium both for and against as a master sniper. He was unbeaten In the challenges and was a superb pilot. He was known for his tactical manoeuvres and springing surprises on the enemy. The Trill took a big sigh as he joined with Tiris. They had a lot to be thankful for.

Bucker didn't make a big issue of the move he knew that the Trill were going up against the Empire and its links with the Linsani. They were first attacked with the Medusa seed. Then they were at the mercy of the Dark Talon. But these Creeping Troopers, he was still chewing over the best way to handle and then the splicing of the Talon and the Trooper. No, Linsani had a lot of grit in the way of Biological warfare. No, they were practically invulnerable. Just as well the Reapers were around as they were the only ones who proved time and time again that they could take on the mighty Linsani Bio Techs. But still these creeping troopers with their cybernetic enhancements, well they were making short work of the hard work.

*

117

James Sanderson was meeting with the rest of the delegates for the new Empire. They had everything to gain and nothing to lose. So, they sealed a treaty. That there would be no back-stabbing and they would help out as much as they could. The treaty was signed by all the heads of the different alliances. Janus Regan, Tarius Jacks, Wade Summit, Jarson Reddit, Terry Reprose and Karin Nova. They decided it was time to unleash everything that they had on the Reapers. They were well aware of the manoeuvres that the Reapers could pull. And seeing as they had bought a new Skirmisher (*The Psyche*), that was just another thorn in the side of the delegates. It was quite the new find for Bucker he had been fond of The E.S.P. But *The Psyche* was a new way to go. She purred and hummed in the cockpit, it was almost orgasmic. Bucker fell for the A.I. and everything.

Smiling as she purred into action. He was to do a small recon around the Linsani home worlds. See where they had all gathered. He noted that the gargantuan hulk had been left just to the right of the main Linsani Tech world. It was left for a number of hours whilst the delegates surmised, planned and plotted, not seeing *The Psyche* as she drew closer to the Main Tech world. She got as close as she could. Bucker had an idea he would pin a few mines on the massive hulk of a ship. Then set the timers and left. He got as close to the main engines as he could with the magnetic plate nuclear mines. He stuck several on the engines then sped out of there. The timers counted down from fifteen to zero, and Bucker was well on his way back to *The Defiant*. The ship exploded and left very little for them to salvage. Bucker knew this of course but also this was only a temporary thing they would soon be hunting *The Defiant* and *The Psyche*.

Bucker was well aware of the situation and knew that they would be hunted and hunted for a good long while. But *The Defiant* and its crew had made deception and stealth a state of art. They had done a number of things that had given them an edge, They, never took anything for granted. If things were too quiet, they would sit quietly and let the cloaking device work its charm. And watch as the various enemies flew on by. Then they would head in the direction that the enemies had just come. This was total subterfuge and worked well for *The Defiant*. Again, they made a Paradox pick up and again it worked out in their favour. They had very little to be wary of. But they knew their luck was running out. But still they carried on their, trading knowing that they were vital to several systems that were crying out for the substance. Tiris smiled as he heard *The Psyche* couple back onto *The Defiant*.

"You did good," Said Tiris and they gripped wrists.

Bucker smiled and said, "I gotta power up my armour, it'll take a couple of hours".

Tiris smiled and replied, "Yeah sure you deserve extra R.R. for that one anyway".

Bucker carried on beaming with pride. That little action would show any and all that *The Defiant* and the Reaper Teams were in it for the long haul. Tiris went back to the helm and looked over the star charts and where they could hole up until they were safe. The Junk Yard in the Orion nebula.

They headed there to the outpost that was a weigh-in station for deserters and pirates. They docked with the station and walked through to the main area. It was a mish-mash of Cyborgs, Trill, various troopers and scouts out to make their name legendary. But that was easier said than done. The various tyrants that were around made it difficult for any trading to be done. They began to really tighten their grip on the various systems this made it hard for the rebels to stay safe. They were constantly being boarded by the Imperium and searched. *The Defiant* though was always one step ahead of them. This had been easy for them to stay out the way of trooper carriers. And ships with the Linsani logos. The rest well they were not too safe when *The Defiant* attacked, leaving junk in space and dead in the waste.

Tiris was a competent and very skilled leader, he had ways within ways. Skills and deception were in his very marrow. He resonated power and cunning. As did the rest of the Reapers as they were always ready to make Tiris' orders as competent as possible. They never shied away from an order knowing what he did was for the best of the two squads. They were completely competent and fearless, you bet. They never challenged his orders and never regretted following them. Tiris smiled and carried on switching down the ship, then when he was satisfied the engine was cool enough, he headed for the main populace of the station.

Putting his skull helmet on and operating the A.I., he was on full alert as if something were bugging him, and yes, he followed his instincts. He knew one thing that more times than not his gut had made decisions that he had to follow. He looked around scanning for enemies and hostiles. He made a full competent sweep with his A.I., looking for anything abnormal he came up nothing.

"Thank god," he, said and carried on sweeping around the main populace. "I could use a break".

Still nothing. He headed for the canteen with his two squads in tow. They settled down to a high energy and high protein meal. And it wasn't slop. No, they enjoyed the meal and didn't say a word to each other, just ate. Tiris still suspicious carried on scanning the room whilst his Reapers had a much needed and much enjoyed meal. This took a lot of the burden off of Tiris. Not that he was worried, he just had to make sure they were properly rewarded for their efforts. I mean the money was one thing, but the fact they were onto a lot of money. This was more than triple a year's pay in the Reapers pocket. And that was being accumulated more each day. But they still needed to be ready in case of severe action and knowing the type of enemies they had, they would need to be rested and refreshed.

Tiris stopped being so analytical and took of his skull, and joined his men in a good, well-earned meal. Bucker stood up, noticing a young boy running from what looked like a group of ghost militia. The young boy had been seen picking pockets and was making a get-away. Bucker left the squads of Reapers and jogged off in the direction of the young boy who was no older than twelve. Bucker stood between him and the ghost militia. The militia seeing the Reapers skull and suit immediately went for their weapons. But Bucker was faster and produced the laser pistol repeater and blew a hole in each of them. Leaving one shot left. He smiled and put his laser pistol back into it holster on his hip. Tiris stood up and said, "Chow time is over, we better head back to the ship".

They all stood up fixed their helmets on and started to head back to *The Defiant*. Bucker pulled up the rear watching his A.I. carefully as it was making sure that nothing was creeping up behind them. They got to *The Defiant* and sat in combat seating. With the heavy plasma weapons first nearest the door. The ship then kicked over into fusion and they flew away into the cosmos. Bucker got up after the initial power surge of the ship. They then headed back to Rygon Five to get more Paradox. They did so very quickly and paid then left heading back to the Linsani regency, where they would sell the product they had just picked up. They made the sell and left swiftly, as they were taking a huge risk selling to the Linsani, especially after what they had just done.

*

Around about this time Janus Regan was tracking them, who were hot on their heels with their four warships which were all loaded with mercenaries and were prepared for a heavy fight with the Reapers. *The Defiant* came out of full throttle and went straight away into red alert as the four warships showed up on their radar. They were straight away fired upon by laser repeaters from the ships. *The Calculas* (The head ship) began to warm up a nuclear side winder. And Bucker ran to *The Psyche* while the rest were using the sand throwers to dampen the laser repeaters as they were aimed at *The Defiant*. They were out maned but that didn't mean they were going to surrender. No, Tiris liked it when the odds were stacked against him. This was when he was at his most resilient and loved the combat. The other three ships began to circle and fire at *The Defiant* but Tiris had been in tighter positions and had a few tricks up his sleeve.

That's when *The Psyche* made her move. Bucker put a laser locking shot at the missiles that were being shot at *The Defiant*. He then fired his laser repeaters as the sidewinders shot forth and destroyed them. Tiris smiled and fired back at *The Calculas* with his heavy plasma cannon, he ripped into the side of *The Calculas*, destroying and sending the ship's engines into destruction. The other three ships began to lock onto *The Defiant* but *The Defiant* had its Guardian Angel, *The Psyche*, who was laser-locking onto their missiles and blowing them to pieces. Tiris smiled as the fight was going their way. The other warcraft's weren't going down as easy, no they were putting up a healthy fight and were firing off their heavy laser cannons. *The Defiant* was handling this with a degree of ease, using the sand throwers to full effect. This stopped the lasers in their tracks. And gave enough time for Tiris to laser lock on the other three. He then shot out his sidewinders that headed straight to the other three.

Tiris smiled as the sidewinders struck the engines of the other three ships and sent the three ships into meltdown. Tiris smiled as the explosion ripped the three warcraft to pieces. He then decided that the best move next was to pick of the troopers that were floating around. This was no problem to Tiris. The laser repeaters picked them off. They then headed off to the old Imperium planets (Hiding in plain sight). They got there and began to look at the nearest planet with enough tech to re arm and refuel *The Defiant*. *The Psyche* as well was needing to be rearmed and refuelled. The cost was insignificant and was a means to an end's, They were rich any how and had no qualms about the cost. They kept up the bad work.

*

Kurt Lidel came across what was left of Janus's Warcrafts, He smiled and said, "Well, well, well" then saw the dead troopers floating out in space. Then he decided to open the Alpha niner channel, "Rip Cord this is Guardian Angel, I've just came across your last skirmish."

Tiris nearly choked on his stogie, "Yes Kurt".

Kurt smiled as the man had more tricks up his sleeves than a famed magician. It wasn't luck, no it was pure skill and tactics.

James Sanderson made it back from the Linsani world with another major load of Creeping Troopers and Talon. He had lost his major warcraft but there was always more than one way to skin a cat. He smiled as he loaded up about twenty cargo ships with about ten Creepers and Ten Talons. He also had at the rear the spliced Creepers and Talons about five Cargo holders.

James sighed a little as the news of the death of Janus Regan had come through. He thought little of it as he was about to see to the end of the Trill. And besides this Tarius Jacks was being his wing man. Him and his half a dozen warcraft with the most bloodthirsty of pirates and troopers. They had never seen a fight that they didn't win. No, he was a severe piece of work and was well and truly in the lead in the war sense.

Tiris had a bad feeling about what was happening. It was quiet out there and he didn't like it when it was quiet he then got an emergency transmission. The Trill were under attack again. This time they weren't prepared for the assault as the last of their home worlds were being attacked by a massive surge of Creepers and Talon. Tiris growled and immediately headed back to the Trill home world. Again, they were witness to the surge of the Creepers and Talon, this was the third planet of Trill that had been under the destruction of the savage creatures. Again, they were left with the only option and that was nuclear destruction. They took as many of the populace of the world as they could. The Trill Armada came into the planets sun side. Now began to warm up their planet killers. Then after setting the timers and firing the huge missiles into the Trill home world, they got out the way as the explosion was huge and almighty. They saved just under a quarter of the population. And that was sheer luck.

Tiris got in contact with the Trill warlord. "Hey cat you know it always brings a tear to my eyes when we have to do an action like that."

The Cat hissed his displeasure at the statement. "You aint the one who has to live with the tail end of the action."

Tiris sighed a heavy sombre sigh. Then lit up his stogie. "Well cat my man, it just getting a little bit par the course, if you get what I mean."

The Trill warlord smiled and hissed, "It would be different if this was happening to your home worlds."

Tiris smiled settled back into his chair and let the statement hit home, knowing that he was right if the Trill were doing the damage to the Empires home worlds. It would be something that they would have to settle but this wasn't the case. Tiris knew his course of action would be to destroy one of the major lab worlds. And that was a mission of utmost importance and also difficult. Very near impossible in fact. But Tiris was confident in the fact that they could pull off another sniper style of action. This meant using Bucker to his fullest and deadliest. Tiris gave a smile and thought,

'How do I get close to their leader James Sanderson?' Bucker came up from the cargo bay and stood at attention whilst Tiris kept reading about how much they were needing to pull of another miracle. The face on Bucker was stone like and he held the most contempt for the Linsani. Many soldiers had vanished whilst under orders by the Linsani tech heads. He was no fool and knew that this undertaking was a major fight back at the Empire.

Tiris had to be sure on the targets that they were hoping to get. He knew that Bucker would do the mission and do it well. The major planet was housing the most diabolical of biological weapons and was also where James Sanderson was housed, in his impregnable fortress, guarded by a legion of creepers and a large number of ghost militia. It was very near impossible to gain access and what lay behind the large iron doorway, well, it may be as close to hellish demons as you could get. Bucker sneered at the questions whether he was clear that this action would and could be tantamount to suicide.

Bucker growled and said, "Yes Sir!"

Tiris looked at the Sniper sergeant and said, "Just making sure were on the same page Sergeant." Tiris smiled and said, "At ease sergeant"

Bucker relaxed and smiled. "I'll need two more men?" he said and wiped the sweat from his eyes.

Tiris smiled "Of course you will".

Bucker smiled and replied, "Dayton and Crassent".

Tiris smiled as he wrote down something that was very important about Crassent and that was that his family had all been massacred by Linsani tech heads, they were testing out a new biological chemical that mutated then killed the people within a forty foot radius. Crassent had managed to get a safe distance but watched as the powerful chemical twisted and contorted all that had been in the blast radius. Then it twisted them into a grotesque shape snapping their bones and melting their eyes. As he grew up, they had come to know Crassent as quiet but loyal. He never took his position as granted and kept himself to himself. The end of the Faith wars had only proved to him that he was one step closer to destroying the Linsani. When Bucker told him that he was going for the head tech and that his skills would be needed. He, as well as Dayton was a demolition expert and this couldn't be a better gift to him as he was seething with animosity and knew the challenge would be well met by the three of them.

The Stronghold was dead centre in the rural area on Linsani world Exelsus, their chief aim was to make and produce as many Talon and Creepers as they could. And they weren't short of troopers to turn into creepers as they were signing up in droves, The sinister tech heads were completely in tune with the diabolical way of the Linsani. They were constantly up grading and making new toys (As one of the head techs had called them), Dayton on the other hand had a true passion about destroying the Linsani techs. They were the only thing keeping the Faith wars going. This mission was, well, it was going to be fun. Bucker took the two of them aside and explained what exactly that it was they were to do. They were to infiltrate and destroy any and all LInsani projects.

Bucker smiled and said, "It's a one way mission". Bucker sighed again knowing that the two Reapers were signed on and signed on all the way. They boarded the skirmisher *The Psyche* and headed toward the war world Exelsus. *The Defiant* kept its distance whilst monitoring the Linsani head tech labs. They flew to the edge of the rural area and each of them switched on the Chameleon suits that were standard issue for snipers in the Reapers corps.

They got to the large doorway and waited for signs of life. They waited three or four minutes then the door slid open and they slipped by a squad of ghosts. They began to advance into the station and prayed that they had the right intel. They headed towards the main area for the Talon to be extracted, they then set out thermite nuclear detonators enough to put a huge crack in the planets ground. Bucker then signalled the other two to head towards the main populace of tech heads. They were to seek and destroy as much as possible, they were at the height of their skills as they entered the main boarding of the Talon.

They set a few more thermite nuclear devices and that was when the fun began, they walked right into a firefight with the ghost militia. Their cover was blown, someone had scrambled their chameleon suits and they were now in full visibility. And the ghost militia were taking no prisoners. They opened fire on each other. There were at least six militia and there were more bringing up the rear. Someone had tipped them off and they scrambled the chameleon cloak on their suits.

They took up defensive positions as best they could. The firefight began. As the troopers began to relay their fire. Taking their time and giving each other a chance to fire whilst taking on a volley of fire front and back. Bucker was firing off his carbine loaded with a 100 rounds of splitters. Dayton and Crassent were firing of high energy plasma cannons, these had proved to be the utmost of sheer energy weapons. They were burning through one ghost and then burning through a second and third. While Bucker shot into the rest with the ultimate lethal strike. The Splitters were exploding into the flesh of the ghosts. Ripping them to pieces. Bucker continued to relay his rounds of splitters into the ghosts who were just firing away and the bullets from their carbines were having no use or effect on the Reapers. They then began to carry on through as the last of the ghost squad was rendered dead. They carried on leaving a trail of nuclear detonators primed and ready. They had enough to orbit the lab and all its contents. This would be in pay back for nearly wiping out the Trill. They laid the last of them then headed back towards *The Psyche*.

They got into the skirmisher ship and headed straight back to *The Defiant*. The only reason why the Reapers had to detonate inside out was the cold shielding that protected the labs from a nuclear strike from above. Bucker flipped the remote switch to prime then pushed the button. There was a loud cracking like the earth and rocks ripping in two then the bang. Bucker and the other two began to whoop and holler as the station imploded and it was wiped from the face of the planet. The mushroom itself was worth watching, and it had been a long time coming. They had dealt a major blow to the Linsani and it was worth every second of it exploding. They docked with *The Defiant* and went straight to the helm where Tiris was sat watching the explosion with keen interest.

Bucker stood to attention as did the other two. "You did well sergeant,"

Bucker looked dead ahead and replied, "Yes sir!".

Tiris smiled as he turned his chair around and said, "At ease Gentlemen".

The three Reapers smiled and waited for the Colonel to continue.

"Yes, not a bad job at all," Bucker smiled.

"Was there much resistance?" asked Tiris.

Bucker shook his head. "No sir," he replied.

"Go back to the rest of the Reapers, celebrate, that was just what the doctor ordered".

Bucker and the other two Reapers went back to the mess hall. They were instantly greeted with howls of excitement from the rest of the reapers. But this was just the beginning of the fight and they all knew it. But they were psyched and ready that they could handle anything that was thrown their way. They were making progress, in the Paradox wars. They knew that they were practically indestructible. The Reaper Armour was performing beyond expectations. They were a charge of immortals, the very epitome of death itself. This was shown in their suits as they were skull shaped and bone covered. They made the most arduous of tasks seem easy. And none of them so far had taken as much as a scratch. They gathered together and ate and drank ale. They had enough time to charge their suits and even more time to rest and get good and shitfaced.

Tiris smiled and thought, 'This was easy really easy'. They didn't have much in the way of competition. But he knew the rest of the opposition would be scheming and plotting. They had struck a blow for the good guys, yet they knew that they still had a lot of opposition and it would take great deal of skill and expert tactics to make it through to the end. They had nearly wiped out

the major opposition, which being James Sanderson.
Tiris smoked on his stogie and reflected on the major
triumphs that they had done recently. Giving himself
a major pat on the back and rewarding himself with
a well done. He then took his armour off and set it
to charge.

The ship was on automatic and heading away from
the Linsani's home planet. They headed back to the
Orgis nebula, which housed the dangerous mutineers
and deserters. The next plan was to go through the
opposition, and I mean go through them. There were
six major players in the game since they had ended
Janus Regan. And they had a good idea who would
come at them next. Tarius Jacks was already heading
straight for them. *The Defiant* knew the kind of attack
they were coming up against and would be well
prepared. They were elite skirmishers, with their two
men to each ship, one running the weapons the other
was piloting the ship and there were over twenty of
these little ships and they were nimble and quick. Using
the speed and light weaponry to full effect.

The main ship carried armament and maintained the
battle with quick refuelling and re arming. Tarius was a
major madman and thought nothing of sending out
suicide kamikaze ships at the enemy. He never ran from
and never quit a battle, knowing that his winning was
the utmost surety and him and his wasp brigade had
never lost. He revelled in battle, he loved the combat,
the action, To look at him, he was a blond with a
wicked hook nose, almost eagle like. He was known
never to smile, laugh or give of any emotion. He was
totally enthralled by the action of combat, but never let
it show. Deep inside he had a heart, but it had turned

black as ash a long time ago. No feelings, as they interfered with his judgement. He was constantly grave he never shouted or raised his voice; no, he spoke and spoke with grave concern. He never had doubt about his leadership and no one defied him. He too was fond of executing, just to keep the pilots in check. If there was a problem, he sorted it with a quick click then crack as the heavy bore pistol blew the head clean off whoever started the initial treason. Nobody envied the man that took the wrath of Tarius Jacks. No, they weren't wanting the same, an iron fist he ruled with.

*

Tiris had a feeling that they were in line of sight with Tarius Jacks. He had heard rumours about Tarius, rumours about the suicide death squad the Wasps, and how they had never retreated and never lost a fight and there had been many. They were heading straight into a stand-off. But Tiris was psyched and wired his face looking grim as it stared away into the depths of space. He knew the Wasps were a major nightmare to come up against. They were busy refuelling and preparing their weaponry. It was a matter of hours since *The Nest* (the name of the main ship) had gotten a radar picture on *The Defiant*. They would be coming up on them any minute now.

Tiris pushed the com link and said, "Bucker how should I handle this?"

Bucker smiled and replied, "Hit, run and hide the old-fashioned way."

Tiris smiled, "an old-fashioned scrap that's what I like to hear".

They began to see *The Nest* and its Wasps flying around and preparing themselves.

"Into the breach my fellow Troopers, into the breach". *The Psyche* un-coupled itself from *The Defiant* and switched on its cloaking device as soon as it got clear.

Bucker then began to tag several of the small Wasps, preparing for all hell to break loose. The Defiant came in range and the Wasps immediately headed straight for it. Bucker and his ship started to fire its lasers and plasma cannons at the Wasps and each target was blasted to pieces. He took at least four of them and carried on sneaking passed the rest hiding and hiding well, This just confused the rest of the Wasps as *The Defiant* put a laser tag onto *The Nest* and readied itself to fire several small sidewinder nukes at *The Nest*. *The Nest* got the red alert and twisted to get out of the way of the missiles but two landed and shook the ship. *The Nest* being more powerful than *The Defiant* began to circle and try and get a lock on *The Defiant*. The rest of the wasps were preoccupied with trying to figure out the whereabouts of *The Psyche*. *The Psyche* nimbly circled the Wasps and began yet again to target several of them. The lasers targeted and again fired taking out three or four of the Wasps. *The Defiant* on the other hand was again targeting *The Nest* ship.

Tiris was well in the fray, and he was doing remarkably well. Then it happened, the Wasps began a suicide run at *The Defiant*. Several of them began to push through the fusion barrier, and head straight at *The Defiant*. Tiris smiled and auto aimed his plasma cannon at the Kamikaze Wasps. There a mighty surge of energy and the cannon fired, tagging several different ships one after the other, then blasting the Wasps to bits. The surge and the kick thrilled Tiris, he shone an evil, yet humorous look onto the region of space where the Wasps were re-arming and re-forming into squads.

Tiris sent a message to *The Psyche*. "Careful Bucker they look worse than they are."

The Psyche, still cloaked in the confines of space decided to get closer to The Nest. Again, he made his presence known by destroying several of the housings that the wasps housed and re-armed in. But Tarius was unresolved by the actions. He had a few more tricks up his sleeve, he sent two beacon ships off to see if anyone else was close enough to give them a hand. He picked up the flagship of Jarson Reddit, he immediately contacted him asking for his help.

Jarson responded and said, "Heading straight to your vector, be there in two".

Tarius breathed in and carried on defending himself from *The Defiant* and *The Psyche*. Tiris felt something was wrong. This was going to easily and Tiris was cautious, smelled a rat. He flew to the outer rim of the battle area and switched on his cloaking device. The two ships were both invisible and they had an enormous advantage over *The Nest* and its Wasps. But like he thought, something was wrong. They began to fire on *The Nest* with everything they had, knowing that they were in the right position to destroy *The Nest*. They circled the ship a couple of times knowing that they could not been seen, then in a strike force of the two of them they fired everything they had, and that took out Tarius and his Wasps. They then headed away just as Jarson and his fleet of skirmishers arrived. They needed to refuel and re-arm. So, they plotted a course to the nearest tech twenty world that had everything they needed. They smiled as they landed in the tech proficient world of Klandine. They set straight about refuelling and re-arming. They knew that there were more and more Battle Generals all hungry for the throne of the Empire.

James Sanderson, was way in lead in the stakes of gaining the throne. He held all the aces, he was a sure fire certainty, but knew he had to cut back on some of the competition. So, he made it painstakingly clear that Tiris and his reapers were to be eliminated with terminal Prejudice. No discussion, no getting a deal and certainly no joining with the Empire. The Empire that was growing through the ashes of fire and destruction that had been made by the Reapers.

No this had seemingly strengthened the malicious intent of James Sanderson. He was biologically making more and more enhancements and coming up with stronger and stronger more efficient killing Talon and enhanced troopers. He was paving the way in biometric enhancements, changing the face of the human race altogether. He was held divine in all aspects and was the sure fast solution to the Faith wars. The people didn't mind their sons their fathers, their bloodlines being genetically enhanced, and prepped for the final battles that were two solar systems away.

They were planning on killing off the last three Trill worlds. And it was a daring strike, an unseen strike, no they had most of the Talon in its pupal stage and the rest of the Troopers were measuring up their cybernetics, with each knowing where their comrades were was key to this massive and unholy strike force, some with

Chameleon suits others super strength enhancements and various weapons built into them. You know, single shot laser repeaters and various other toys and shields and grenades firing from their arms. To say these troopers were ready was an understatement. They had a great thirst for blood and no fear of dying. The Talon trooper hybrid, well that was just psychotic to say the least. Them, like the Reapers were practically immortal in every way. They would take up the rear and be used in the most bloodthirsty of ways. They would carry on finishing of the Trill indiscriminately. And not having any remorse or any feelings they finished what the troopers and the Talon had started.

The cargo ships made their way under the guise of food and water. Somehow during the last Talon attack they had managed to severe all foods and medical supplies. And it was having the most catastrophic effect. The Linsani sent the signal to say that they were entering the atmosphere, with meds and foodstuffs. They then, all of a sudden, realised that they were being invaded by the blue skinned troopers and the dark as hell Talon. They gave no quarter. And took no prisoners. The chameleon suited troopers began to use their suits to the fullest of their potential. And began to cut down the Trill like wheat. Laser shots went off from the unseen corners, Talon detached itself and began to devour the Trill. Getting hungrier and hungrier.

*

The Defiant heard once again the alpha niner channel opening up, "Rip cord, rip cord this is the cat we have got huge problems".

Tiris switched the Alpha niner on and replied, "This is Rip cord how can we help you". The channel buzzed then clicked as shots were clearly going off in the ear of Tiris. He grimaced then spoke down the channel. "Cat man, do you copy?" He could hear the laser repeaters being fired off and plasma cannons but he knew they would be too late for the attack. Tiris snarled at the dead end of a channel. "Okay reapers we got a purpose!"

They then strapped themselves in and headed straight to the Trill home worlds. Not that anything could be done at this point. The Trill battlecruisers flew away as many of their race as they could get. But this had only saved a small number of their race. The rest were slaughtered without any remorse, they were consumed by the Talon, and the Troopers just kept on going into the Trill leaving their dead stacked up in piles so as the Talon wouldn't starve. Tiris got to the last home-world of the Trill. He saw as they landed and detached the cargo holds onto the planet, straightaway he warmed up an air to surface nuclear missile and fired. This smashed into the big cargo pod and blew it to smithereens. Then *The Psyche* detached itself and went straight into high alert. It too had a few things to show the Linsani. And this was a perfect way to seek and destroy. He began to target the cargo pods but waited until they detached themselves, then he was in prime position to destroy the cargo in its entirety.

The ships of the Linsani began to head back to the Linsani space stations and home worlds. They were planning to hunt down every last feline humanoid. They were more than capable of doing this. But as they gathered together more Cybernetic humans and Talons

The Defiant appeared in their vector and began to target the various cargo ships and troop carriers. *The Psyche* released itself from *The Defiant* and immediately put its cloaking system on and began to target the several large craft that were just waiting and refuelling he smiled and said, "adios" dirt bags. Then fired several sidewinder missiles again at the pods that housed the biological engineered creatures. *The Defiant* then pushed through, it's cloaking device on and shielding on. They then flew straight by Linsani ships and dusted the area with sand then began to release the mines, both tactical and nuclear mines. The sand disguised them and the Linsani ran right into them. Explosion after explosion as the cargo ships destroyed themselves amongst the sand and metal. After that was done *The Defiant* plotted a course back to the Trill to secure as many of their royalty as could be saved. They were needing good news, as-well.

James Sanderson had taken the first wave as luck would have it and he was going to use all his strength to come up with some sort of win against *The Defiant* and *The Psyche*. He hurried together several battlecraft and went out into the marches following *The Defiant* the best he could. But Tiris had a plan to string out the fuel and weaponry on the Warcrafts. It was simple, take them on a fool's hunt. Only showing up on their radar now and then. Giving them the appearance of battle weary and needing refuelled. But this wasn't the case, they were highly stacked with both fuel and weapons. They showed themselves two or three times and figured that they were on a good thing and the head of the Linsani James Sanderson he thought but didn't realise, that this was the best cat and mouse game in the

Marches, and Tiris had taken lessons from the Cat himself (Cascoe).

He and Cascoe had discussed at great lengths the cat and mouse tactics. Tiris had come away a hell of a lot smarter. Knowing that they were the most treacherous but simple and effective. He planned rigorously knowing that nothing came from nothing and that Cascoe was truly one of the great militant minds in the Marches. Tiris sighed a little at the loss. He had no idea what sort of contingency plans James Sanderson had. But it was going to fail and fail, hard and fast. He kept on showing himself in distances that only appeared short. He smiled as he shot round the rear of the Linsani knowing all he needed to do now was throw their weaponry out the ship so to speak. They came up behind the Battle crafts and began to wear them down. They did this by slipping between the eight cruisers and short ranging them. Making them hit each other as *The Psyche* flipped and twisted around the ships causing great confusing amongst the small but already struggling armada. Tiris had one more ace up his sleeve. He was going to use his laser repeaters and aim at the engine room and the fuel tanks. That were housed on either side of the ship. He had spent many a night looking over the ship plans and studying them looking for the weakest areas. By the time they caught up with them they were floating on fumes. And their weapons were out matched by *The Defiant* and *The Psyche*. The battle that ensued was epic in proportions and just as they thought they could get away the Trill appeared on the star charts and they began to finish off the Linsani. It didn't take long as they had all the trump cards up their sleeve. They were definitely ahead in this battle. And they weren't going leave until their honour was satisfied. And James, well he was helpless in his endeavours He tried to escape but not enough fuel he saw his end and decided to finish himself. He put the big bore pistol into his mouth and blew his brains out. This was getting to be a trend for future Empire leaders. He rather die than face the torturous thinking that came with being caught.

*

Wade Summit who was watching at a distance had the lonely thought of being the next Emperor. This didn't sit well with him, he had enough humanity in him to know that the Throne was fool's gold. But he knew people would be relying on him trying to see if he would pick up the old mantle. If indeed he had the grit and the savagery to run the Empire. Well, Wade was a little apprehensive to say the least. He was held back and nothing, not even the surety of the troopers and all their might was giving him the courage. He sat there close to panicking and decided he would be better elsewhere. The other side of the Marches and the known Universe. They would be better off out the way, as after this the Marches were an open book and he knew one thing only a fool tries to secure something that was falling apart. And there were a number of them who were on the short list for the Empire. Four to be precise. But Wade was stricken with cowardice. He had no loyalty other than to himself. And this had led him to stay out of the fray and keep himself in good health. This was a sobering thought, he knew that he would have to face The Reapers at some point and this sat cold in his guts. But he was resilient enough to know that he had time on his side. He saw how the

Reapers had handled themselves and this had made him fearful. He wasn't a coward by nature but he had enough sense to know that he may inherit the Throne but then he would have to face the Reapers. And he wasn't looking forward to the confrontation.

*

Tiris headed back to the Orion Nebula. As the Trill finished off the last of the Linsani. They made sure that things were settled with the Trill and the Linsani. Then kicked their engines over and headed back to the Orion system. They got to the junk pile that was mainly around Orion and settled into the Orgis station. The main network of the resistance received a hero's welcome and again they enjoyed every second of it. They had proved themselves time after time that they were seasoned soldiers and that it was a mistake having been blessed with the Reaper armour. But this was all too late as the two previous Emperors had found out to their demise. Tiris smiled and walked through to the sleeping quarters and put his suit on charge. He then bedded and slept for two cycles, a much needed sleep. The rest of the Reapers did the same after celebrating the end to the Linsani company. They left and put on the A.I. to guard them. This was a good thing as Jason Reddit, Terry Reprose and Karin Nova were all heading towards the Orion nebula. Tiris never suspected the three of them were joining up and that it could lead to a great showdown.

Tiris went onto the alpha niner channel and spoke to Tooms. "Tooms my man, can I count on you in the next three or four weeks?"

Tooms hesitated as Tiris had never needed help at all. But Tooms knew something was spooking the Reaper team leader.

Tiris sighed, "I think this next fight is coming right at us".

Tooms snorted a short sniff as if to say (You definitely are desperate). It was a small part of his brain that functioned with empath and he could tell that something was up with the Colonel. His wavering voice and small talk only reinforced the thought, he's scared. He has actually come to the pinnacle of his power and found the whole being relied upon to wave free justice, was well not so much a matter of instincts but he really had the Empire in his grasp and he saw what it did to the last two Emperors. The greed the lust, the power the whole universe was at his fingertips, and he knew it and it weighed heavy on his shoulders. He realised of course that the other guy's greed was a major piece of paranoia. But he would stand his ground and rely on his two squads of Reapers to keep him, and their graces and at the mercy of the rest of the known Universe.

The Marches was a vast and well-travelled Universe. And once he was ready to ascend to the throne he would cast out the demons and unnatural creatures. The ones that held the balance and kept him on his toes were left to a spell of indignation. Where they were purposely overlooked, then when the time was right, they would be dealt with personally and purposefully. He had no Illusions these were mad Troopers, with nothing to lose and everything to gain. But Tiris was a well-trained and state of the art Reaper and no one could refute that. He still hadn't lost a man and knew that things were getting dicey. And he would one day be in the battle of his wits and soul with steadfast Reapers that sent the marrow to chill.

No one could deny him his legacy, he was one mean machine and knowing that the light of the universe shone through every encounter he had and showed no possibility to him ever slowing down. He would weep as the Marches were his to rule over with surety.

Tiris puffed away on his stogie and settled into the rhythm of cathartic rest. His bones ached for peace as did the rest of the reapers. But hail and heartily they awoke the next morning, there troubles seemed a lot more in perspective. They received food and grave nourishment. Each Reaper wore a scowl, each Reaper grinned the deadening upside-down grin of a man who was just about to make legends out of themselves. They grimaced and ate their sustenance. They were really going to make the way for Tiris and the rebels that were swarming to help them, this was a true test of courage each man would be set apart they would be both black and white both bone and spirit, they would carry courage and help each other, the old ways of the faith wars brothers in arms. Knowing that they were truly in a state of readiness, smiling as each trooper put on his Reaper A.I. helmet.

The whole of the Orgis region was suddenly filled with troopers from the last three Generals in the Empire. Jason Reddit, Terry Reprose and Karin Nova. Their ships huge hulk like Battle cruisers entered into the Orion nebula with a swarm of smaller ships who were only in it to see if the Reapers would stand up to a full Imperial.

"Here we go," said Tiris, as the swarm of small cluster ships attacked *The Defiant*. Bucker let the couplings loose and flew straight dead on with the one who would give them the most trouble. And that was Karin Nova. She smiled, a many scarred face and headed straight at *The Psyche*. Bucker was going guts to beggar and flew straight as an arrow at her. She grimaced and set all the fire power to unleash straight at *The Psyche*. But Bucker twisted through space and avoided the majority of laser weapons and majority of their energy beams. He lay a blanket of sand whilst turning and setting off a couple of sidewinder tactical nukes.

"Chew on that Bitch," he said then flicked his cold fusion on to protect his engine. Then he flipped the switches to put on his cloaking device and vanished from sight, twisting and turning and sending his laser cannon blazing at the ship that housed Karin Nova.

"You hungry, bitch?" he said then twisted and came up on the rear of her hulking battle cruiser. Looking at the planet killing housing for Orbital strike missiles. He smiled and shot forth into the close proximity of her hulking battle cruiser. He sent a couple of A.I. mines to stick to the missiles housing, then flipped a rip switch and blew four of those missiles up ripping the hulking ship to pieces. Then he sent another barrage of missiles to blow the rest of Karin Nova into particles of infinity.

Her last words were, "Aww fuck". Then she began feel her insides getting ripped out of her.

In a split second Bucker looked on and said, "No time for a prayer Bitch".

He then hid amongst the debris scouting and picking of the Skirmishers, Meantime *The Defiant* was head to head with Jarson and Terry. Tiris' A.I. was going mental "proximity alert, proximity alert, take evasive actions". He skimmed the ship at the forefront of the attack. And shot up as the two hulking Battlecruisers tried to barrage *The Defiant* with laser and plasma fire. They shot up after *The Defiant* made the clear proximity clearance. And the two hulking beasts of ships realised that Tiris had them both in the palm of his hand. As he ascended *The Psyche* shot down through *The Defiant's* Ion trail and straight at the two Battle cruisers. They were firing at empty space but *The Psyche* was one jump ahead of them as was *The Defiant*. They spun in each other's ion fields and the rear plasma cannons on *The Defiant* shot a full barrage of laser and plasma at the two huge ships, whilst it did that

The Psyche sent forth after locking onto the engines on each ship a full assault of sidewinder nuclear missiles. Seven missiles four on the ship of Jarson and three and a barrage of lasers onto the ship of Terry. They hit and hit the mark well.

"Fuckers," was all the reapers heard in their skulls. They all smiled as the ships were reduced to absolute junk. The engines imploded on the ships as the missiles struck again and again. Reducing the massive ships to junk. The Troopers on board each were left in the icy confines of deep space. Floating and gasping for breath as the limited number of bubble suits were used by the ranking officers. This just left more playtime for Bucker and *The Psyche*.

The Defiant was all hands-on cannons and was also destroying as many as it could of the troopers who were just floating outside *The Defiant*. And skiffs, well they were also an easy target for both ships. They began to blast the small ships and pick off the troopers in bubble suits. Leaving the ones that had no gravity suits to freeze in the carbon freeze of the universe. That was about as merciful as Tiris was going to be and Bucker, he just didn't give a fuck. He had seen too much and been through too much, no, he was playing fish in a barrel for the next few hours, knowing that most of the men he was destroying were hard core troopers of the Imperium and had it coming.

The Psyche attached itself back onto *The Defiant* and Bucker joined the rest of the Reapers. They smiled as Bucker headed towards the helm of *The Defiant* where Tiris waited, knowing that the Sergeant had done an exemplary job. He had made junk of the three hulking battle cruiser and hadn't even broke sweat. Tiris turned his chair round just as the sniper specialised Reaper walked through the doorway. "Bravo, bravo, well done soldier".

The Sargeant, a true man at arms, couldn't help but smile as the Colonel patted his back. "You are truly a weapon of great skill and you will not be forgotten. Your name will be held legend. You are out there amongst the stars, one of the most deadly and affluent of weapons that has ever been my pleasure to work with." Bucker beamed with pride his scars on his face taking that sheen of gleam on them. He knew he had done the job and done it well and to the liking of Tiris. It was his hour.

*

Tooms on the other hand was still heading towards the battle, knowing that he was too late. As he could hear the laser cannons repeating themselves and the missiles hitting home on the three colossal ships and ripping them to bits in the fury of fire and laser. The missiles exploding onto the engines and the housings of their missiles.

"They never had a chance," said Tooms who then sent an all clear from the rear of the battle. Then several Trill warcraft entered just as Bucker and Tiris were finishing off the rest of them. Their long-range scanners picking up the fight as they drew nearer to the Orion Nebula. They got the picture as *The Defiant* and *The Psyche* took out the last of the Imperium, Throughout the Universe Troopers were giving up their positions, were power was absolute, The powerful were turned into helpless pawns that were no longer needed any more. They gave up their decorations of honour and fell silent as Tiris began to free the war torn prisoners on both sides and they had proved that they were an absolute power to themselves and that resistance was futile. Tiris stripped the generals of rank and made them commit suicide. This was a public show of power and Tiris was raised high in ascension and he was truly a pragmatic leader.

Tiris retired about thirty years later and no one succeeded his station. The Imperium was disbanded and left in a diplomatic show of strength to the people to decide on a parliamentary rulership. Holding all things in a diplomatic stead, a democracy to be honest. All of the Linsani worlds were destroyed and all its xenomorphic studies were brought to a halt and all were destroyed and turned to ash. The Linsani codex for all things it created were destroyed and no one could ever make those abominations again. The Universe settled and both the Trill and the Humans were at last at peace with each other. The Universe was a grateful place the drug paradox was banned and treated with the full swift hand of justice, Piracy was stamped out and Paradox was criminalised with the death penalty being implemented if you were caught with the substance. The Trill signed a peace treaty and Humans were able to go into their worlds, Not a shot fired by the Humans and the Trill as they co-existed. They never offended each other's principles and kept to the laws that the two races wrote in honour of the dead and the living. This left the two sides on an even keel, the Faith wars being honoured by both races.

The End

ROCK AND ROLL REFUGEE

Johnny Ebb and the Silver Wing, were finishing up their world tour. They had everything, money, fame and drugs and they were one of the most adored bands ever. Their hard rocking reputation couldn't be better. Johnny Ebb, the front man for the band the Silver Wing, was a slick singer and a poet to a point. When he smiled it was charisma and he lived a twister of a life. But he was about to feel the raw edge of power. The drugs success were going to change and he was about to get a lesson in the macabre supernatural world that was tearing into ours. The demons of hell and the devils were awaiting, the portents that were dawning in this world and sending our world into the fiery cataclysmic dimensions of Hell. Johnny Ebb was to be our saviour. But even his fans couldn't see his fate,

It started with a trip to Scotland; the band were about to appear in Aberdeen and Edinburgh. He and his band had journeyed to a small, cruel, cold fishing town Anstruther and it was a cold, wet and dull day. That was where Johnny met the first of the six witches. Davina. He smiled as he glanced at the raven haired, pale skinned woman who's striking eyes met his. He felt confused yet totally attracted to her. The moon was waxing and she was drawing him into a sinister and horrific game of chess, where both good and evil were going to clash and set the dimensions into a careering cataclysmic event.

The band were hanging round the hotel bar and Johnny and Davina's eyes were locked onto each other.

"Perfect," she said as she approached the handsome, lithe yet muscular figure of Johnny Ebb. She kept her eyes on his as she got closer, she began to recite a small spell to entrap him in her power, "Catina shich gea". She walked over and as she drew closer, she pulled down the veil on her dark gothic hat. This was to mesmerise him.

Johnny dismissed the rest of his band and sat down with Davina. He ordered himself a rum and coke and asked, "What can I get you, Darlin'?"

She smiled lifted her veil and replied, "Bloody Mary".

Johnny smiled as the drinks were brought over. "My name is Johnny, Johnny Ebb".

She smiled her most charming smile and replied, "I'm Davina".

Johnny took her hand, warmed hers with his. She nibbled a bit at the celery, Johnny sipped some of his rum and coke. "Well love where you from?"

She smiled took a sip of her drink. "I'm local." she replied.

Johnny smiled and she continued, "You had a number one. *Blood runs on the three of clubs?*"

Johnny smiled, "Yes it was top for four weeks.".

She smiled and sipped her drink. "I love the bass rift in that song, which one of you plays bass?"

Johnny crunched a piece of ice and answered, "I'm the Bassist". He crunched another piece of ice. "You want free tickets love?" She smiled and replied, "Yes and a T-shirt please?"

He smiled and walked away saying, "Coming right up".

The small spell had just started to take control. It was a small spell but dark and inviting. Jonny came back after a quick word with his manager. The T-shirt's had a big metallic wing on them on a black backdrop. He gave her four of them. And four front row tickets at the Playhouse in Edinburgh. He also gave her backstage passes, another four in total.

She smiled as he handed over the merchandise. "You want another bloody Mary?"

He asked, The grin that could win never left him and she was receptive in the offer. He got himself a pint of Caffrey's at the same time. She finished hers first and they made small talk and got to know one another. Johnny smiled as the conversation continued and Johnny made sure she didn't put her hand in her pocket. They exchanged mobile numbers and Johnny gave her a peck on the cheek. Then said, "I got to go and sleep of this drink, the next concert is in a day and a half".

She smiled and pulled the veil down over her face. "Thank you, sweetheart," she said then left. Johnny was used to meeting and greeting fans but this woman, well she was fascinating to him. And he wasn't aware of her magical ability. But still he was charmed and spellbound by her. But that was her plan, she smiled as she left. He had no idea that he was an unwitting pawn in the fabric of space and time. Heaven and Hell were wrapping round his very conscience and drawing him into a battle for the Earth and its purity and paradise. Johnny slept on with the dark spell growing more and more, in his soul. He woke the next morning and headed to his touring bus where the rest of the band stood around smiling. The drummer asked the million pound question, "I take it you didn't bed her?"

Johnny smiled and said, "I'll see her again".

Just as they were readying to depart and head for Aberdeen a sullen old man stopped Johnny and said, "You be wary of the dark lady she has plans for you".

Johnny sneered and replied, "Aren't you too old to be Jealous?"

The old man gripped him and gripped him tight and replied. "She is more devil than you think".

Johnny sneered again and walked onto the bus, dismissing the old man's warning to be nothing, but foolish superstition. The bus gunned into life and the band sped up north to get to Aberdeen. The spell that Davina had cast was slowly but surely gaining strength. He dismissed the strange feeling to be lust, yet it wasn't gripping him that way. It was stranger, more satisfying, more unique. It was like he had won a major prize. He had a smile on his face and was looking forward to the Playhouse concert. The rest of the band were well they were non-plussed in the affairs of Johnny Ebb. They had seen him with many groupies and much revelry. He could have been an Olympics athlete going for the medal, which was his appetite and he had a ferocious hunger when it came to the lusting and intoxicating, himself, he never needed coaxed into a night of orgies, drugs and alcohol. But somehow this lady was hot on his mind, and was totally taking up all his time, he was enrapt with her. He couldn't shake the spell so he decided to crack open a bottle of tequila see if he could drown her image but alas no, he was just giving her more fuel in the intoxication of him.

He swigged away on the bottle of Tequila. The rest of the band were getting their weed on, smiling and joking. The band comprised of four other members, The first being Carl Rex the drummer. Then the lead guitarist Ronnie Sidling, then the rhythm guitarist Sean Wiseman and last the Keyboard player Ray Colding. They were sat toking and snorting drugs. Smiling and having a good time, Johnny stayed at the back of the bus and he drank his Tequila and smoked some cigarettes. But nothing could stop him from thinking about the beautiful and intoxicating image of Davina.

*

Davina smiled to herself and thought how such spells really affected the rich and the famous, she began to set about the task of vanquishing her enemies. She sang a little chant that would bring about a sudden heat spell that was actually hell opening up its mouth and breathing on the little town of Anstruther. Then her and the other five in her coven grabbed the old man that had tried to warn Johnny about her. They then prepared the man for sacrifice, he was conscious during the whole sacrifice ceremony, after being drugged with a high dose of amphetamine and forced to witness the whole macabre ceremony. He was screaming but the mansion they were in was within a good mile of landscape. First, they cut out his heart and nailed him to a gate to show the world that they meant business. They nailed him to the Vicar's gate, his entrails and heart being fed to a pack of hungry dogs.

After they had finished with the old man and they had nailed him to the local vicars garden gate they began to create a sudden fever throughout the town. It was caused by the drinking water, they had put a dose of a substance that really put the towns folk at the mercy of the witches. Everybody was hallucinating, some were coming down with a fever, an intoxicating one that left them at the mercy of the Witches. They struck down most of the major townsfolk, killing the public officials and cutting out the hearts of certain clergy. Then offering up their pure souls to the Demons and Devils of the planes of Hell.

People began to vanish. Davina was more and more powerful every day and the hallucinogen was tearing through the small town. The chip shops were closed, the museums were also closed, everybody was under the curse. The body of the old man was set as a symbol. But most people were oblivious as they were in a fervour of fever and hallucinating. They began to obsess with each other and no one was safe. It was paranoid delusion and sudden fear and anger that gripped them. They were at each-other's throats and nobody was taking prisoners. They were in a psychic and spellbound storm of dark satanic power. And no one had the ability to control the spells and curses that were flowing. Everybody drank the tainted water, nobody knew what to do about the feverish way and sudden grip of fear, it was too strong to be vanquished and, as I said, the clergy were first to be sacrificed to the Horned god's of hell.

Two more days and Davina and the rest of her coven would be at the concert in Edinburgh. Two of them would stay back at the hotel where they would prepare the magic for the lead singer Johnny Ebb, They were needing his power as a singer and front man to cast a mass inducing spell on the crowd. That would lead to a predominant rise in satanic spells that would cover the world in a cloak of evil. Then they would bring forth the unholy army of zombies, ghouls, vampires and other assorted undead. Then the devils would be ready to take over the Earth.

*

Johnny finished his concert in Aberdeen and headed backstage to the Bucket of ice with the Budweiser in it, he smiled and opened the bottle with an opener on his key chain, he smiled as the liquid refreshment went down real smooth. He gave off an, "Ahhh, that hit the spot," and took another bottle for later on. The rest of the band joined him and they headed away to the Hotel to relax and blaze up a few joints. There was nothing more satisfying than kicking back with the various groupies and dealers of narcotics. They were in Shangri la. A complete and utter heavenly state. They spoke, recounting the various tricks with rifts and musical solo's. They were doing a complete and earth shattering explosion of a tour, this was what they did.

Whilst preparing to bed down they saw the news about the unholy massacre at Anstruther and also the poisoning of the water that sent the towns inhabitants into a ghoulish frenzy of murder and mayhem. Some were even given over to cannibalistic tendencies. They also had ritual ceremonies at which the local clergy were sacrificed to various Devils and Demons. Johnny and the band watched the report with their mouths open. As they showed various bodies of Kirk elders and patrons who had succumb to the poison and toxins that were flowing freely through-out the small town.

"I take it we left just in time," said Ray.

Johnny pointed at the screen and said, "That's the old man that warned me about the woman." The picture of the man who was nailed to the large wooden gate with a huge gash in his chest where they had obviously removed his heart.

*

The six witches were preparing for the night after next when they would have Johnny Ebb in the palm of their hand, so to speak. They would then complete the ritual and Johnny would be the opener of Hells gate. His sacrifice would be enough to bring about the unholy apocalypse in the world. They needed him to shine a light on the very gates to hell. Davina smiled as she saw into the future. She wouldn't fail and her evil life was full of unholy purposes. She had left the Town of Anstruther in the midst of cataclysmic turmoil and yes, she was proud of herself and the other five witches. But nothing was set in stone yet. No, they needed the world's finest chanter to make the locks on Hells gate rust and break. She smiled through her veil and spoke softly to the rest of them.

"We must prepare the way for our unholy chanter" The spell had four more days until it reached the maximum power then he would be a true vessel of evil. An antagonist of sinister proportions. He was the unwitting pawn of evil the other five witches agreed with this, knowing that all darkness would eventually consume light. The other witches were the point of a star, the morning star. With Davina being the middle the focus point of all evil. The points clockwise were. Susan

Grimes, Lorraine Thompson, Carla Knotsford, Shia Lucia and Anne Lowe, who was repeatedly taken by the demonic forces, and was somewhat a treat for the beasts and evil powers of Hell. They each had a mad, cold stare that you never took in or you would feel fear. Most people who had succumb to their cold as steel glare were suddenly bit by a cold wind that ran through the persons soul and body.

Sometimes, and this was only sometimes, they paralyzed the person who had caught their evil stare and was left in despair and hopelessness. This would lead to one of two outcomes, one death, the other a temporary paralysis. This being a reminder that there are powers in the Universe, sinister powers, that few could control. And these six witches had come to be the most sinister and archaic of witches. They had left the town of Anstruther in a blurry state of turmoil, with no regrets about the total evil in its aftermath. They headed to their luxurious rooms, where the place was ideal in space, but not in a way to luxuriant. They began with a salt hexagram, then they boiled a black cat to erase the luck that was imbibed, then they began more spells to make sure they were prepared for anything. Not luck and not goodness were present in the room.

They drew the curtains and began to rock and chant, a very slight chant of murderous words and every now and then they would hiss and sound an insane curse that only devils and demons knew. They were burning toxins like hemlock and arsenic. And various weeds and berries that were poisonous in the edibility. These would be fed to their unwitting pawn who was going to seal the worlds fate. They carried on chanting and creating a rift in the fabric of Earth this would remain open for six days and six nights, by which time they would have the songster Johnny completely full of evil and demonic powers, then using the magic he had been empowered with he would break the locks onto which the Gates would swing open and the world would feel all hell breaking loose. At which point the end of days, as the pits and charnel places would empty and well, Hell on Earth.

*

Craighton Lake woke the morning before the concert. His biblical peers had gotten him a ticket for the concert and right then the news of the small Scottish town was all over the telly. They had HASMAT and chemical engineers taking away the toxic water and testing it for various toxins chemical substances. They were sketchy at first knowing little about the substances only that they were close to hemlock as you got these days and it had sent the entire town insane, murderous and cannibalistic. They were still uncertain as to the body count, but over two thirds of the population had succumbed to the chaotic poisons. Craighton Lake had surmised from this that it was a small but very evil coven of witches. He wasn't sure but the portents and scrying of Davina had led him to believe that the Satanic Coven were in the process of a spell that would break the shackles and chains on the gates of hell's. This is what he believed.

The portents and charms were pointing at the rock group Johnny Ebb and the Silver Wing. He gathered himself together and headed towards the Playhouse on the edge of the city centre, where the band were playing a one night only gig. Davina and three other witches Susan Grimes, Carla Knotsford and Shia Lucia entered the gig venue and headed for the front of the hall. Craighton arrived sometime after the witches had and the auditorium was filling slowly. He too had gotten himself a backstage pass as he posed as a magazine writer with *Mojo*. He thanked the lord for duplicity. And held it dearly that things were really amiss. The whole chemical remnant of the fishing town. Well, it still had an ominous stench in the air. And more and more bodies and remains of bodies were getting dragged out into the light of day. It was very hot and the air hung with decay and desolation it was October and yet so stifling as the air hung and was blisteringly hot. But it was weather that was usually mid-summer temperatures. The peak of summer.

Craighton carried on into the auditorium of the playhouse theatre. It was vast and deeply cavernous 'brilliant acoustics' thought Craighton as he heard the pin drop as the fans began to gather in a slow murmur that was steadily getting more electric as the auditorium, began to fill. He spotted the four witches as well; well they weren't hiding the fact that they were witches of the dark magics. They each wore veils over their heads and they were there with a purpose. They glided silently of the ground but this was hidden in the dark folds of their dark dresses. It was as if they were immune to the laws of physics. Gravity being a firm footing for most, but they were in the respect of their Devil overlord and he was fond of granting them the evil book of black chaotic deeds. This, or as known in the witching world as a Grimoire, a pitch-black book of evil spells and cursed chants. They were chaotic and black as the pitch devil blood of fire. They had only their servitude to lean on and that was only when the moon was at the pinnacle and then they had to sacrifice.

Children were the norm, especially with their virginity intact. They especially liked teenagers who were at the beginning of puberty. They found females especially were a must to their Devil masters, the horned ones had an evil and enticing grip on them. And favoured them at the outset. They sacrificed once a month at least and every time they did so they were imbibed with deathly evil spells and curses if you heard some of the cursing that went on in those summoning times your body would boil in the fasting fires of hell. And no one felt the frenzy of a devil like an innocent; no, they were particular about the innocence of the world being ebbed out of itself. Slowly giving rise to the bloody chaotic plane of Hell.

The music struck with a loud whining of an electric guitar in a high toned piercing scream of metal. Then came the bass walking along as the rhythm guitar sent into the playhouse. "Mmmm back tack a lack. Johnny is home and that's a fact smiling, sending lights and praise. As you know Johnny was left in a daze". He smiled and continued. "Ahhhh sugar pop my name is top, reckon you know about my ways, smiling watching and shaken this malaise". The song carried on and the audience was mesmerised. He did a full set of about ten songs and no renditions. Then the music stopped and he smiled, "Thank you everyone you've been great!" then bang, as the metal hit the ground. Then the stage went black and Johnny smiled and headed to the exit on the stage. He was stunned as the auditorium went silent then a cheer as loud as the wind hitting ninety miles an hour.

It was the most appreciative thunder he had ever rolled into. He popped the cap on a bud and smoked a joint of a different kind of bud. Then the backstage was opened up for those with passes. And Davinna settled her gaze once again on the handsome, smiling, charismatic Johnny. This time the spell really took hold She murmured another slight spell of dark enticing delight. And Johnny was spell bound by her. He didn't see this coming; Craighton watched from the wings of the stage. Noting Davina as the head straight away, as she had more spirit about her. He smiled and watched as her and her coven were greeted by the band as they passed them by, all except Johnny who was powerless over this witch. That word never came up and he had really fallen for the head witch. He walked forward and spoke to her. The other three were giggling like schoolgirls. But there was something off about it, they seemed too eager. To excitable.

Craighton smiled and said, "That Grimm Bitch". Then he walked over with his press I.D. and said to Johnny, "I'm Craighton J. Lake, I write for *Mojo*. I was told that you were on the greatest achiever award" Johnny smiled and said to Davina. "Head out back to the tour bus I'll only be half an hour".

Davina set the last of the spells alight with the stroke of her hand. Then her and the other three glided away. "Okay Mr Lake. You got my attention, And as you can see, I don't have much time".

Craighton smiled. "Well Mr Ebb, I won't keep you long".

Johnny smiled and mopped his brow with an adidas towel. Then he said, "Fire away Mr Lake".

Craighton smiled and produced a small digital recorder. "I see Mr Ebb that you have a building of power on the stage".

Johnny smiled and sat down, "Yip we are pretty intense".

Craighton carried on recording, "You don't seem to be on an ego trip either Mr Ebb?"

Johnny smiled and continued with an answer, "I give the audience and fans what they want, and that is pure talent".

Craighton smirked at that answer. Johnny smiled and said to Craighton, "Carry on my man".

Craighton continued, "Does your pop bubble gum poetry that leaves girls and women in general satisfied is it a part of your routine?"

Johnny smiled and said, "How can you ask a question like that when you already stated that I wasn't on an ego trip, that sir is a contradiction in terms."

Craighton smiled and said to himself. "You have no Idea Mr Ebb".

Craighton began to ask some standard questions, "is the next album another Tour de force of heavy blues, and sparkling connections that you seem to have with your fans worldwide."

Johnny gave off a small laugh as if the question itself were redundant. Then he replied, "Well man, the thing with my music is that it is deep in my soul and that is why the connection with my fans is so powerful."

Craighton smiled and nodded. "I know I know," he said as he started to remember the questions. This went on for ten minutes. "And last but not least, Do you agree that sometimes and I mean only sometimes, that your music is detrimental to your fans".

Again, Johnny laughed "I don't know what you mean Craighton," Johnny smiled, and Craighton finished by asking what the next album was called. "We haven't come up with a title but it's in the works we are told by the manager and a lot of pundits that there may be three or four top ten's on it".

Craighton shook his hand and felt the subtle flow of what could only be a small magic spell course through his hands. "Well talk again soon," Said Johnny and he headed away towards the rest of the group. Craighton looked at the way that he headed. Then he boarded the tour bus and sat next to Davina. She smiled her most charming smile. Then they began to talk.

*

Craighton on the other hand was following the bus at a safe distance. As it headed back to Sheffield. He watched carefully knowing that he had just gotten a sense of the four witches. The other two were preparing another offering to the Hell mouth. This one a small girl, she was terrified as the ceremonial dagger was raised, then the child screamed. and blood, as her heart drained into the bottom of the table that was used by the coven. The blood had stained the oak and I mean stained, as the more they sacrificed the darker the wood got. The unholy spirits and demonic forces were gradually getting released. They had been at it for a number of years, so the wood as you could imagine was blacker than pitch in certain areas. They then went about the task of empowering themselves by cooking the child's heart. Lorraine took the first bite and cackled as the warm muscular flesh with what blood was left went down her throat. And she began to feel the unholy powers that were coursing throughout the room Anne felt no attention at all but was ready to let the evil spirits into her vessel of a body. Then the room dimmed as the candles went out and the air began to crack and pop, Lightning flew with sparks then lifted the body of the child and dragged her empty carcass into the Ninth plane of Hell, forgotten innocence. They then began to murmur as the spell was coursing through their bodies and doing its malevolent best. They knew that soon when the moon bled that they would have an opportunity to send earth into the hellish planes of evil. This was the nightmarish plans that well all evil and malevolent forces were trying to do.

Craighton felt the shift in power and called on his Archangel Darrius. He needed guidance and he needed to help Craighton out. Darius smiled and the wings of the golden angel were beating slowly around Craighton.

"Yes Craighton?" came the question from Darius.

Craighton smiled and said a small prayer in the hope of being worthy of the gifts that he was well, imbibed with. Craighton smiled and replied. "Holy one can you see into the future?"

Darius smiled and light shone onto Craighton. Darius spoke, "I see you are trying to stop the apocalypse from happening." Darius gave slight, but deep in his chest, laugh almost like a groan.

Craighton smiled and said, "Do you know how long until we run out of time and the dimension shifts out our favour?"

Darius sighed and thought, 'as always we are needed to protect the flock of brethren', He then beat his wings some more and said, "You won't like this, Hunter".

Craighton grimaced a little and the Angel smiled and replied, "You have six days counting this one".

Craighton smiled and thought, 'never enough time'. Darius drifted away and headed back to the gates of heaven. Knowing that he would be needed. And time was short. He smiled as the altar shone, on to which his piety was celebrated. And the children of god surrounded him as he entered singing hymns of love and peace. He grew quiet and sombre yet holy and satisfied at the same time. Darius lay in his feathered bed of pristine glory and thanked the maker for some rest.

*

Craighton on the other hand was in trouble and knew it too. He had to gather a team of Demon hunters and he had only a short time to do so. He phoned over to America and got in contact with Father Clayton. Father Clayton who had vanquished the Soul Collector and had made sure that the summoner who had been trying to end the earth was punished. And not by Holy means either.

He smiled as he picked up the phone and said, "Ahh Craighton how's the assignment going?"

Craighton was very abrupt and made the next comment a statement of absolute fact, "I need you over here man, they've already wiped out a small town".

Father Clayton smiled and rested his rosary beads on top of his Bible. "You want me to bring Carlos?"

Craighton smiled and looked at the scars on the underside of his arms remembering. That day and night he had drowned the evil demons in a holy lake, Their nails had raked and burned Craighton's flesh and scarred and seared the arms. Craighton spoke after a brief pause. "Yeah man that would be aces".

Father Clayton smiled a sorrowful smile and said, "I'll get in touch with him today, How many days did you say we have?"

Craighton breathed a shallow breath and replied, "Six including today". Father Clayton hung up the phone and set the arduous task of gathering a hunting team. He got in contact with Carlos, and also Robert Crufax. He knew that there was virtually no time to act and that the scales of justice didn't even come into this, its evil and I mean evil incarnate. These Witches were gaining so much power in the known universe that they would do either of two things, one destroy the earth or destroy themselves trying, but when they destroyed themselves, they would usher in something so diabolical and evil that most of mankind would be torn asunder and destroyed. Either way it would be mass destruction. Craighton knew this of course but held the holy belief, that he and the rest of the hunters would vanquish the Witches and send them into the hellish dimension where they would know suffering for all eternity. Robert and Carlos boarded a plane and headed for Edinburgh Airport where they would meet up with Craighton who was getting that cold feeling again.

*

The four witches, sat on the tour Bus of Johnny Ebb and they smoked a little reefer and did a little ching. They were quite comfortable and their hardened looks took on a gentle glow. One that would easily beguile the most intelligent of men. But they kept up a psychic link with each, hissing and cursing at each other as though things were perfect for their paths of diabolical deeds. They needed though, somehow to get Johnny away and into a den where they would prepare his immortal soul for sacrifice. They hissed and laughed as the whole bus were having a great time in their heads, they showed little thought for the mind state of drugs and alcohol. They were completely immune to their effects. But the Four of them made it look good.

Then when the bus settled into a sleep like state the four of them began a small chant, a small psionic chant that was only noticeable to the recipients ears and that was Johnny. The rest of the bus slept on. Johnny looked at Davina with a spellbound stare. He then closed the gap between him and her, slowly like a man with nothing other than purposes.

Davina smiled and hissed as he got closer. "Ahh Johnny," she said with the power of her mind. Johnny's face was impassive and totally spellbound. "My Love!" she continued, "My Heart's desire…"

Johnny was at her mercy and no one else knew this more than Johnny.

"You are the one we seek" Johnny Stood looking at her. Transfixed, mesmerised and as powerless as a baby. Then the bus eased to a halt and they sat at the junction. Johnny's face was impassive straight and to the point. She carried on, "We have plans for you plans that will change the world."

Johnny was blank, motionless carried on staring into her cold dark eyes. Her whole expression changed into a sharp craggy-faced stare, one that shone like an animal a starved angry animal. But still Johnny stared at her, locking with her black as pitch eyes. She scowled at him then hissed. The rest of the bus aside from the other three witches were in a comatose state. Davina hissed again and spoke another dark spell. Johnny was totally under her power.

Susan smiled and said, "What now Davinaaa?"

The other three witches looked at her knowing that only one matter needed tended to and that was, the rest of the band and the bus driver.

"Cut their throats and let the blood run free".

The four witches screamed in glorious unison knowing that this was the most glorious part the examples. They even drank a little blood as they carried on with the diabolical task. Then they exited the bus and the other two witches who were right behind them parked a minivan into which they all climbed. Headed back to the hotel room that was now a sacrificial room.

*

Craighton came up behind the bus with the corpses of the Silver Wing and the bus driver. He walked gingerly to the open door of the bus and noticed the blood seeping down the stair. He knew the worst had happened. He pulled out his mobile phone and phoned the police. They arrived promptly in vans and jeeps with forensic investigators. They were lucky to get the ones that were there as most of the force were up in Anstruther. They arrived and Craighton greeted them with his sombre impassive stare, the grave and only stare that was his in times like these.

A detective Monohan was first to approach the Demon Hunter. He took the man's hand in his and the first thing the detective noticed was the scars on Craighton's arms. He knew this was no coincidence, no he was obviously an expert in occult findings and this just made Monohan's job that little bit more, tricky. Knowing that it could and probably will get diplomatic.

Craighton sighed, the man smiled a straight smile and asked Craighton, "How come you are here and what part do you play in this?"

Craighton smiled, "I'm an occult detective from The Vatican and I hold degrees in psychology and para-psychology".

Monohan gave a small laugh at the sheer cheek of the hunter. Monohan then pulled on his rubber examination gloves. "This isn't an Exorcism, Mr…?"

Craighton shook his head and said, "Lake, Craighton Lake".

Monohan smiled at the frame of the man who was easily controlling himself.

"They took the lead singer Mr Johnny Ebb," said Craighton. "Yeah, I know the man well that is to say my daughter is a huge fan of his".

Craighton looked in the doorway of the bus. "They weren't leaving any witnesses," Craighton sighed, a thought that was well clear and decisive.

"They are Satanic Witches who are responsible for the Anstruther incident."

Monohan looked at the man with a serious frown and said, "Go on!"

Craighton smiled and watched as the men in white suits began to sort their way through the carnage. "They are responsible for over fifty deaths and that's just in Europe."

Monohan looked at the Hunter and said, "I take it this isn't about money?"

Craighton shook his head, "No this is definitely not about money".

Monohan silenced himself letting the last piece of information settle into his thoughts. Then he asked, "Is there anything I can do to help you in this matter?"

Craighton smiled and replied, "Just let me have a quick look, then leave me be, I've got a couple of specialists coming from across the pond". He then boarded the bus and looked around looking at the cuts that were on the band and the driver, he noticed that the cuts were expertly done and done with coldness and really sharp knives.

"Not your average Butcher," said one of the Technicians.

Craighton gave off a "Mmmm" and held himself deep in thought. The four of them must have enjoyed it he thought. You can tell by the way the cuts are situated that they were in the throes of a blood lust. Enjoying every single minute of the acts of carnage. Taking time to quell their bloodlust as it happened upon them. He stepped of the bus and headed straight to his car, a silver Volkswagen Golf. He then headed off towards the airport as their plane would be landing in an hour. It would take him half an hour to get there. Then he would be at full strength, the three of them would take up this arduous task with great power knowing that when the dice were thrown, they were on the Lords side.

*

The six witches tied Johnny to the sacrificing altar and table and held him gagged for his honour. They then went about preparing the sweet bread and other Devilish foods, They had a large cauldron in which they mixed various poisons into the human flesh and organs. They did this with purpose and exacting elation, enjoying their work and sacrifice. They held slight their cannibalistic tendencies, knowing that they were easily leant to the habit of eating human meat. And a blood test had often captured a cannibal. The bacterium condition when searched for in the blood had captured a few of the brethren. It also gave the brethren a slight greyish appearance that was a tell-tale, on something that they had to hide. Thats why the Veil. The dark colours. The whole living in shadows.

Now your average vampire, it could be well, caught as pale and wanting for fresh blood, A ghoul, they had that slight greyish tinge and that wasn't just because of the consumption of human meat, it was the poison also a poison of exact lethality. That even a small taste of the sweet breads would kill in a matter of seconds and this to them was called Merrick. And was used in the curing of human flesh. Also, the flesh was kept at a chill level, some frozen in pots and used as the ghouls wished. They then after killing several children they prepared the meat to be transported to a den of ghouls, whom they had a small treaty with. Davina wrapped the parcel of cured meats into a large sheet of brown greaseproof paper. It was thirty kilos of flesh and fifty kilos of organs all soaked and prepared for the ghouls. The head ghoul was a demon called Sattrani, a Romanian ex pat now over here as the pickings were slim in his home country. He smiled and sat down as the parcel was brought to his door of his freezing ice cold apartment. After Sattrani there was a golficous his right hand and as strong as four men having his work cut out for him by carrying what is known in the world to be dead weight. There were three others in this den, Persin,

Moult and Fenway. They had a voracious appetite for sweet breads of all kinds. Especially children. No one had met these ghouls and lived to tell the tale.

*

Darius had come upon one or two ghouls but he made sure they didn't survive meeting him. He was a holy Avenger and kept score and when he needed to, he would exercise his holy and divine powers then would deal with the problem. He saw the ghoulish parcel getting hoisted into the back of a refrigerated van and flew through to the other end of the town in Edinburgh. Darius poised waiting to see the location of the van. It was 3 am and the guy wasn't holding any prisoners and sped to the ghouls lair. Darius followed, his golden armour flowing into the air was darkened, his eyes were fixed and he was sure of one thing that their time would come.

He would get back in touch with Craighton when he had a good look at this parcel as it was exchanged into the lair of the Demonized Ghouls. They unwrapped part of it, then Sattrani tasted a small morsel. He breathed in after ingesting, waiting for the cold poison to give him that kick of evil power. Darius watched waited for the ghoul to hand over the money for the Unholy parcel of meat then Darius snarled and flew to the church house where the three demon hunters were located, the vicar an Eli Patronage was finishing off his sermon. Darius walked into the small quaint cottage and drew holy breath, then spoke to Craighton.

"There are Ghouls in Edinburgh and they have an allegiance with your Satanic Witches."

Craighton whispered a small prayer then came off his knees and replied, "What do we need to do Darius?" The question was quiet and calm.

Darius lifted his golden sword and replied, "It just complicates matters Craighton"

Craighton smiled and lit a candle for his wife and young daughter who had fallen victim to a group of vampires. He sighed and carried on speaking to the avenging angel. "Where are they Darius?"

Darius shifted slightly in the ethereal plane of existence. And let the calm beating of his wings cool the mind of Craighton. Craighton said a few prayers then headed to the back room where there was a holy armoury sat there. He lifted his preferred weapon, which being a Colt 45 special with hollow points to make sure that the bullets mushroomed and flayed in the body of whomever it hit. He was in the advanced ways of hunting and had heard the calling to arms for the Lord soon after his daughter and wife had been left bloodless, and dead.

Craighton carried on pushing bullets into the revolver's chambers. Six in total. He then filled his leather jacket pocket with at least twenty of the bullets. He remembered when he had first encountered Darius and how he had helped to ease the pain of loss. Then after a few days vigil he was asked if he would like to get pay back on the demonic forces that were spilling into this world. Craighton had been wary at first, but as more and more he saw into the heart of evil and darkness, the more he watched the more he disliked what was growing more and more in power in this world. He knew he had to do something that was when he first met Father Clayton who explained some of the ways which they used on Demons, Devils and the undead.

He had a strong affinity with the way of the holy men that he had come to respect. He had met other demon hunters, all with a similar calling to the vanquishing of the evil that was growing more in strength and getting bolder in the calling to destroy the Earth and Heaven. And all this over Jealousy, the pandemonium where Lucifer sat with the other demons, devils and evil forces. Was growing strong and getting bolder. They were getting more supporters into their armies. More and more they were growing and more and more the followers of the holy and divine were getting sacrificed and used in the Dark one's purposes. Unholy deeds and possession of a pure soul was happening more and more.

Craighton then picked up his Bowie knife and slid it into its sheath. Carlos and Robert Crufax were also in the armoury loading their weapons and saying prayers. They had a solemn but much needed task and that was to save Johnny Ebb. And stop the malevolent forces from opening the unholy Prison of Hell. If this happened the world would be made a sacrifice, zombie's and various other undead would rise and the beautiful world that we know will be a bloody and chaotic mess. People will die in their thousands, ancient demons and devils will swarm over the human race, there will be so much gorging and feeding of flesh and bone. Child, adult, handicap, will suffer like nothing ever had suffered before. Craighton finished blessing the weapons then gave it a light drizzle of holy water.

*

Davina sighed a little as the sun rose and they fell into their cursed sleep. The daemons and demons that were looking at the six satanic witches as they carried on their slumber knowing that they would rise just as the sun set. They smiled and licked their bony lips with their lizard-like tongues and hissed and said small devilish curses that were aimed at the six satanic witches. They laughed as the spells made themselves a matter for all diabolical needs. They hissed and left. The witches grew more in power. They knew that things were strong in that season of death. The cold, cold bite of winter was truly in their favour. They saw one thing and one thing only and that was Pandemonium's victory.

*

Robert smiled as the dawn drew upon, them he could feel his spirits being lifted as did the other two. Carlo's lifted his serrated machete and also his sawn-off shotgun, these weapons too had been blessed. Robert had his silver bulleted Uzi nine millimetre with several magazines holding forty rounds each. They then jumped into action, straight into their Volkswagen Golf and headed to the ghouls lair. They were set in purpose and knew that this was the best course of action. The ghouls were a powerful enemy and had strong evil links to hell. But then so did the witches. And fealty was the name of their methods. They had true paths and true evil incarnation was flowing through them.They had everything to gain and well the only thing they would lose would be their mortal coil. They would be free.

Sattrani rose, sensing the hunters coming closer, he had a feeling that this would happen. The ice box of a house was split into to two parts, one was dining, the other preparation of the Iced flesh and poisons, Merrick rose from his cold slab of metal that he had made specifically to keep him cold. The air hung with a bitter smell of arsenic and other highly deadly poisons. These were constantly pumped into the house. And no one had entered and survived. The hunters arrived and the first thing they noticed was the seal along the bottom of the door. It was a refrigerator seal and a bloody good one. It opened inwards, this being the only difference. Craighton produced his tear gas mask as did the other two. They then tried to gain entry; this was a difficult process but they had a good crack at it. They produced, from out the boot of their car, a large crowbar, that they wedged into the sides of the door.

Sattrani was standing just at the side of the lobby, waiting for the three of them to get closer, he then just as Robert was closing in popped round the corner and dug a deep knife wound in his abdomen. Craighton held him as he fell. Carlos shot the ghoul with both barrels. Sending buck shot right through the head ghouls neck and chest. His black blood pumped onto the floor as he lay their dying of holy buck shot.

Sattrani looked at the two hunters and said to Craighton, "You're too late blessed ones, the witches have already moved lairs."

Craighton took one look, as the last of his thick as pitch blood, bubbled on the ice cold floor. He then did what was necessary. He cut the ghouls head clean off with his Bowie blade. They then set about the task of killing the other four. They left the wounded, Robert at the front door just in case any of the ghouls got past them. Robert cocked the Uzi and waited feeling nothing was as it seemed. They cut of the heads and blew holes in the hearts of the rest of the ghouls. They were kind of assuming the poisonous air would finish them off. But the hunters were prepared and they knew there was little the ghouls could do it being daylight and they were in a deep cold, sleep.

Craighton and Carlos, after doing the deed, hoisted Robert and he limped back to the car. They then drove him to the local hospital. Where they made sure he was stitched up and sorted out. They did their duties (the nurses that is) and Craighton explained that the blade may be envenomed. The sister who was in charge that night made sure that the appropriate blood tests were done and the poisons were treated. But Robert would be out of the game for a number of weeks. Craighton knew this was uncontrollable and well, well he and Carlos were a force to be reckoned with.

Carlos said as they went back to the church, "We have got to get those witches"

Craighton shifted the car into gear and they headed to the Church. He didn't say a word all the way there. His look said it all, it was cold and ironlike. No emotion other than sheer rage that had been building up for a number of days now. He smiled as he thought about where the coven were. Then laughed, he knew who could be the best person for that information. Ammanda White and Christine White, they would have to get across the water to a small coastal town Aberdour where the two sisters owned a charming shop and Craighton had often taken the sisters in his confidence, knowing that the two of them were powerful with magics and nature. Amanda White, the younger of the two had helped Craighton track down a group of wamphyre. She had been of great help to Craighton and when the phone rang into their little shop, she had known who exactly it was.

"Hello Mr Lake!" came the statement.

Craighton smiled knowing who it was that picked up the phone, "Hello Amanda".

She smiled a winning sunshine smile and he could feel the heavenly vibrations pour down on him, his Chakras beating and giving him unmovable spirit, then the smell of lavender. All the luck in the world including protection came from the sensory perception of smell and the nose.

"You need help Craighton?"

Craighton smiled and huffed at the same time. "Yes Amanda," came the response of Craighton.

She drew a quick charm in the air and her sister Chris invoked a candle with a circle of life.

"We need the whereabouts of a coven, a satanic coven".

Chris smiled, no sparks the spell was cast.

Craighton waited a moment or two then Amanda continued. "Be at our shop by midday"

Craighton smiled and Carlos and him headed straight to cross the Forth and arrive at the small seaside town of Aberdour. It only took an hour.

*

The moving of Johnny Ebb was of course necessary. They had to find the bloodiest of Ley lines where evil had interrupted the grace of angelic coming. It had been a fierce and bloody battle on a small piece of land deep in the highlands where Fae folk and goblin had grown up together only to end up as bitter bloody enemies. This was where the last of the unicorns had come to lay down their life with the holy protection of the Lord. They had seen to another enchanting way and will with Paladins and Holy Clerics had fended of the Demon hordes as they gathered and started to rise up with the might of what they had built, Pandemonium.

But Grey Hawk who had travelled from his world had cast a mighty hand in the vanquishing of Demon, Devil and all out evil. As soon as he had seen the last of the Paladins going to hell and never being saved, he knew that he had to act. And gathering the party of knights, barbarians, monks, thieves and clerics. He saved the last earthly Paladin and the Barbarians had vanquished Beelzebub. Throwing his gigantic body into the sea.

The witches stood at a ceremonial point, Where evil had been vanquished, now they would open up that old wound with a chanters voice and delivering his soul to the Lord of the Underworld, Satan himself. Where he waited, ebbed in black and blood of many a pure soul was giving to him to dine on. Davina called on the unholy powers of hell to come forth and sleep a while in her dark black ebony soul. They had four days left and knew that the closer to the pinnacle of power the more that things would gather in absence of good all evil would prevail. Darkness would ring out across the land with evil and malevolent forces growing more powerful. Sending where fresh virgin souls lived into all Hell.

*

Craighton arrived at the Green Witches shop with Carlos; Robert was left behind to heal and surmise the best laid plans. What he was hoping for was the exact plan of action to stop the six diabolical witches, destroy them and save the day. He had a rough idea what was needed and had sent a text through to the sisters so as they wouldn't fall short. He needed several wax angelic candles, and several ,myrrh anointments to bring forth the power of the Lord Jesus Christ, who had vanquished many demon devil and other underworld deities.

Craighton and Carlos arrived and were handed the summoning tools that they needed. This was to let the avenging angels of heaven right at the witches of satanic rites. And the benevolent forces of heaven would send them reeling back into hell. But nothing so valuable and needed was easy to come by, they stayed and spoke with the two white witches and were told the proper process for unleashing heavens holy avengers whilst the archangels stood back and waited for the hells gate to open. They would then vanquish the armies of the nine planes of hell and send their planes deeper into chaos and further from the heavenly abodes. This had been stewing between hell and heaven for thousands of years. They knew that if they could control earth by sending it into unholy chaos they would be close enough to finish the heavenly planes and win the war that had been raging since, well forever.

God was well pleased with Craighton and Carlos knowing that they two had been powerful in this extremely sensitives time. The rest of the Vatican had been impressed by the demon hunters that had been quick to the calling of God. Knowing that there were many white souls on the face earth who were not just eager, but had been given gifts to help the heavenly angels in this, what was an unholy war against Lucifer and all his demons, devils and daemons.

*

Carlos smiled as they spoke to the two sisters who were eager to help.

"I Know this Amanda," came the curt reply from Craighton who was needing to justify why the urgency as according to Chris and Amanda, "The moon hasn't hit its bloody fullest yet". Amanda Craighton smiled as she wasn't through with her point, "You see they may have more than one opportunity at opening the hells mouth." She stated quite blatantly.

Craighton shook his head and returned, "I know it peaks twice in this cold winter's moon, A hunters moon and a zenith of blood a blood moon".

"That follows the Hunters moon." She nodded and smiled back at the Hunter. "You are missing the point Craighton," she replied.

At which point Christine piped in, "If they can make his sacrifice last through the two moons they will unleash a surge of infinite evil, one that would take a millennia to recover from and that will make the devils and demons practically immune to heavenly ways and words…"

"Then," Amanda butted in, "that would mean we would be in an almighty scrap with the unholy forces. They would gain so much power that it would be an out and out fight".

Craighton looked on after the lady finished.

"That's why they pay us the big bucks," said Carlos.

"You need to save the singer Johnny Ebb," said Chris. "If their plans fail then hell will weaken like I said but remember they have the two points to aim for and they will be going for the bloody double."

Craighton laughed a little and said, "We only have two more days to find them". T

hey then started to look over the requisitions that they had and needed to vanquish all evil, that was surging up from the Ley lines and easing out as cosmic magic from the stars and moon. This was growing more in power and Craighton knew this he had to find the singer Johnny Ebb before they began the long slow painful sacrifice at which point he will give off an unholy scream that would chill the marrow of even the hardest of souls. Then the portal would open Johnny would be swallowed into hell's mouth and bang all hell will break loose. Energies were aligning against the hunters and it was looking more and more grim.

*

The six witches began to draw on their unholy powers. They prayed in a most unholy way, each offering their bodies as vessels to the demons and devils. They anointed the clearing with blood, both theirs and various children that they had grabbed and made them suffer with various torturing devices. Bleeding them all slowly, Johnny sat down and shivered as the cackling and profanity of the witches seemed to grow fiercer and fiercer. They partook the sweet breads and drank blood like it was wine. Offering up dying children that were screaming in pain. Knowing that this was as evil as it got and they were not going to be saved.

The smell of burning innocent flesh and the smell of hemlock was circulating the clearing. Johnny carried on shivering to the pit of his soul, he had given up all chance of freedom and knew there was little he could do to reason and stop the satanic sisters of blood and bone. The six witches carried on murmuring and chanting. Every now and then one of them would cackle an insane hollow cackle. Johnny squeezed his eyes shut and stopped crying. Nope this wasn't going to end well but something was in his mind something foreign yet benevolent. It was offering a spark of hope; he smiled a little as the voice was distance yet there. It was Darius, he was holding out a semblance of hope. It was distant yet near, a small light of a pure candle, unto which he held the rock stars soul with a minor semblance of hope.

The angel smiled and the rockstar gained a little more hope. He cocked his head and blanked out the screaming and murmured chanting that was diabolical and wouldn't shut up, it was tearing his head to pieces. But the holy light of the divine angel was weighing his soul down like an anchor and settling his soul. The last of the children were sacrificed and it was the third day and devilish night with things becoming more and more insane. He was, at one point, up until the angel contacted him, well, he was a gibbering wreck. The eye of the lord had been well placed onto the forehead of the young rockstar, lucky he was a catholic and had been christened.

*

Craighton began summoning forth the powers of heaven, Carlos held the candle aloft and they began to say the Lord's Prayer whilst burning myrrh. They knew that they didn't have long to go, one more day and night and they would have to stop the satanic witches. But this was a problem in itself as they didn't know where. Darius then got in contact with the two demon hunters.

"Craighton," said Darius. "I know where they are".

Craighton Smiled and muttered, "Thank you Lord".

Darius continued, "They are further north in a clearing next to an old black tree. The one in which they had sacrificed the Last Unicorn".

Craighton sighed a little and said, "Where Darius and how far?"

The avenging angel smiled and beat his wings. "Closer than you think."

Craighton smiled and Darius showed him the way. It was a good three to four hours away and they had to hurry.

*

Meanwhile Chris and Amanda carried on their benevolent spell casting, hoping that they would be able to send a holy barrage of divinity at the witches. This was taking up more time than they had, but it was necessary and time was changing a normal day with its divinities, into a cold dark night, with the bloodiest moon that they had ever encountered. The six satanic witches had obviously grown in strength and diabolical power. They must have made the correct sacrifices to the lord of devils and demons, Lucifer their master. But Amanda and Chris both had a sense of hope, so they carried on chanting and reciting magical charms that were full of light and hope. The hunters carried on heading to the clearing, they could see that the place was shaded over and turned to darkness nothing good was alive and it left a rim of malicious weeds and deadly poisonous fungi.

The creatures who hadn't made it out the clearing in time were choked and starved of air and died. Such was the nature of things and things this tainted were strong in dark magic and evil abominations hid in the shady clearing, next to the great dark oak tree. The six witches carried on their unholy vigil. Each one of them inviting demons and devils into their black souls. To take over and hold all hell in their sway. The possession of their souls well it was of no major consequence and they were cursed enough to know that they were truly malevolent, truly evil and they could see the dawn of hellfire come closer.

The fourth day was approaching and Craighton came upon the rim of evil that was polluting the very idyllic forest. The roots were being chewed up from the roots of the great black oak and the poisonous energy from the curses were enveloping the whole forest. Craighton looked at the dead animals and birds. They had turned black with poison and the very ground was a grey cursed colour. He could see the black pumping itself along the various tree roots and flowers which were wilted and dying. They too were turning black, with evil and malicious intent.

"If this aint, cursed," said Craighton. "Then I'd hate to see the end result".

Carlos rested his shotgun on his shoulder and replied, "Looks like we are just in time".

Craighton smiled and poised over a dead rabbit that had rotted in an untimely way. "Just goes to show that the most unnatural thing would destroy the most innocent and beautiful thing, leaving the thing to rot and die in the cold light of day."

Craighton shushed Carlos as he heard in the distance the macabre chanting of the witches. He could feel the cold unearthly magics of hell as a curse of old was growing stronger, he could hear the witches cursing and chanting the evil diabolical language of hell. The smell of decay was all around and very stifling causing Carlos to wretch some. Craighton breathed out his lungs and took small shallow breaths knowing that whatever killed the local animals was obviously in the very air they breathed. More dead animals but they were getting blacker the closer they came to the Oak tree. The sinister murmuring was growing slightly as they closed the distance, that's when they saw it the human totem pole of children some killed others were left to rot and various organs and orifices were open and parts removed to either appease their hunger or for the sheer pleasure of torture.

They had made an ultimate sacrifice to Hell and they now had the last one to go. Johnny smiled a sad small smile as he was staked to the ground and placed on his eye lids were the flesh-eating purple worms. Then they cut his wrists and ankles and began to bleed him slowly all the while keeping up an unholy murmur. A chant that chilled the very marrow of your body. There was no way out, Johnny cried a little and did a little begging, seeing if he could reason with the six cannibalistic witches, he was already beyond the point of terror and he really could see his life ending at the hands of the demon worshipping witches.

'Black as pitch' came one of the demons voices through the empty vessel of a witch. 'We purify with blood' came another voice this time from a different witch there were sparks and sudden drenching in bloody rain. Johnny closed his eyes after a minute or two. Each witch was possessed by a demon or devil. They were bucking and braying, contorting and twisting into unnatural shapes whilst they hissed at Johnny as his blood was slowly draining away. And this was the demise of Johnny, he smiled a little and began to sing one of his songs 'Blood on the three of clubs.' There appeared to be no way out of this situation.

Then again, the Angel spoke to him with a calming voice. "Be still my song master".

Johnny let a tear drip off him and held it together as the chanting and squeals of the possessed witches was getting louder and more sporadic. As the rhyming and evil event was beginning to heighten every now and then Davina would call on the horned ones to subjugate their offering with all the powers in Hell. They were indeed into the very mouth of the Hell planes. That day passed into night then into day again.

*

The two demon hunters were lost in that forlorn, desolate wooded glade where everything looked like it was turning to poison. The very roots and plants were stained black, from the ground up to the treetops. Birds and animals were running making a desperate attempt at survival. Most had already ingested and breathed in the unholy diseased evil that was getting stronger. Most died at the inhalation of the dark magic that was engulfing the majority of the forest. And killing off the inhabitants. This was only becoming more and more powerful, more decay, more desolation. It grew dark for the two hunters who by surmising the rate it was spreading were not hopeful about curing it. They knew that if they didn't stop it soon it would spill into the urban towns and villages. But nothing. Craighton smiled and noticed several dead birds and a deer. Lying decaying into the black bracken on the floor of the forest. He realised that some-how they had come full circle on themselves. They were lost in this grey and black dying woods,

*

Amanda and Chris sat waiting for the dawn to rise. Knowing that the spells they had just used had had little effect. But they still held out hope for Craighton, knowing he was a formidable adversary and had been known to bring about divine intervention. A miracle from God himself. A sure fire way to clean things up. He rounded back to the unholy Totem pole of dead children. Their faces twisted into scream as they suffered an agonizing death. The thing was a grim reminder of what would happen if they failed, They, had one more night. To come and then all Hell would, break loose and they would be powerless to stop Hell engulfing the whole planet. They needed time but that wasn't possible it was running out and running out fast.

Again, the chanting and evil murmur of unholy chants and curses. They were only just hanging in there; the Myrrh had anointed the Blades of each of them and holy water was in an army issue flask. They were prepared but they must hurry. As time was ticking away leaving the last sunlight day before they sacrificed

Johnny. They carried on listening, seeing if they could gain an advantage over the six witches. They sidled up to the edge of the clearing, where sparks flew out and evil cauldrons bubble out the remnants of the dead children. They were again twisting and contorting whilst the air hung heavy with blood and terror. It was looking like they had appeased the evil ones as the air hung heavy with death and feastings of flesh and bone. They were in their element.

*

Christine was holding her crystal ball to her third eye. And watching the curses noting to herself where the angels of heaven would be at a greater standpoint in the chaotic war that would be the earth's only chance at redemption, after the evil that has been released will take many lifetimes to dilute and send back to Hell. She carried on watching as hells power was released in an untimely manner. It was evil incarnate that was what they had begun to bring forth, Amanda smiled as she saw the Bowman himself appear into the chaotic remnants of the woods. Then Apollo, then the heaven sent avengers, seven in total. They circled the six malevolent witches and Craighton felt the rush of goodness then saw the seven Archangels and also Apollo.

Carlos looked around and caught a glimpse of the Bowman ,lord of the hunt. Tarregen was his name and a more deadly foe they will never face. Craighton sat down and laughed feeling a little drunk of the sheer magnitude of the odds being with them. The witches carried on fearing nothing, they hissed and spat, cursed and screamed. That's when Darius appeared and changed the outcome of their evil. Darius smashed into Davina and began to scream, "die unholy defiler and eater of innocent".

She pulled out a ceremonial dagger and sliced along his armour. Craighton smiled and thought 'I didn't think you would just sit this one out' Then Shia Lucia was struck in the chest with an enchanted arrow, caving her body and turning her to dust. The seven Archangels began to close the distance between them and the satanic witches. Darius was having a struggle with the head witch, Davina. But that wouldn't stop him from seeing the task through to the end. They grappled and Darius lifted the witch into the air and dropped her she screamed a high pitch scream and landed with a hell of a thump. The bowman was aiming a second arrow at Anne Lowe; he aimed and waited for her to line up in his eyes. He closed one and fired as soon as the opportunity came. This hit her in her shoulder and sent her reeling back screaming. It was a mortal wound but was not enough to finish the screaming satanic witch. The seven Archangels began to descend on the last five witches. But Davina had a few tricks up her sleeve.

She began to summon a shadow demon calling out its name and demanding it to help them out. She stood up and held her arms aloft. Shouting a demonic curse and holding out her arms then all everyone heard was a devilish laugh. Then it appeared and started to attack the enemies of the witches. Whilst they were in the fray with the shadow demon, Maltzare the five witches made a break for it. The Bowman fired two arrows and hit the van just as the witches got in. They then drove away at a hellish rate. Darius then focused his attention on the shadow. The shadow demon toward up towards the trees and the angels and the Bowman were caught in a fray with Maltzare. They used the lights of their weapons knowing that they only had a few hours unto which they could kill the demon. Whilst they were fighting Maltzare. Craighton and Carlos cut the bonds that were holding a pale Johnny Ebb. They hoisted him to his feet and took him quickly out the shady grove of trees. Where their car awaited. The battle that was ensuing was one of epic and huge proportions. It would seem as though the heavenly angels were tried and tested but still they would not let the shadow demon win. Darius was using spells of his own, and the Bowman, Terragen, was firing beams of light at the demon these were keeping the fight in their favour. Then Darius struck his warm sunlight sword a (broadsword) of holy vengeance slashed through the demons chest, piercing the shadows heart. This had sent the demon to the ground where it was vanquished and sent back to Hell.

*

Craighton floored the small Volkswagen Golf and they sped off to the local hospital. That was in the city of Dundee. Johnny kept fading in and out of consciousness, muttering and coughing a soul racking cough.

"They must have poisoned him," said Craighton.

It was getting near night-time and they were up against the clock. They got to Ninewells Hospital and the nurses immediately put him onto a gurney and he was wheeled into the Emergency Room. Immediately they put an I.V. into him and began to sew the wounds shut. Craighton, who was relieved that they had made it this far, sat down heavily and weary. Carlos stood and watched as the nurses ran around the station he was lying in. But still they couldn't get him to wake, he fell into an unpleasant coma. The nurses were rushing around making sure he was saved. The doctor and the nurse came through after a half hour of him struggling.

"He's alive." Craighton looked on exasperated, the doctor continued, "But he was lucky the wounds were severe and he lost a good sixty percent of his blood. And the poison was an exotic one, we still don't know what".

Craighton looked at the doctor and said, "He'll live?"

The doctor smiled a little and replied, "Yes".

Craighton smiled a sincere smile.

"He is going to be in a coma for at least a week, and considering the amount of blood he's lost, he's lucky," continued the surgeon.

Craighton nodded his head.

The surgeon asked the million-pound question. "How did he come to be in this state?"

Craighton looked at the doctor and replied, "Don't ask".

The doctor looked at the two men severely and carried on, "I'm going to have to ask, I'm afraid."

Craighton looked at Carlos and Carlos shrugged his shoulders as if to say, 'Why not'.

Craighton nodded his head, "Well doc, we are occult investigators and have been on the trail of a group of satanic witches for a number of years now. We got lucky in our information and I arrived just as they kidnapped the great Johnny Ebb".

The surprised doctor went, "Ohh."

Craighton then explained how they were lucky in the task and it could have been a hell of a lot worse. The doctor listened to Craighton who spoke for forty-five minutes. Then Craighton gave him the number to the head of their order and how he should phone to check them out.

He left, as did Carlos who at next to Craighton and said, "Do you think he'll buy it?"

Craighton snarled and replied, "Couldn't give a fuck if he does".

Craighton and Carlos booked themselves into a local hotel and hung around for the next three four days. At which time they contacted Ammanda and Chris. They smiled at the good news and as they hung up Craighton laughed.

"Those two will never change".

Carlos laughed and said, "We would all be damned if they did". Craighton smiled an inward smile. Warming himself and giving himself a pat on the back.

*

Davina cursed the very daylight of that day. She was a bit battered and bruised from the fight but she was glad that she had saved herself, her and the other four, Shia had died and that to them was an angry point, they would want revenge and revenge they would get. Johnny was in a hospital somewhere in Scotland. And they had not finished with the sacrifice. They soured their faces and carried on eating sweet breads. Davina hissed as the meal was nearly finished, "We must prove ourselves worthy of Hell, we must find the two demon hunters and destroy them".

The other four witches grimaced and looked out in cold, stark, evil insanity. Sinister, you could say that, they were going to have to bring more chaos into the world. Davina was starting to plan and formulate a way that would save them face and would get them more in tune with Hell. They had failed, yet she was not letting this thing go, no, this was salvageable. If she could finish off Johnny she would be back in the favour of the Dark Lord. She smiled as a plan began to formulate in her mind, she would carry on the hunt, looking to finish the young rockstar. She knew he couldn't be far and they were getting noticed around about the west of Fife.

They had grabbed a couple more children and they dined fresh that evening and the next four. Then she smiled as she saw into the hospital that Johnny Ebb was lying in, he was comatose and he would be an easy target. So, the five witches cast aside their usual glamorous clothes and dressed in nuns outfits. They headed towards the hospital in Dundee, Ninewells. His heartbeat was steady and he had a room to himself. But the coma wasn't just going to dissipate. No, this would be like shooting fish in a barrel. Davina produced a large leather satchel filled with purple screaming flesh eating worms. That which they had starved for the last four days. They entered and spoke with the nurse who was sat in front of the room reading, it was quarter past two in the afternoon. And nothing gave them away. The glamour covered over, the Hellish worms screaming for food. They spoke, telling the nurse they were sisters and were here to anoint the head of the poor unfortunate rock star.

The nurse looked at the clock and counted how long was left on her shift. At this point, the five nuns entered and began the semblance of a holy duty. They closed the room door and closed the curtains. Then Davina hissed as she poured the fat purple worms over the unconscious rock and roll star. They tore him apart, and they revelled in the satanic act the flesh eating worms eating him, devouring him as the five witches looked on, savouring the unholy act. After they finished him, they headed out and the flesh eating worms were satisfied with the meal. They picked them up knowing they would come of use later on. They headed out into the Ninewells car park got into their van and drove off cackling and screaming hideous blood curdling screams. Laughing and tearing into the human flesh they had been saving for the celebration.

*

Craighton and Carlos exited the elevator and heard the young nurse scream. They headed straight to the room where the remnant's, of Johnny were lying, as the flesh had been stripped from him, all that was left was the marrow and bone of the young rock star. Even his eyeballs had been eaten. Craighton opened the bony jaw on him and saw the last, remaining purple, fat, flesh eating worm. He asked the Nurse for a specimen jar. She went straight away and procured a small specimen jar. Craighton put the worm that was squirming and trying to bite the flesh of Craighton into the jar. He then went and looked around the bony skeleton that was seared of all its flesh. Making sure there were none left, he approached the nurse who was getting hugged by the Porter.

"You okay sweetheart?" asked Craighton. "Who was the last to come in here?" He asked.

She stopped shuddering and said, "The only people who have been in were the five nuns".

Craighton said, "That was five satanic worshiping witches" and they had moved very quickly into the hospital fooling everyone. The nurse who was baffled asked, "What do you mean? I take it they weren't Nuns."

Craighton gave a dry laugh, "No sweetheart you were just beguiled by five of the most sinister witches in the world".

She smiled and said as the body was taken down to the morgue, "There was nothing I could do".

Craighton smiled as the bones were shifted.

"Well, he's at peace now," said Carlos.

They then headed straight to the Green Witch in Aberdour. Amanda and Chris again spoke a quiet spell as Craighton walked through the door. Carlos laughed as they had done what was necessary and that was stop the rites, the satanic rites, from gaining a foothold in the world. They were to be awarded with a large bonus. It was a couple of million each. Carlos asked if Robert was any better.

The Two sisters smiled and replied, "Yes he is fine, they drew out the poison from his system".

Craighton smiled as he blew on the mug of coffee that he was just handed. He sipped and continued the conversation showing the two sisters the purple flesh eating worm. Chris looked at the thing and opened the jar, at which point it screamed a deafening scream out of hunger. Chris grimaced as the scream carried on for about a minute. Amanda smiled and said, "close the goddam jar".

Then she screwed the jar shut and the worm wriggled and tried to eat its way out of the glass. Craighton looked on at the thing and wondered how many it would take to eat through a full adult male. At a guess it would be at least five hundred of them. He went through to the back room with the specimen jar and looked through the ancient texts and magical creatures, malevolent ones and got a good picture of one in an arcane evil summoners text used to sacrifice the flesh of a human to Asmodeus the Archdevil of insects.

He read the texts, noting down how long they had been around and how many a human had found out to their peril that these things were ferocious eaters of flesh and left nothing but bone and marrow. Craighton continued to take notes whilst Carlos was having a smoke of a cigar outside the front of the shop. He smiled as he finished the cigar. He came back in as Craighton was still in the back library looking up the deadly flesh-eating worms. Witches had been using said demonic worms since the dawn of time, they were in common usage in the hellish scheme of things and the more he read the more he disliked. He was transfixed by the text on them and he got a cold shudder down his spine as he carried on reading about them.

He also came by a cousin variant of the species, the rot grub. These were a little smaller in size and didn't shriek when they were hungry. Also, they weren't purple. They were the colour of maggots but with razor sharp teeth. They burrowed their way under the flesh then ate from the inside out. Starting mainly on the organs, then popping through the flesh. Their appetite was ferocious and they didn't leave much in the way of leftovers. They too were used in certain satanic rituals. Carlos came through and laid another mug of coffee in front of Craighton. Craighton looked up and gave a half-hearted smile as if to say this is interesting. Carlos peered over his shoulder and looked at the picture of a ceremony unto which the covered a child with the starving flesh-eating worms. The picture showed a small baby also being devoured by the worms. This kind of ceremony had been used for centuries in the summoning and asking for evil rites to help the world know that hell was real and that the world would someday come closer to Hell and evil would rule the hearts of men would turn black and servitude to the Satanic ones would be there only cause. Not that they were worried, no good had produced the most reassuring of actions, with the likes of Craighton and various demon hunters stopping the evil from getting a hold on the earth.

The phone rang and Craighton carried on reading. It was Robert Crufax. He had recovered from the knife to the guts and also the poison.

"Am fit, I can help," He said to Amanda. Amanda just smiled and replied, "well you better get here fast, as they got Johnny and finished him with flesh eating worms".

Robert sounded startled and asked, "Purple ones that scream?"

Amanda laughed, "You know them?"

Robert replied, "Yeah I know them, I encountered them a few years back when a brood of vampires had decided to go hell for leather in an idyllic town in Romania" He growled a little "We were unprepared and the town got slaughtered. The children were sacrificed using the worms, very little trace of them left, bones mainly".

Amanda stared out into the distance.

"They are a formidable satanic weapon," said Robert. "I'll leave right away".

Amanda hung up and Robert grabbed his jacket and also his Uzi nine millimetre. Things were getting interesting. Craighton came through after his studies of the purple, fat, flesh-eating worms. They were simple to kill but if there was a lot of them it was different matter entirely. The noise they made whilst they fed was disturbing to say the least. Craighton sat next to the open coal fire and warmed the chill in his bones.

"Was that Robert?" He asked.

Amanda smiled and replied, "Yes and he is on his way".

Craighton rubbed the heat into his bones after reading what chilled him to the marrow. Chris smiled and lit another angelic candle. Trying to give hope to the Demon Hunters.

*

Darius let his wings beat warm hallowed air into the small but homely shop. The witches and the demon hunters were needing all the blessings in heaven and Earth. So, Darius watched over them for a good seven days. Unto which he just learned of Johnny's unholy demise at the teeth of the flesh-eating worms. Robert arrived the very night that Darius began his vigil over them. They discussed the possibilities of where and when the witches would strike next. They watched on the news as the town of Anstruther was getting tended to. The Emergency services were swamped from Dundee to Dunfermline. It was an unholy epidemic. And it had shocked the world in its desolation. Giving the world an insight into what was decaying the world of mortal man. They had never experienced an unholy outbreak of its magnitude. They carried on their discussion and Darius carried on quietly watching over them. Things were turning strange and more sinister Darius smiled and gave a laugh as he was summoned by the Prince of Angels Michael. He traversed through the Earth plane and into the Heavenly realms where Micheal was waiting for him at the Gates.

*

Davina smiled as they took a ferry toward France, there they would meet up with several servants of wamphyre, who were planning an all-out evil scheme that would leave the world wondering WHY! But the answer was simple and that was because it's in their nature to cause chaos, to damn and desecrate the holy and the divine. To cause such evil that world would go numb with shock and block out mindfully all the evil that radiated from their unholy ways. They were planning something big and that was to exact unholy terror in the city of Paris a great plague and evil sacrifice. And then they would see if Hell were as weak or just lying in wait.

Davina smiled as they followed a small convoy of cars into France and northern to Paris, where several broods of vampires had taken a small district in the poor quarters of Paris. They arrived a couple of hours just before sunset. And as the sun set, they saw why they were so feared. The broods murdered and drank the blood of everyone in the area, joggers, dog walkers, people going home, they fell on them as night started to descend on them. Davina loved the cold and deathly way that the Broods had made their presence known and people of the area were disappearing. This had given the five witches the confidence that they needed. They felt at home with the diabolical brood of vampires. They seemed to have purpose, direction and well they were planning on causing as much havoc as they could, they welcomed Davina and her coven into their fold and Davina made diabolical promises to the brood.

The head of the six man brood was a devilish looking Ferdand, who was very powerful and very sinister. He had worked his way up the ranks to master vampire and done so coldly and methodical. Next there was Siesko a young Chinese vampire who had been hand-picked for his martial arts attributes. Then Carey, Carey was a tall six foot two inch greedy vampire who left little if anything for the rest of the brood, he was the one who watched and sometimes he would play with his food. Gholis was a pale good looking vampire that liked to charm his way into homes and finish entire families. Carmden was a young British who claimed to have killed over six hundred men women and children. And last but not least was Samwey, evil incarnate, he was savage and raw and no one, I mean no one, could watch as he dined on the blood of an innocent. He was bloody and furious.

Davina walked into their nest and they lay there sleeping in cold deathly silence. Davina hissed, smiled and began to make room for herself and her coven. She dined that day on a small child she had snatched whilst it was playing. She began to cook the child in a large oven that was wood burning and gas. The rest of the coven dined also on the flesh of children. But they were noticed. Then divinity, the local divinity had noticed a lack of locals and many children had gone, missing. They were unassuming, cold and methodical, but they were being tracked by the Archangel Michael. That was the reason for him to call on Darius and tell him of the nest of vampires and also that Davina and her coven had crossed over into the broods lair and hunting ground.

*

They sat perched with impassive faces watching as the Coven did their evil deeds, summoning, sacrificing, calling all the devils to bear witness at the offerings of the satanic coven. They knew when they were in the graces of hell, as they felt an immeasurable amount of power surge through their bodies, wracking them, twisting them, showing them what they felt was normal burning pains and twisted brains. They sat and dined whilst the brood were in their deathly cold slumber. They then went on the hunt again, looking for fresh blood for the head vampire Ferdand. He rose, his black, slicked back hair and long bony fingers clutched at his first snack.

Davina screamed as the vampire slit the young thirteen-year-old child's throat. He hissed and cackled knowing that his feeding habit was twice the amount of the rest of his brood. Of course, Davina knew this and was prepared for a long time of hunting, not just for the master vampire but also themselves. Ferdand smiled after he finished with the young teenager. He looked with black as coal eyes at Davina and thanked her as he needed to dine fresh at the beginning of the night. The rest of the brood woke a short while after Ferdand had fed. They smiled and hissed at the five witches knowing that in the diabolical scheme of things they were of grave importance. Especially their summoning and sacrificing skills. Ferdand gathered his Brood together and hissed at the vampires, "See I told you she would come."

Siesko hissed next, "Saw what you did in Scotland, a good way to get in Hells favour".

Davina cackled and the other four witches joined in. "We will call you our master until we have done our deeds, with your help of course," Davina said.

"We will receive all the evil rewards of Hell," Said Ferdand. They then got on with setting up an unholy alter of evil.

*

Craighton smiled as he sat down in the Church house and drank some coffee and ate a lite lunch consisting of a tuna sandwich and a plate of fries. Father Clayton had come across from America to make sure the next part of their holy mission was seen to. Robert and the rest of them finished off their meals and started to plan and plot the best way to get at the Satanic coven. But nothing that evil was vanquished that easily and there were several places they could be. Throughout the world anyway. The five witches would surface somewhere and it would be their duty to stamp out the evil and malicious force that they were. Craighton was sullen yet full of hope. He just had to be patient they all did. Amanda and Chris who were guardians of nature were scrying to see if they could find them before they gained enough power to destroy another town, knowing that they were ferocious flesh eaters, enjoying the human meat raw and cooked. They carried on scrying waiting for something unnatural to happen. Then they saw them in Paris using their evil glower to set people paralysis. They did it several times to replenish their foods and also to send a message to the holy and the divine. They weren't just going to roll over and die. No, they worked for the lords of chaos and they didn't care who came at them. Chris smiled and said, "Got them," then she began to note down where they were. "France," she said. "And I think it's Paris".

Craighton got straight on the phone and booked first class tickets for all of them, Father Clayton included. They were on the next plane to Paris. They had Interpol to thank for the Firearm Licences, with which they were allowed to take guns because of the nature of the beast. The six of them exited Paris' main airport and went straight away and got their two hired cars, two Vauxhall Lagunas, one white one silver. They then went and checked in at the side of the motorway hotel. They were to wait a couple of days and then head to the local église where they would be blessed and meet up with the leno dupre (Priest) his Christian name was Antione Salisver and when they had rested and rearmed their weapons they headed to the chapel where Antione was waiting for them.

"Hello, my fellow demon 'unters," He said with the sideways way of an accent. "You are well prepared and well rested I assume?"

Craighton took the man's hand who had a smile that said, 'well, everything was going to be okay'. It shone in the gentleman's eyes. Hope like that was hard to come by as most of the world was living in the fact that nothing evil was real, and the Devil and God didn't exist. This was the way of the world. But Craighton and the rest of his demon hunters knew different. They had spent the majority of their lives hunting and destroying the evil demons, devils and gods of chaos. Unto which most of mankind were deluded into thinking the devil and his minions didn't exist.

Craighton laid his kit bag with all his weapons in down on the small church house floor. The rest all did the same. Antione put the kettle on and made them all mugs of coffee. Cream and sugar were on the tray for them to help themselves. That's when Craighton showed the specimen, the flesh-eating worm that was wriggling and trying to escape the container that it was in. "Have you ever come across anything like this?"

Antione looked at the thing "No I have not come across them but may I make a note of it in my Journal?"

Craighton smiled and handed the jar to him he took a picture with a polaroid camera then went and got his journal. The Priest smiled a small, contented smile that was warming and very friendly. He wrote a couple of pages and Craighton filled him on the details of the flesh-eating worm, you know, where he found it, how much it was used in the satanic covens rituals. Craighton didn't spare the details and went to great lengths about why they were used and just how many there were of the worms. How they lived and how long they lived.

Antoine was fascinated and copied down every word about the flesh-eating worm, and how long they had been in this realm. He was totally, enthralled by the history and how the Satanic witches had used them for evil rites and unto which they had gained more malevolent powers. More strength.

"I think," finished Craighton, "That they may be more a turning point than we anticipated".

Antoine. "So, I should send the specimen to the Vatican?"

"Yes, post haste!" came the curt reply from Craighton.

The Parisian Priest jumped right to it and sent the Worm straight away by Fed Ex to the Vatican.

"Now these witches," came the statement from Craighton, who was really wired and psyched by the whole thing. They then had a long discussion on tactics, who was most use and who was best to take up the rear. And that was Chris and Amanda. The weapons again were blessed by both Father Clayton and Antoine Salisver. They finished the rites in Latin. They also filled up on Holy Water and sharpened their Bowie knives and over sharp instruments. But what they thought was a minor problem was going to be catastrophic in nature. They had never encountered at the same time a brood and a coven. They got round to the large mansion that looked like it came right from New Orleans. It befitted the area as this was a poor area

It was always the way of things, the rich right across from the poor, as if they ogled the poor, taunted them made them feel inferior. But since its new inhabitants were slaves of Satan then they were twice as malicious and twice as deadly. The Coven were eager to start their satanic rites and begin filling on evil enchantments and sinister powers. Continuing their cursed existence. Hoping some-day to raise hell itself. They had come close a number of times but were thwarted by the demon hunters and their kin. And this time they knew they were coming, so Davina waited for night to end where she and her coven were ready for the hunters. They waited patiently as the hunters parked a little way off from the mansion. And began to head into the area where the blood was washed away by the springtime rain. And the chill of winter was subsiding and turning to summer. They had decided on a daytime plan of attack as the Vampire numbered same as them. But this didn't sit well with Craighton, who was of the feeling that the Coven were well aware of them. Craighton looked around the area noting puddles that were filling with the blood being drained.

"Yep, awash with blood," he said then carried on looking for a back entrance. The row of spikes that kept the garden in was well, unkempt and it soured the whole neighbourhood. Not that there were many people left in the neighbourhood. No, they were walking into a vampire feeding ground. And Craighton could feel the evil emanate from the large house, they were obviously waiting for them

They got round to the back of the house, noting where the windows were and where the other doors were positioned. They started to jemmy the back door when they got a sudden attack of nausea. This was caused by the flesh rot that the witches had left, in which there were several people hung up on hooks, including a number of children. The smell was sour and of rotten flesh, a pungent mix of death decay and inhuman poisons. It took all their strength to stop themselves from gagging and being sick. They each covered their mouths with bandannas to stopped the acrid smell and decay from taking hold and ruining their constitution. They walked by, looking around the large kitchen and noting the meat cleavers were still bloody and the blood was fresh.

Craighton snarled under his bandanna. They had obviously been doing this for a while and the victims were never in control of what the witches and the brood were going to do to them. Some had wandered up to the door under a dark enchantment, some were grabbed off the street whilst passing the macabre house of hell. None survived. They were drained of blood and sacrificed in a pentagram of evil drawn in blood. The bones were used to make incense and every now and then they gave their pet worms a body or two, to keep them satisfied and abate their screaming, a screaming that was noted in the area.

People crossed themselves and walked fast along the street, some knowing that the place was evil and the house was somehow channelling a demonic universe. This was why the witches had come to the house they were sacrificing all the time and doing ritual spells to summon the blood gods and the demons, devils and other malevolent creatures, showing them the door so to speak. Seeing if any of them were strong enough to come through. Some were, some weren't, but most felt appeased at the offerings they were given. Craighton came upon the bathroom, in the bath were several thousand flesh eating worms, He reached into his coat and produced a can of lighter fluid. He poured said fluid then lit the tub up. Then he shut the door firmly to keep the noise down. They were screaming as they burned and popped, crackled and snapped.

They then followed through to the main study that was where there were several demonic possession books and ancient blood soaked books that housed the very incantation of evil. The room adjacent was their ritual room and it was cold as a well-digger's ass. It only heated up in the hottest of summers and because of so many sacrifices it was constantly dark and cold, only heating up a degree or so. They trashed the place, poured holy water everywhere all over the pentagram and altars that held a human child's eyes. Craighton's face turned sour again at the evil design that had shaped this room. He was used to seeing all sorts of desecration but this one was the worst yet. Amanda stood at the doorway as they began to say prayers in Latin and the five witches who were on the hunt for more fresh souls, were oblivious to this. They then saw the basement where the resting place for the vampires was. They carried on down, hoping that they had come in time, but something was wrong they could all feel their skin crawl as they got further into the basement, again it was cold, they opened one coffin hoping that they had caught the vampires, but no they were empty and they had all vacated that mansion. They were heading deeper into France. So just to make sure they covered the coffins in holy water and marked them with the sign of the cross. Then they searched the house to see if there was anyone alive. But alas no.

*

The Coven travelled knowing that they had made the right move carrying the six vampires to a safe town where nothing was what it seemed. No, it was a dark village that housed many things not of this life. They would, after a while, head into Romania. This would be a pilgrimage and evil pilgrimage to possibly gain more strength. And get more clarity in the rituals seeing as Romania was as close to the daemon lords of Hell, you know Dracula and such. They laughed as the metal caskets that the coven had purchased for the daemons was very much appreciated. They all knew that the hunters would be fast on their heels. And had little to concern them on their journey. The village was on the French side of the Alps. And was quiet and dark when they entered its folds. The metallic coffins were unloaded into the main town house and put to earth so as the vampires could rest. The witches went straight to the main sacrificial point and began ask for forgiveness in the way they had left the Mansion in Paris.

But the Lords of Darkness were not easily satiated and demanded a double sacrifice so as to cover their folly. And gain the respect of the dark lord. They carried about the task straightaway and gathered two infants from a neighbouring village. They then cut out the two babies hearts and set them on fire. They then waited for their Lord and at that time of year it was Asmodeus and he had a particular taste for children. The hearts were tossed into the fire as it grew and out of the flames came the dark lord. He hissed at them, his bug like eyes, much akin to a fly focused on the five witches. "Make this the last time you call on me in failure". The witches all replied, "Yes master".

The coven carried on chanting and lighting up flames in their hands. They then began to hiss and moan. Every now and then crying for the death of Shia. The devil lord smiled, "she was a fine meal for me and my friends".

They began to cry all the more, begging for more power in their ways. Asmodeus was still displeased with them. "You must understand that it won't be long until the light of Heaven breaks down our gates in Hell and we will be vanquished forever. You are our unholy servants, and by our will and the will of Hell you will do as we bid you. are we clear on that?"

The coven again cried and begged for mercy.

"Mercy". He shouted then hissed again, "Mercy you have nothing but my pity and everything else, well it is just luck".

Then the flames surrounded him and he was gone again. Davina stood straight up and looked at the other four witches in sour regret. "That's it ladies, show more willing, we have a long way to go and the next time we summon a dark lord it may not go in our favour".

The four other Witches began to wail in hopeless dread.

*

Craighton smiled as the rest of them settled down to a meal. The Vatican sent a team of monks and other Library scholastics to go over the large evil book collection in that mansion. They hoped to gain a good footing on the daemons and the coven, and that library was a good place to start. They must have been warned, but didn't have enough time to gather their literature. Craighton smiled and drank some red wine then headed into the study to carry on reading about the flesh worm. He felt that they might be a key clue there in the use of the worm in sacrificial ceremonies. They may have overlooked the blatant fact that they were gathering more and more macabre demons and other creatures of the night. And in turn the lords of Hell were getting more and more strength and more and more people were looking to hell for the answers. This being said it also made people hug their Bibles and pray more. Not that there wasn't anything to gain from the religious belief and its system, just that bit of comfort, which reassuring feeling that we weren't alone and that well, that as bad as it gets, we always win.

Craighton carried on drinking his red wine. These witches were proving to be more than a little difficult to handle. No, they were sure fired and cocked, armed with evil and satanic ways. They had been a major pain in the hunters arse before and after Anstruther. Yes, they had stopped the ceremony from taking us all into Hell, yes, they had killed one of the satanic witches and yes ,they had gathered enough of the damned vampires and well, the demon hunting team was left in a bit of shock. They knew not where the coven and brood were heading, Chris came and stood by Craighton, "You know we can always Scry again"

Craighton smiled and let out an "mmmm," as if in deep thought.

She carried on, "We just got to keep our chins up and keep hoping for the best".

Craighton smiled and replied, "The Lord will deliver us in victory".

Chris took his hand and warmed his hand with a small breath. Robert came and saw the two of them. It wasn't affection it was friendship. And she needed to show just who's side she was on and it was the hunters. Craighton in particular, she had a small crush on him. But Craighton was aloof of her attentions. But love was something that they didn't have time for. So onwards and upwards.

*

Darius meanwhile was having a long conversation with the Archangels in their place of practice. Where spells were used and divinity was held up most. And thoughts of evil well they just disappeared no angel had the time to think like Satan, never mind turn like Satan. As when he had turned it was ugly and I mean ugly, it split the heavens in two. Fractured the very essence of angel and devil. The Lord had enough of the petty argument that was jealousy. Michael smiled as he drew his golden sword and balanced his shield, he was in golden armour and his dark curly hair was glowing with gold through it. His wife Delphi ,had taken care of him always had, always will.

Darius smiled as they faced each other in the sunlight Micheal had never been defeated and Darius knew this, so he didn't say a word to the prince of Angels. They faced each other and began their melee. A number of hours they fought never backing down to each other but still the two of them smiled. Darius lunged at the prince, who brought down his shield and practically disarmed Darius. Michael then swung the sword at Darius nearly taking his throat, but Darius had seen it coming and backed away. Then the two of them began to circle one another levitating a couple of feet of the ground, the two of them showing great wind control with their wings, wings that beat a wind of warmth at each other. If they chose to, they could beat a tropical storm at their enemy. That and attack before the wind settled. They laughed and started to position themselves in the air. Combat like this could not be underestimated, and all the angels in heaven knew it.

The Lord God had many Angels but these two were his prize, his elite. Darius picked up a spear and threw it at Michael, Michael dodged it easily and the spear imbedded itself into the rock wall behind him. Michael smiled and asked, "Are you quitting Yet?"

Darius let out a boisterous laugh. One that only he could control. Michael then picked up a spear and used it to attack. Darius balanced his gladius and shield and began to defend himself against Michael who was just warming up. Darius was on the receiving end of the attacks, a good twelve thirteen minutes. They were evenly matched both at skill at arms and using the environment to its fullest potential. They stopped, realizing that the two of them had never been through half an hour of intense combat. No, they were well and truly well matched for each other. They finished and saluted to each other before they put their weapons away.

Michael came up to Darius and said, "Well done Archangel nobody has gone more than ten minutes with me!" The Lord sat and watched as the two tried to outwit and out match the other. He was satisfied with the result, Michael smiled as they drained their water skins and ate some passion fruit and figs, holy breads and cooked ham, Darius then asked a question that only Michael knew how to answer. "How can I better serve the demon hunters?"

Micheal tutted a little and thought about it. "No, there is little you can do about the flock. Especially the ones that guard and tend to the flock." He then began to dine again and Darius asked another question "But how am I going to help if man has to be his own saviour?" Michael smiled and chuckled a little. "I too have qualms about this, sometimes I worry about the state of earth and that is when they need me the most."

Darius smiled and carried on eating delicately. Then Micheal spoke again, "They need to learn from their own mistakes and leaving it to rot well that just isn't good enough" Darius nodded his head and began to sip some wine. The conversation went on until Morning light.

*

The vampires woke that night with nothing other than blood lust and they were dire in need of a feeding frenzy. Davina and the witches were summoning the night to carry the vampires off and protect them from all that is holy and divine. The demon hunters were still left wondering where they were. The vampires flew of in search of blood and they wouldn't stop until their thirst was satisfied. And this bloody night would leave a new mark on the moon. And all hallowed and evil would know that things were just right and that they were set upon the task of creating Hell on earth. Ferdand, Siesko, Carey, Gholis, Carmden and Samwey flew about their murderous mission desolating a small village, killing man woman and child. Leaving the place desecrated and ruined.

The thoughts that the parishioners of that village were, "Why Lord? did we do something wrong".

They were some of them set symbol, but most drained completely of blood. then left to rot in the summer air that hung heavy and foreboding. They flew back to the village where their metal caskets awaited them. Davina heard them coming back laughing and joking about how the earth would soon belong to them. Davina hissed at the moon, turning part dragon. She had black faith and would turn this world in on itself. But she knew as night followed day that the hunters would be along soon. And they were a match that she must not underestimate. She gathered up her sacrificial knives and daggers. The Coven began to fill the cauldron that they had with sweet breads and bloody vows that each of them had taken.

Lorrain began to summon a demon into her soul, panting and frigging herself and making huge orgasmic grunts. Then she doused the blood of a goat all over her screaming and panting. Davina was tending to another shrine of evil, one unto which was the brains and eyes of a fourteen ,year old, blonde girl. They would devour the child's eyes and brains during the next bloody moon. And that was in two days' time. Then the other three Satanic witches began to murmur and chant whilst Lorrain began to moan and decry god and all the apostles, as well as the angels. She calmed down and began to let the demon use her body as a vessel.

She finished went still then it spoke, "I'm Cantor the nether demon what is it you wish?"

Davina cackled a great laugh and said, "Success, you are truly in the demons favour."

Lorrain lay still for a second or two then the demon became impatient. "What is it you wish?"

Davina snarled then spoke hissing the words, "We are here to do your bidding Master Cantor"

The demon twisted Lorrain a little bit more her bones cracking and her mouth groaning as she struggled for air. "You are not worthy of my biddings." Davina gulped as the body that was writhing was now being twisted in torture and damnation. "She will come with me and never call on me again or the punishment will be more severe". At this a crack of lightning hit her body and she evaporated into thin air. The witches had just learned the golden rule of Satanic verses and that was don't trust the demon as it can turn on you in a split second.

*

Craighton smiled as the last of the light shone on the crystal ball. And they saw the town where the witches coven and the brood are. Antione Salisver was sceptical about the whole searching through the ether and mists of time. But the two sisters were perfectly adept at the scrying and seeing. They had clear crystal vision and they had learned magic and power. Spells and enchantments. Ways of old and ways of new, seeing was a speciality to them. They let the light shine into the orb that was blessed with the egg of a dragon. It was found centuries ago in an old cloak of leaves and greenery. It was passed down from white witch to white witch. They had held its power for over a thousand years it was the oldest Crystal ball in existence. None, other than that one had lasted this long. And they had kept it in mint condition only using it occasionally. They preferred to use tea and holy water for most of the time. But when it was something special like the finding of a lost soul they used what they call the sun orb. They had caught serial killers and a lot of people who were just corrupt and using good honest folks scams the police often came to the shop when they were baffled by the case facts and couldn't get a clear picture, missing children and of course seeing if love fitted the two people that were courting. And whether to treat a jealous rival with kindness or violence. Never the latter though.

*

The brood and coven were in the little town next to a lake in the range of the Alps. Closer to Sweden than they ought to be. They had come to know this place, as a dark shadow hung over their vision of the place. And nothing right was in place, no holy chapel, no church, no school, nothing, just a very desolate place, it was out of character for France but it happened when two evil parties got together and wanted to destroy something pure. They had littered the place with bones and skin and then crucified the men and the women they deflowered and ate. They were evil incarnate.

They had set symbol the towns parishioner who was really advanced in his years He cried out to Jesus when they castrated him. The place was amidst an unholy war. The two sisters had viewed all this whilst remaining sane, most normal folk would have turned into gibbering, foaming at the mouth, imbeciles. At the thought of sacrificial witches and vampires, lord knows that they weren't supposed to be real. But turning from God, well who knew what could happen and then the other undead that plagued the cities and the various towns well they were known throughout, the Vatican had made notes on every case where things weren't as they should be, possessions and exorcisms were becoming more the normal way of life for Priests, even certain rogue demon hunters were known to have a crack at exorcisms. But they generally fell short most of the time in the litany and they were constantly reminded that the pros have all the angles figured out. But this didn't stop them, some even claimed to be of the cloth, Craighton at one point had broken a man's jaw and sent him reeling back and into the arms of the ambulance service. Even they pointed out that. "See the likes of Craighton are old pros at the demonology game"

The man drank his dinner through a straw for several months, this went on and he ,through no fault of his own ,realised that the Vatican were all over it and the priest that was at that particular case showed him the 'As should be motion'. Holding out both his hands after the exorcism and saying the demon was late in his apparent reunion with the rest of the demons and devils. The house and young child were clean of all sins that had attracted the Lord of Chaos and Darkness. To her in the first place.

*

They began to make preparations to head towards the village of the damned. They loaded a shit load of silver and crosses and holy water. They were figuring on finding them whilst they had the power to do something about their state of affairs. That meant a night-time excursion into the village where the odds were against them. The Priest stacked up a load of wooden stakes seeing as he was only one who saw sense and suggested a daytime attack. Craighton couldn't fault the facts but they had one stark staring reality and that was the coven. They were waiting on the hunters and knew that they would try and get by them as they were constantly sacrificing and constantly chanting, but they had to sleep some time. And Craighton put a small wager on the fact that they were pure lunar and did everything they could to keep themselves awake and in the thralls of an ancient evil rite.

They were sending evil out and out and invite to the ritual unto which they would need all the curses and magic of the Hell planes and as many daemons, ghouls and undead. They needed to turn this war into their favour. And they would start with summoning the soil for more purple flesh worms. Then they would call on the black dogs of hell. The ones that wandered the earth visiting homes with dog flaps and young children. That's when most of the world got a cold shudder down it's spine, especially at a newborn which they would steal away and devour. Sometimes they travelled in packs, sometimes in solitude, but they were very near impossible to kill, you had to do a lot to even to scare them off and when you got close enough, they became the most ferocious animal ever faced. They never backed down and never give up and ran, you were in it to kill or be killed and believe me that dog was a killer. There is no feeding and getting them on your side. And definitely no metal pole to have them under restraint. No, they snapped three out of four of those poles and if it was a pack, you were about to have a run in with hells teeth. When it bit, it locked its jaw and carried on the grip right past the point of blood. They were the black dogs of hell and sometimes they acquired an owner, someone who could feed and see to the dogs black behaviour. They were loyal to evil incarnate. But mainly they were loyal to themselves and if the tide shifted and the master was useless well, he would leave then come back sometime later with a whole pack of black dogs and finish the ex-owner. Be it vampire, ghoul, warlock or witch.

*

The village was a beacon of evil and it was just getting started. It was offering up an unholy carnage fest, in which they would start to raid village after village. Then with the power of the plague bearer they would begin to sell the soul of earth and send it straight through to Hell. But this was easier said than done as the demon hunter had a good grip with a holy power, and well, it was just needing to be done. Warlocks and other unholy subjects of hell were becoming more, confident and cocky, arrogant and flamboyant, often teasing the Vatican with Satanic verses left at the unholy rites they were doing more and more.

The Vatican were doing everything to keep the world from slipping into chaos. And Craighton's team were the best at what they did. And their skills were about to be truly tested. The seven of them were a holy barrage of hunters and they had never been short of failure and were blessed with exalted deeds and goodness. They made the journey to the small village feeling and seeing the unholy carnage as they got closer, men women and children crucified, some with their hearts ripped out, others skinned and set symbol. The closer they got to the village the worse it was. They appeared relentless in their butchery and you know that they were dining on the flesh of human, child, woman or man, they had no particular preference. And only the pure were truly a treat on the plates. Craighton looked very cold as they got closer to the village it was dusk and he was sure they were waiting on them to somehow ambush and try and destroy the hunters. But they were well prepared and ready for anything. Robert was smoking a large Cuban cigar. That was keeping him from gaging as the air hung rich with decay and poison. And it was quiet the further it got into the village.

"The best way to deal with this is from the heart of the village and work our way killing everything Unholy," said Craighton as they gathered around.

Antoine said just before they started this unholy cleansing, "We must say a prayer for the fallen populace." They all bowed their heads and said the Lord's Prayer,

"Our Father who art in heaven, hallowed be thy name, thy Kingdom come, thy will be done in this world as in heaven, Amen" They were suddenly lit up around them with holy pristine light.

"God is with us". They all felt the power of goodness and knew they wouldn't fail in this so holy a task. Father Clayton wrapped his rosary beads around his fist knowing and feeling the Lord's presence and power of heaven, they were truly blessed, Nothing was going to stop them from making an example of the unholy, evil and malicious. Craighton produced his sawn of shotgun that was loaded with silver and holy herbs. He had a full pouch on his belt buckle filled with shotgun shells. Robert was packing a small Uzi with twenty mags of silver and Garlic in each bullet. Carlos was sporting a .357 Magnum, also with silver and garlic, he had about seventeen quick loads. The ladies had a nine millimetre Berretta each with a total of thirty fifteen bullet magazines. Also silver and garlic.

Antione was carrying the steaks and rubber mallet. Father Clayton was also carrying a Colt 45 with about seventy shells, all silver. It was quiet and I mean really, quiet. It was unnerving to say the least. They started to cleanse the village of the damned. They looked up at the church cross and saw the castrated Priest aloft. The sight soured their minds and reminded them that these things that inhabited the village were the worse that they had been up against and the mess was a constant reminder that the holy hunters were up against evil and evil that had been brewing for centuries.

"Do we cut him down?" Came the question from Antione Salisver.

Craighton sighed and turned as he shook his head. "No, we do that after we clean these god forsaken creatures". Carols, who was scowling at the sight, "Mother fuckers," he said.

The light still stayed with them. "Where do we begin?" Came Father Clayton's voice. Craighton whose face was stoney and sombre replied, "First come first served". They then started to pick their way through the buildings. Looking for the brood who were about to rise for another night of blood and power. Ferdand opened his casket with his long bony fingers. The rest of them followed suit. Craighton heard them whoop and holler to each other and they began to rise from the basement that they were occupying.

Craighton didn't wait a second he ran at them and fired of a shotgun shell at the first and that was Samwey. The blast ripped him in two. Ferdand flew at Craighton, but Father Clayton had seen it coming and fired his Colt 45 with a huge cracking noise, the bullets hitting Ferdand in the chest he fell staying motionless. The remaining four were hissing and screaming seeing their master fall, with two ripping wounds to his black as pitch heart. They light began to glow fiercely and blind the other four vampires. At which point the hunters saw their chance and they seized the opportunity to destroy the full brood. The seven hunters all opened fire on the last four vampires. It was divine retribution for them but there was more to this than just vampires.

No, the witches were still somewhere in this village. Craighton beheaded the vampires and covered them in holy water that disintegrated the vampires and left nothing but bones and dust. Now they had to find the Coven who were by all accounts sleeping of their ghoulish feeding habits. They were also being guarded by a pack of black dogs. Who were good at keeping unholy things safe and guarded. There were six of them all sleeping as they were used to being on guard duty. They never saw it coming to them. The light again blinded the hellish animals as the hunters got closer to them to really exact the Lords punishment. They woke with the piercing and divine light of retribution it sent them braying in pain.

The Coven woke instantly at the piercing shrieking of the dogs getting punished by the Lords light. The hunters then saw the door open to the Hotel that they were slumbering in. They began to set their eyes on the hunters. This was part of their unholy gift. But somehow it wouldn't wash with the hunters. Father Clayton stepped up to Susan who was a dark haired stoney faced woman, who thought that her Malevolence was more than worthy of the dark lords she served. But Father Clayton married her to a 45 bullet at point blank range. This lifted her head clean off and sent a whole pile of blood all over Anne Lowe.

She snarled at this her tongue seemingly snake like, licking some of the arterial spray, which had come from her sister. She then produced a sharp ceremonial sacrificing and whipped it across Father Clayton's chest leaving a nasty slice just beneath his left nipple. Robert aimed his Uzi at her and fired a spraying pattern at her. The bullets ripped through her and she jerked as they landed all over her torso from belly up. She fell with a splash of black blood.

Davina and Carla were the last two of her Coven. And they began to beg for mercy. They hissed and contorted saying, "Spare our lives it was all our masters doing, spare us, spare us"

Craighton looked at the two women and said, "Nope, you must join your sisters in the confines of hell". Then he stepped forward and put the double barrel to Davina's head and shouted at the point of pulling the trigger, "Burn in hell bitch". The buck shot disintegrated her head. The other witch was cursing and crying she was cursing the devils that she had once held in high esteem. Craighton sent her the same way as he had sent her head witch. Both barrels. Bang. They thought it was over but nothing that evil was alone, in its ways. They headed back to the centre of the village when something happened that shocked and sent the hunters on their last battle in that unholy town. Zombies they came pouring out at them.

Craighton looked at them shambling along numbering in the hundreds. "Nothing is plain sailing not when it comes to the purging of the wicked". They formed a circle and began to fight the Zombies, knowing that their aim had to be expertly used. (aim for the head). They fired of as much as they could. Taking out most of them.

"Where the fuck did these fuckers come from?" asked Robert spraying at the heads of three or four at a time. The light shining around them and giving them enough light to aim at their heads. They were beginning to lose heart at the number of Zombies that never seemed to end. But the lord was answering their prayers that night. And sent Darius and Micheal down from heaven to set thing's straight.

They arrived with a blast of pristine light, the two of them landing and an explosion of holy light destroying the majority of them. Then with holy avenging swords they began to lift the heads of the Zombies that seemed to keep on coming. They were just in time to as the hunters were running low on ammo. Craighton smiled and said, "Trust in god and he will deliver you from harm".

The two White witches were first to run out of ammo. Then so did Father Clayton. Then Robert then Craighton. Carlos was doing the right thing and swinging his machete at the things and Antione was using an axe that he had procured on the way back to the centre of the village. He was cleaving and cutting with the thing. It was a fire axe and it was useful. The battle went on until the next dawn. And Darius and Micheal were doing the task at hand and serving up the flesh eaters righteous and holy destruction. The zombies began to taper off. Fewer and fewer of them. Craighton wiped the sweat off of his brow and had been using a bowie knife to its maximum usage. They had cleaned house and now they were going to find a quiet place to go and eat some food before they head back to Paris. That was when the holy Vatican arrived and began to clear up the mess.

The End

THE SOUL COLLECTOR

Mary Beth woke from her gentle slumber, smiling to herself as she washed and dressed, it was one ritual that she had struck an accord with. Anyway, her hygiene was important to her as she was a nurse in the cancer patients ward in the local hospital. She had slipped into the job with relative ease and was flabbergasted at the way she handled the patients, she was a natural healer and had a close net of friends whom she mingled with and got together with. She had an optimistic view of her life, and nothing perturbed her in the ways of living. Her friends included several nurses and two porters, who she lived to meet with, Charles was her favourite, he often found himself alone with her at the end of a get together. Christian was the other and was a complete heart-throb. He was fond of the gym and he and Charles went together at least three times a week. The female beauties that hung around Mary Beth were truly sensational, in both their looks and their attitude. They often crowded together and giggled when someone new came into their fold. No, they weren't cliquey, no they had morals and those were kept in check by the sister superior, Elaine.

Elaine was a raven haired beauty whose smile would make a holy man horny. She kept her sisters in check. But she knew that this balancing act of beautiful power was only for show, at night, when she wasn't entertaining, she was a reader an avid reader. Of all kinds of literature. Sometimes she would even read the Bible. She wasn't a diehard Bible thumping puritan. No, she was a mild, sensuous lady who had a flare for the dramatic. Clara was the other nurse who had a kick ass body, which would be summed up by the way she swung her hips.

They were having a meal together that weekend in honour of a couple of patients who had successfully come back clear of lung cancer. This had pleased Elaine no end, they had little reason to dress and be jovial, so they enjoyed having a night on the town where they could celebrate their rejection of death and the beginnings of a new life for the two patients. But someone was watching them as they gathered in a local Indian Restaurant.

He was a tall lithe man with dark hair and darker eyes. He had plans, supernatural plans. He was working with the ancient magic of Hell. He had opened the doorway to the other side a number of years ago and had come to experience power no mortal man was fit for. At first it had drained his energy and he had scrabbled around in his basement choking on the atmosphere of the planes of Hell. The fire the brimstone. The blood that was in his veins was congealed and gave him a sick pale ghoulish look. He wore glasses in the daytime to help him with the reading and summoning of various devils and demons. Every so often he sacrificed a small animal to Lucifer, who in turn responded by filling him with devious acts of hellish nature He belonged in hell and knew once his mission had been finished he would Join the damned and evil spirits in the new world order of Hell.

There was a whole network of Devil worshiping witches and warlocks. Some of them were in hiding, others well, well they were caught and ended up incarcerated in prison, with no access to their grimoires and candles. Some had been caught sacrificing children and various other holy animals, goats and such. He had a way, a skulking slithering way that could not be dressed any other way than evil and loathsome. His Name Mark Candace, he was enjoying listening to the conversation and cheering of the group, he was in the preparations of several mystical spells and ways that he had been studying from his skin covered grimoire. He had taken to personally hide the book with the skin of a young girl child.

Mark sneered as he drank some of his Cobra Lager and tucked into his Lamb Dopiaza, with rice. He nearly missed the five of them leaving as he was meditating, concentrating onto what he was to do next. And that was a true act of treachery. And would need all his cunning and guile. But he had faith in the unholy power of the pandemonium and the evil devils that ran Hell. He paid for his meal and wandered off in the opposite direction to the five hospital workers. He had some candles to anoint with various herbs and tinctures, to prepare the way for the soul collector. This demon had not seen any action in the earth realms for the better part of six centuries and would take great skill to enable it into the Plane of Earth.

He had been caught and sealed over in space and light shone on his bonds, as they were impossible to sever, the holy chains of light. But Mark had to show the way to the Greater Demon. But needed a six person sacrifice and an unholy act of carnage, and these things

,well they needed balance and meticulous rites and also, they needed the moon to be at the right stage in order to show the way to the Soul Collector.

To release his bonds. It would turn the world into great darkness and shadows. Then the damned would find a way to destroy the mortal shackles and a new day would dawn. a day of shadows and evil. Of a thousand tortured souls exacting justice on the world, not Buddha, not Allah, not Jehovah, not the Greek, or the Viking gods would hold the power to destroy the Soul Collector. And the end of its incarceration in the light, well it was fast upon them.

*

Craighton Lake woke that morning and walked to his sink, running his hand over his balding ginger hair. He had been seeking a demon that was hiding in the souls of the pure. It would latch onto the psyche of a nun then dissipate into the soul of an altar boy. Then when it got brave it would cause the death of one or more holy victims. These victims were arch-clergy and were obviously targeted for some sort of weakening ritual and bringing forth a chaotic evil force that was unrivalled in the earth domain. He called Father Clayton who was a strong pillar in the community of the city of Bently. They had kept their distance from the ethereal demon, knowing that it would be a short time before it needed to possess another Holy host and then they would perform an Exorcism and banish the spiritual into the Ninthe Plane of Hell.

They needed to capture the demon as the dead were mounting up. "Hello Father".

Father Clayton smiled as he responded, "Yes Craighton. Is it nearly time to set the trap?"

Craighton smoothed his balding head that he shaved most mornings. Leaving it smooth and easier to maintain and concentrate from. "Yes Father, the plan is in full swing and I've already organised an area that is being blessed as we speak."

Father Clayton was a well-built man who enjoyed the pleasure of construction work. Brick laying, carpentry and of course labouring. He had callouses on his callouses. The manual work was his way of staying pure. And his way of connecting with god's holy work. He would help in the building of orphanages and also hospitals. This was his way of healing and keeping fit he was in his early forties, was rugged and handsome and had a smile that was shining in his eyes every waking moment. He had stuck through the vow of celibacy, knowing that sex would destroy every moral he had.

"Okay Craighton, I'll see you in a day or so".

Craighton gave a small content laugh, "Yes Father".

Father Clayton put the bag of tools and a sledge hammer in the trunk of his '69 Dodge Viper. He had restored the motor from a rusty shell. He got in and drove to the Hospital that was for children and was well on its way to completion. He got straight down to business. The foreman knew exactly why they were blessed by the Priest; he was twice as strong as their youngest and fittest. Father Clayton carried on smashing the ground that was rocky and desolate. He had made progress; more progress than half of the young construction squad. As you can imagine the strength that he had come to need both spiritual and muscular were constantly needing recharged. But he found the solace of the Lord and the strength of the Lord were practically going hand in hand. He was constantly in shape physically and spiritually he was at ease. He kept the good book close to his heart and managed to pull a stubborn shift on the sites where he was constantly engaged in the physical laws of strength. And was glad to be pulling the shifts that he could. It kept him patient, quiet and above all things grateful for the energy. Sometimes whilst engaged in the hard craft of manual labour he could hear the angels speak to him. And this is what he meant as hand in hand. The angels sometimes sung to him whilst he slogged it out with the concrete and muck.

The demolition side was a particular favourite of his. And the angels knew it. It was the main time his storm was focused. And was a favourite time for the angels to sing to him as he was particular about his anger and discontent. He loved sermons as well knowing that his flock had never abandoned him. As was well meant as they constantly kept the various charities that he was fond of in check and those other things, the darker side of Humanity, were constantly under watch by Craighton Lake, Carlos and various others who were on the ball when it came to vanquishing the Hellish foes.

They had just cleared two nests of vampires and were now concentrating on a spirit demon who was causing all sorts of bedlam and chaos. He had been the cause of several young altar boy's disappearances. They found its lair and now the demon was exposed. They were now laying a trap for it. The lair was full of grotesque trophies from the dead altar boys and also several young nuns and a priest. The place it had come to know as it's lair was a decrepit old townhouse

which had its electricity rigged and never was thought
to hold the grotesque evil trophies that the demon had
dined on. He had kept it secret for a number of years
when Craighton, who had just destroyed two nests of
vampires, had quite by chance stumbled onto the
whereabouts of the Spirit Demon. They poured for
months looking for the name of the demon but alas no
name was attributed to it. No, he was stumped but he
knew that thing was incredibly cunning and was
cautious when it came to his quarry. It had the police
department stumped and several private eye firms
totally confused, with one private eye blowing his brains
out after discovering that it was a demon. (Something
that regular people thought did not exist).

The other private eyes had been spooked by the
sudden death of the detective, a man renowned for his
clarity and his wisdom in detection, knowing only that
the simplest explanation was generally the correct one.
But when he had stumbled onto its lair he was robbed
of all his faculties and went spiralling into insanity and
bang, blew his brains out. Craighton had seen this
coming, knowing that the dead that surrounded the
demon were evil and pure evil at that. They liked to dine
on fresh virgin souls, the younger the better. Craighton
scoffed at the thought of the demon turning him insane.
He had seen many chaotic devils and demons and none
had survived the light of the Lord.

Craighton was a hard-core demon hunter and had
destroyed many an evil spirit, spectre and ghoul. He had
never failed in the detection of one, but this case was
strange. It was a simplified fact that whoever this demon
answered to, was a true devil of pandemonium. The
Ninth plane of Hell. Being the worse of the devils,

demons and daemons. They were planning on something big and this minor blip in the paranormal world was causing a healthy ripple that was leaving a stain in the retched humanity. Craighton, had been around since the Occult Wars had started. As a child he was taken to see various, hoo doo holy men and priests of vast power's. They had been channelling the world's vast and holy powers. They were keeping the seals shut and Hellsgate closed. But every now and then a demon or a devil escaped causing bedlam on the planet.

Chaos was, as it seems, hard to capture and even harder to restrain. Craighton smiled as the candles of pure spirit were lit and the local priest, who was a man in his junior years was shaking at the thought of what may come of this. He was to be the bait, a fresh twenty-one, year old, who had just passed out of seminary school and was still rejoicing. His name was Robert Cruz and was on the fast track to the occult side of the church. Showing great courage in the dealings of the undead and also several type one demons, whom had silently and cunningly made the treacherous and often deadly way into the earth realms. He had vanquished one with the power of the good book and another with an ancient crossbow that was supposedly used at the very beginning of the occult wars. The crossbow had been blessed by Saint James, patron saint of the lost cause, when he had destroyed the slithering mass of teeth and tentacles.

He really enjoyed the warmth he was greeted with by both nun and priest. Robert took to the arcane studies like a duck to water. He had come forth with names and sacred paths that could only be traversed by the Holy and the blessed. No Robert was a true demon hunter.

Craighton Lake had become a very skilled ally, with Robert's nose in a book and Craighton's muscle and blessings. They were unstoppable and true enemies of chaos and evil. They were also being watched over by one of the Archangels, Darius. He made sure their path was clear and pure and that nothing went to pot in the hunting of daemons and demons.

Darius had intervened once or twice, especially when it was ghouls and their feast of poisoned flesh, this really revolted Darius and the Lord Himself. But more and more sinners were turning into demon and the undead. It was a no lose situation for some, others it was well, they wanted life to stop on their marvellous world, see how many benevolent people would survive the end of the world. No, Witchcraft of the blackest order was coming into its own with more people wanting to join the legions of the damned. They were usually criminals and the dregs of society. Nobody kept an eye on the dwindling amount of homeless and poor. The priests were the first to notice the amount, of poor were just vanishing.

This was part of the reason that Father Clayton was sent to the mission in Bently. The first person to make his acquaintance was Craighton Lake. He had been known for the hunting and destroying of several summoners. This led back to Bently where he found that there was more going on than met the eye. The house was dishevelled to say the least but it was ideal for them to make a trap. They had Father Crufax's head over the bath tub and waited as they murmured the satanic incantation to summon the demon. They carried on for nearly an hour then the demon appeared. It was all black even its horns that was because it lived in the heat and the shadow. It flicked its snake like tongue and wettened its lips. He hissed at the figures of both Father Clayton and Craighton who were in ancient demon summoning robes and were just going through the motions. It began to sidle down the side of the apartment staying as much as it could in the shadows.

Father Clayton was first to strike as he gripped the thing by its roasting hot horns that seethed and hissed as the Priest gripped and ripped the thing off balance. The demon roared and tried to scratch the three demon hunters as they grappled and gripped the demon of the night. Craighton produced a large ceremonial dagger and thrust it through the things heart till blacker than pitch blood pumped out of the wound whilst Father Crufax wrapped a long slender cheese wire around the things neck. Then with a quick Jerk he took the things head off of his body. They then doused it's body in holy water and cut it into pieces so as to render it useless Then they took it away and buried the thing in several blessed places in the city. Craighton smiled after finishing off with the digging and Father Clayton blessed and anointed the earth. They then headed away to a local diner to discuss how the thing had made it to the world in the first place.

*

Mark was in the middle of his ceremony of the dog; it was mankind's weakness that had turned him on to the house pet and he was known to sacrifice a couple a month. He knew they were well received in the Planes of Hell. Them and cats. The true guardians of the world dogs and cats. They had been the death of many an imp and goblin. The ferocious fights that had been seen and heard at night between what looked like two cats was in fact a changeling trying to assimilate a cat and the cat was truly in trouble, but more often than not the cat had won the melee and sent the demon back to hell. But this was only occasionally and often the cat had been severely wounded, that was why they get nine lives to protect them and their owners.

Dogs on the other hand could sense when something was wrong, especially at night, they were blessed with canine sense and they knew how to alert their master when something foul was in the wind. Mark carried on with the ceremony and the young black labrador was unconscious in the middle of the pentacle which had come from the blood of other sacrifices. He raised his arm with the sacrificial knife and struck it deep into the heart of the unconscious dog. The dog gave off a whimper before silence as its energy drained and the blood collected at the base of the pentagram and the fire and brimstone that showed itself when the ceremony was in completion.

The corpse of the dog vanished into the Hellish Plane of hell. Obviously, whatever it passed onto was hungry. Mark could now concentrate on his chief goal to raise the Collector, but this was no easy feat. No, he had to corrupt and change the very paths of the lives of the nurses. This would take time and patience and a degree of evil skill. This was not to be underestimated as he knew said incantations would show the demon hunters his lair and that would be dangerous. He sat and pondered the question, how could he deceive the hunters, show them one thing then on the other hand do another. Then it occurred to him he could acquire the help of a group of ghouls. He knew of one lair; it was a long shot but it was his only chance at getting further forward with the summoning. He carried on his ceremony with blood red wine and a feast of sweet breads. He smiled as he dined on the corpse of a young runaway child. As he dined, he felt awash with evil spirit and malicious intent. He was hopeful in the execution of his next spells. He was relying on the sacrifice of various animals and certain runaway teenagers.

He carried on dining on the sweet breads. He also had to calculate the next full moon and when blood would be prevalent on the moon. Various other portents such as a Banshee scream over the entire city, it was seen as portent of imminent catastrophe on the full city of Bently. Demons would rise and send the holy towns into chaos. They would summon the dead and turn the dying into fearsome creatures of the night. They would rise up and destroy the clergy and its flock. Turn the holy into unholy undead and ghoulish with the young and the lame being first to be devoured by the creatures of the night. It was chaos and destructive forces that would engulf the world from the hell gates, pits, and bowers. The evil that had once been mythological was coming into being. He carried on his feast. And smiled as the human meat he was enjoying was washed back with blood red claret.

*

Craighton smiled sullenly as he lay his head onto his pillow. The night had been a productive one and Craighton and the rest of the demon hunters had struck a blow of immediate satisfaction in the Holy Wars. Craighton fell into a deep comatose sleep feeling the prayers of the blessed giving him the courage to do as much as he could. Which was only as much as he could bare in these blood-soaked times.

Father Clayton smiled and rested his hand on the Old Testament gathering his strength and aptitude. Fortifying and conditioning his soul. He took great solace in the way of the Lord. And knew no other way was possible other than the Lord.

Father Crufax was in conversation with one of the other demon hunters. A great ally called Carlos. He was like a bull and knew exactly how to handle demons and daemons. He had twelve years of hunting and had always been grateful for every day he was a demon hunter. He was a great adversary of the Hell spawn.

Robert and he were in quite a good conversation about the rise of devils and demons. "Yes, Carlos this was the worse one yet".

Carlos smiled and extinguished his match after lighting his cigar. Then he replied, "Robert, you didn't phone me to tell me the fact that I'm already aware of. No, you need me, something really sinister is happening and you need my help".

Robert took a sip of his coffee. "Well one of the two Vampire broods we destroyed had a black Bible, a wiccan and devil summoning a piece of old ways, a way to summon an evil devil that could well, destroy most of the world This would leave the world to Hells pandemonium. But it was a risky chance they took as this would also leave the world to its oldest of protectors the Archangels. Who were not known for their subtle ways."

Carlos smiled and puffed on his Cuban cigar. "And there we were all hoping to be thorough in the extinction of Devil, demon and daemon. You will definitely need me then".

Robert smiled and replied, "Yes, Carlos, we definitely will need you".

Carlos finished puffing then put the phone on its cradle. Robert knew that he had done the best he could in assessing the situation. Robert smiled as the dialling tone rang off. One of the most reliable men he knew and that was Carlos. He figured that he had two days tops to get to the bottom of this devil incantation. The book had been drenched in poison and written in blood, virgin blood. It was a remarkable find and he was continuing to unravel its secrets. He needed to sleep, as the past day or so had left him exhausted and he would need all his energy to bring about the end of these demon cults that were growing more and more ferocious, as if they had gained the forbidden knowledge that had given them , when he would inspect the grimoire, and hopefully discover what powers it truly had. He knew he was going to have to study and study hard at the cold light of day. He would call the rest of the demon hunters first thing. This was going to be a cold hard trial of both the hunters and the daemons that were closing the gap between Hell and Earth.

*

Craighton was first to arrive at the small house adjacent of the church. He rapped on the door gently and Robert answered, he was still waking up and saw it was

Craighton. "Morning Craighton, how are you?" He said as he opened the door letting him in.

"Yeah, I'm fine Father, you sleep well?" Robert smiled and pointed down the hallway. "The book is in there," he said.

Craighton smiled, "I take it that it is poisoned and inked in virgin blood?" Asked Craighton.

Robert gave a short scoff and replied, "Yep the usual".

Craighton nodded his head and replied, "Any new handlers written in the book?"

Robert followed Craighton as he went down to the study. "Not as of yet".

Craighton looked at the wretched evil manual. "Are you hoping for something new?"

Robert sighed, "Yeah, well I was but it turned out to be a dead link with one of the vampires fitting the linguistics".

"Ah so it was a close call which turned out to be a waste of time." Craighton put on a pair of examination gloves and lifted the thing off its rest. "And why did you suspect it in the first place?"

"Something it said about a soul being due, and that it would summon a collector, a malicious demon that would not be stopped."

Craighton sniffed a small laugh and said, "So why did it come to nothing?"

Robert took the book from his hand, "It was positive but then it reconciled itself with the fact that said demon was in chains and there was no way of releasing the demon as it would bring about the demonic apocalypse. Everything evil would be destroyed as the Lord would wake".

Craighton smiled, "so it's just that little bit far-fetched?"

Robert nodded his head and put the black Bible back in its place, then continued ,"I've so much more to study and I've a strong feeling it gets darker in Moonlight".

Craighton sat down and said, "When is Father Clayton coming, and I take it you phoned Carlos?"

The far off looking father smiled, "Yes of course I phoned Carlos".

Father Clayton arrived later that afternoon while Craighton and Robert were pouring over the relic. The evil relic, it was fascinating to them as they found more references to The Soul Collector, But the further into the devils Bible and summoning tomb they got, the more about the pure soul and the sacrificing of that soul would bring about the end of the world as they knew it. Father Clayton smiled at the two of them as they were engrossed in the black evil book and they were both of the opinion that the Blood on the Devils moon was soon. And that they needed to somehow stop the wretched night from reaching its pinnacle, but the two of them had no idea as to who the pure soul was and how to protect it from the evil ones malignant plans.

*

They had lunch and spoke until late into the night. It was a puzzling thought and they had no idea who was cultivating this plan and who it was that had the other chapters of the book and why it had been so cleverly found at the Lair of the Vampires. It wasn't coincidence it wasn't luck, it was fate and if one thing they all held precious was that nothing happened for no reason. No, fate was on their side. And they knew it played a huge piece in the mechanics of the Occult wars. Tomorrow Carlos would arrive and they would have a new prospectus to the grimoire. A fresh set of eyes and a new way of viewing the grimoire.

They slept the last of the night away in the confines of the priests home. Craighton was having a light sleep that evening and found himself going over notes of old conquests. Seeing if there was any connection to be made. He thought he was onto something with mentions of the pure soul. But had only led to the fact that the pure soul was a pillar in the community. This was leading him in circles. He still carried on the search for the Soul Collector. A thing that they were having a difficult time in pining down. There was no name to the Soul Collector and no name to the pure soul that needed sacrificing in order to free the Greater Demon. With all the powers of hell being drawn to the Soul Collector.

They just had to hope that the heavens were alarmed by the mention of the Soul Collector. But still no name and no sacrifice to which they could only hope as a good sign. They slept until mid-morning, when the door was rapped on by the huge frame of a demon hunter Carlos. he smiled as the door was answered, it was a small wry smile that only made his charisma all the more engaging. His build was a strong muscular man with a large crucifix tattoo with the words 'Only God Can Judge Me'. When you first met the man, you were overwhelmed by his gigantic frame and dark Italian eyes. But when you saw the tattoo and figured out what kind of statement the tattoo gave off you knew that this man was not to be messed with. He had done his iron warfare and continued to do so three times a week. Many a demon had fled at his frame as it came forward with a Bible in one hand and a gun in the other.

*

Craighton smiled and they immediately hugged as it had been several years since they had been together.

"My man!" came the statement from Craighton.

Carlos gave Craighton the once over and said, "Yes my friend we have trouble's, no?"

The question come statement made Craighton smile all the more. They were close and that wasn't a cheap friendship, it was years of fighting the Occult wars and having each other's backs. Knowing how each other operated and having the time to spend resourcing the evil doers of this world. Father Clayton shook his hand next, then Father Crufax. They then went and sat down to breakfast. It was a fruit salad and eggs to begin with. But the question that was burning in the Dark Italian's head was 'The grimoire' And where was it how much was there left to translate.

Robert after finishing his meal beckoned Carlos to join him in the study. They went through as did the other two. Father Crufax put on his examination gloves as did the rest of the hunters, they had to be careful as not only was it brittle from being around for a thousand years but the poison that the dark relic had been dipped in was a potent contact poison that had long since been lost to the world, That meant that it only needed to be touched briefly and would cause an agonising death, a long slow incurable death. Its handlers didn't need gloves as they were already dead. There was also some chapters missing. And the chapters that had been cut out of the book were done surgically. And no trace of them except the huge gaps in the translation of the grimoire. They all agreed that the chapters were missing from the evil bible were obviously so important that they had removed them with painstakingly accuracy and that they could not find a single clue as to who had the remaining pages.

The soul collector stirred in its deep dark prison. He had seen his return to the earth realms and was pleased with the results so far.

*

Mark was at this point taking pictures of Mary Beth. And holding a long look at the rest of her friends, Charles and Christian were going to be difficult, as Mark noted their strength and size but there was something almost magical about Charles, an inner glow that shone around and through him. He had to wonder whether the man was an Angel, but of course that would explain why only he could see his inner glow. Yes, the man was angelic. And that spelled trouble, especially since he had never gone up against an Angel. "Tricky" He said as he took some more pictures of Mary Beth. He then unscrewed the lens and packed away the camera. Smiling and fixing his stare on Mary Beth as he did this. He had little in the way of surprises for the five of them, two for the altar, one for the ceremony and the other two were well he was going to get complicated sending them into an undead pit of flesh eating zombies. He turned the steering wheel and headed back to his lair.

*

Craighton and Carlos were pondering on what type of Demon was in charge of the Soul Collectors summoning and subsequent release. Carlos was positive it was an arch devil that had been hiding amongst them since the very dawn of time and had been hiding, showing no sign of what it was. They had no lead to whom the pure soul was, only that they were well thought of in the Christian Community. But that could be any number of a hundred people. They sat the next three hours pondering the fact that they needed to save the pure soul.

Craighton had a brainstorm. "Davina." He said enthusiastically. "She can Scry for the whereabouts of the pure soul".

Carlos smiled and lit a cigar. A long thin cigar. "It's just a matter of time," he replied.

That's when Crufax remembered something, something of major importance, "Blood on the devils moon, its four weeks away," He said. "The Devil worshipping conclave have worshipped this night once every five years".

Craighton sighed and listened.

"They call it blood dark on a devils moon. They do their honours of the demons devils and witches who have achieved great macabre success".

Craighton stood up and said, "I'll get Davina and she can try and find the pure soul. But it'll take some doing".

Father Clayton smiled and said, "Great the marvellous Davina Green, and sure she will have a host of theories into the destroying of the Soul Collector".

Craighton Lake walked over to the landline and phoned Davina.

She said, "I have to prepare the spells and incantations".

Craighton laughed at her a little it was a goofy laugh. As the two of them had romantic history. Craighton had called it off because he needed her as an ally and the two of them would just end up treading on each other's toes, juggling a relationship and cleansing demons at the same time would prove to be treacherous. Anyway, she said she would be ready in the next day or so depending on the portents and signs.

*

Craighton hung up and re-joined the rest of the group. They were joined by Davina a day later as she had to do the sacred bathing ritual in which she had focused on all things holy. But this may have been for nought, as she knew that they were looking for a needle in a haystack. There was five million folk in the city of Bently. And only a small percentage of them were demons and daemons. And the rest were well; they were just food for the beasts and devils. But she remained hopeful she had a strong inclination that the medical profession was hiding both good and bad.

She set up the crystal orbs and lit the incense of true seeing. She inhaled in and started to murmur the prayers for the lost souls. Hopefully this would show her a vision or a bright mark on the pure soul. She knew she was onto something when she focused on the Hospital with its goodness and selfless acts of compassion. No, she was in a ward in ethereal form and it showed her the pure soul, Mary Beth, who was coming to terms with another fatality on the Ward. Davina heard her superior Elaine talk to her, "Mary Beth it's a lotto draw in here you know that".

Mary Beth sighed, but there was never an excuse for the immediacy of a crash cart that went wrong. Davina stayed a while then headed back to the house she flew at the rate of the fastest bird. She arrived back and the energy crackled as her body began to jerk and twitch as her soul swam its way into Davina.

"You find her?" Craighton asked as she began to regain consciousness. "Yes, I located her.

Craighton wrote down the woman's name and where she worked. "I'll go and scope her out tomorrow". He said.

Father Clayton smiled and said, "I take it she's a definite pure soul?"

Craighton helped Davina straighten herself out. She thanked him and Craighton had one other question, "Was she being watched? Was she marked magically.?"

Davina sighed as if the answer was going to make or break the mood. She had only her intuition to keep her free from ridicule.

*

"No, she was just there and I knew she was a pure soul, nothing has marked her or hindered her in the holy light that keeps her pure". Craighton smiled and said as he lit a candle in honour of the dead that were needed to help them in the battle against Hell. It was going their way or so it seemed. Craighton wondered whether the four weeks were enough to combat the Soul Collector. He had to approach Mary Beth and knew that it was going to take all his charm and confidence to persuade her that she was in grave danger. If it didn't work, well they could say adios to the world. But there was no way this could happen, he wouldn't let such a thing happen, he was true to the cause in the right way. He went away that night saying that he had a suspicion that the demon summoner was going to try and get as close to her as possible.

Craighton returned after doing a service for her. A service that just may make or break him and all his spiritual powers. He needed to be sure that the young nurse was safe. So, he began to ready himself to try and convince her that she was in grave danger. He held hope that she would come into the hunters realm where he could be sure of trapping the demon summoner.

But Mark had other plans, he had already swooped on one of the five hospital staff. He had Clara in the trunk of his busted Oldsmobile. She was terrified in the instant of it happening she gave a small squeal as the chloroform was put onto her mouth. She collapsed and Mark threw her in the trunk. She was going to the Zombie pit. The only tricky part was the sacrificing of the Matrons life as well as the unholy sacrifice of Mary Beth.

Craighton woke the next day with a slight headache. Davina and he had parted after they had a small quaint conversation in which they had agreed to meet after all this was through. As it was a tough challenge and Craighton had all kind of fears. The mysterious demon summoner was a major factor in this but no one fitted the bill. And Craighton was growing short of two things; one was patience the other was time. He needed results and needed them fast. He had a plan to use the C.C.T.V. coverage and search back to any Lurkers or Stalkers. He noticed one in particular a young dark haired geeky guy with glasses, arriving just before Mary Beth and sometimes a short time later. Mary Beth needed to be approached and Craighton took the number of the old car and went straight in to see Mary Beth.

He approached her calmly and not saying to much smiled and asked, "Your Mary Beth?"

She smiled and carried on waiting for her friend who had been late two days now. She was beginning to scare herself. "Yes, I'm Mary".

Craighton smiled and pushed his hand out to her "I'm Lake, Craighton Lake."

She smiled as she took the young demon hunters hand into hers.

"I know you think I'm pulling you."

She laughed and said, "Am I that obvious?"

Craighton smiled a short smile that really lit up his eyes. "No ,listen I got to talk to you?" he said.

Mary Beth smiled ,"I tell you what, I get off shift at about three, three thirty, you meet me at the parking lot then and I'll be all ears."

Craighton smiled as she walked away, "Three, three thirty, I'll be there". He had handled the situation superbly and knew that the major part had been dealt with the ice. He just had to trust his instincts and lay it on her. Of course, she would be sceptical at first (Well who wouldn't be) It's a pretty major fucking thing you were laying on her. So, he had to be careful when engaging the subject. He smiled as he waited for her to finish her shift. She smiled as she approached Craighton who was of the opinion to just lay it on her. She could only do one of two things one was walk away dismissing him as a total lunatic. The other to follow him down the rabbit hole praying that it was safe and that he meant her no harm.

Mark watched from a distance as the two conversed in what was the only thing they could be talking about and that was him. He was a little nervous not knowing whether this had a satisfying ending in which he could trace her back to her house then under the cover of night kidnap her and prepare her for the devils moon. Only one more puzzle piece remained and that was Elaine Fox. Who had been non-existent since Clara had gone missing. Christian and Charles on the other hand were doing their nightly workout down at the gym.

As Craighton and Mary Beth got cosey they headed away to a local diner where pie and coffee was on the menu. Craighton ordered a nice slice of traditional apple pie whilst Mary ordered a slice of banoffee pie. Then after they had finished Craighton went for broke and decided to tell her what exactly it was that he did. She listened intently to his every word than after he finished, she smiled and replied, "Just when I thought I had scored you turn out to be a flake".

Craighton laughed and responded, "It's true, we are a group of paranormal investigators and we hunt demons, vampires, ghouls and devils"

She laughed a small sardonic laugh and said, "Did Elaine put you up to this?"

Craighton smiled and sipped some coffee. "No, she did not." he said.

They carried on talking as she was genuinely curious about Craighton. "How did you find me?" She Asked.

Craighton smiled and said, "A witches spell".

She laughed at this, "Oh come on your trying to tell me that the Clergy hire witches to hunt for, what was it again a pure soul",

Craighton smiled and said, "Believe it or not it's true".

Mary Beth smiled and asked the waitress for some more coffee; she had a feeling this was going to be a long night. Then Craighton explained how the malicious beings had already homed in on her and they had just over three weeks left until the Devils moon. She had heard it all now. She had attracted weirdos before but this guy, shit, nuts out of this world, gone. She hadn't a clue what to do so she went along for the ride.

"Okay Mr Lake." She smiled, "where do you intend to go from here?"

Craighton smiled, "I'll guarantee your safety and you will remain safe until we track down this demon summoner and kill him" Mary Beth gasped on the next question, "What happens if he gets me?"

Craighton drank some more coffee, "Game over sweetheart".

Mary Beth was really drawn into this scenario. It wasn't the way Craighton talked it was how candid and lucid he was. He didn't even break sweat. This was impressive.

"Okay," she said, "where to now my knight in shining armour?"

He smiled and sat the coffee cup down "To my other team members house just adjacent his parish."

"Okay I take it you are all Clergy?"

Craighton smiled and replied, "They are, I aint"

They then headed to Mary Beths car and sped off into the night.

*

Mark was heading to the zombie pit where a lot of problems the demons had were solved with the problem being thrown into the pit and torn apart by the flesh eating undead. He dragged the kicking and screaming young nurse into the derelict building which housed several dozen of the flesh eaters. He picked her up and threw her delicate body into the pits where the zombies fought each other over her. Ripping the young nurse apart and devouring her organs and intestines. The feeding frenzy lasted a good ten minutes and wall to wall guts and bone with flesh flying in every direction. He enjoyed the frenzy then left. He had nothing more to do but plan the next incantation where he would truly set his sign and mark.

*

Craighton and Mary rounded the corner to the pastor's house. And Craighton rested the engine of the car and said, "This is not your regular Catholic home. There are things in here relics of both demon and angel, Heaven and hell. Please do not be shocked as one hand washes the other".

Mary Beth smiled thinking, 'Psycho-ville'.

Craighton told her exactly what she thought, "We are in it for the species".

Mary nodded as Craighton opened the door. "If one thing upsets the balance then the world and heaven would be in grave danger, and this is why we do what we do," he smiled and she crossed over the threshold and into the sanctity of the hunters.

"How long has this battle been on going?"

Craighton smiled and said, "Too long".

Then father Clayton put in a word, "Since the dawn of time".

She smiled at the two priests who both shook her hand.

"Davina gone home?" Asked Craighton who was hoping to see her again.

"She needs her rest as that particular way of scrying takes a lot out of you and the more you immerse yourself in it the more exhausting it becomes".

He knew this of course but sometimes a gentle reminder of limitations kept him in check. He smiled and sat down. Carlos was next to introduce himself to Mary Beth.

"Hi, I am Carlos," he said with a slight Latino accent.

She giggled a little, took his hand, and shook it, "You guys are for real".

Carlos smiled and laughed, "Yes sweetheart we are for real".

Again, the slight Latin American accent.

She blushed slightly at the man and how smooth he was. "Well, I guess I'm safe with you".

Craighton laughed a little and replied, "Safer with us than anyone else".

She was then handed a mug of coffee and again she blushed, "You are all such gentlemen".

Carlos smiled and said, "Yes, why were you hoping for something else?"

She drank some of her coffee. "I didn't know what to expect".

Craighton smiled, "I thought so".

Then she sipped again, "Well I guess you are telling the truth, I mean two Priests and a Latin American smoothy and my knight in shining armour".

Craighton smiled and got himself a coffee, He then began to discuss who they were up against.

"Ahh," said Father Clayton, "I thought so, a demon summoner".

Craighton walked through to the study and sat back down, "I may have a way to get eyes on the Fiend".

Father Clayton sighed, "I bet you do".

Then Craighton went over to the computer and accessed the camera on the car park and took it back forty-eight hours previous. He then focused on the car that had been following Mary Beth into the car park. He noticed it once then twice.

"And three times a lady," he said as the car arrived a third time. Just as Mary Beth had gotten out and headed into the main building. The old rundown motor had turned into the parking lot. He focused on the driver's side and smiled. "Got Ya". Then showed the rest of them the focused picture of the tall, lithe, greasy-haired sinister looking dude.

He smiled as he looked at the camera, showing no fear no fear at all. They all took a good look.

"Oh, he knows he is made," said Carlos.

Craighton laughed, "Yep".

They knew that this was a major turnaround. They now had a target to focus on. Craighton drew a copy out of the computer and pinned it on the wall next to the black Bible. They sat down to a group discussion.

They talked most of the night, into early hours in the morning. They then got onto the discussion on what may have happened to Mary Beth's friend, Clara.

"If this guy is as evil as we think then we must assume the worst-case scenario."

Mary gave a little choking cough and said, "She's dead, is that what you are saying?"

Craighton sighed. "Yes, we must assume so," he said.

Mary couldn't help but draw a tear. "I take it the rest of my friends are going the same way?" She asked choking on her sorrow.

Craighton passed her a hanky, "You know we may get him before he completes the evil rites on the Devils moon".

She took the paper hanky, smiled slightly with great sadness and asked, "When is it the Devils moon?"

Craighton relaxed, "Two weeks".

Mary Beth smiled a sad smile. "Then what are we waiting for?" she said.

Craighton admired that in her, a fresh perspective on the whole fucked up situation. She was cottoning on to the whole thing and was not short of ideas on how to best deal with the whole mess. They settle down just before dawn, and they each of them fell into a sound sleep. One of the angels had taken it into their own duty to comfort Mary Beth. Whilst she slept, "Well child I have been waiting for you to come close to our doorstep". She smiled as the angels eyes warmed her with tenderness. "You are truly exceptional".

She answered silently, "Thank you".

The angel smiled and showed her more warmth. "You are perfectly safe child".

She smiled and murmured a small, "Thank you".

*

Mark decided the next move to be one of true evil. He would grab the young porter Christian and feed him to the Zombies, then he would begin to cite the unholy rite of the Soul Collector and knew it was close to the Devils moon. He knew the hunters had sighted him he smiled at the thought of how he was going to deal with them, but first Christian. He knew his nights when he was at the gym and tonight was one of them.

He parked close to the gym and watched as Christian walked around the corner and entered the gymnasium. He smiled as he paid for his hour long workout, he was true to the cause and that was no pain no gain. Mark waited for nearly the full hour then exited the car and slid into the shadows adjacent to the gym. Christian rounded the corner unaware of who was waiting in the shadows. He went to put the key into the lock of his car and bang the lights went out and he was unconscious. When he woke, he realised that he was heavily roped and secured to a chair. He was also blindfolded and had little room to move his hands.

"Who the fuck do you think you are?" he asked.

Mark gave a deep throaty laugh and said, "I'm your fate. Your whole life has led you to me".

Christian snarled, "Who the fuck are you. You will not get away with this.".

Mark snarled back and went, "You have come to the end of your journey and it is fate and the Dark Lord that have guided your path."

Christian growled again at him, "You have no Idea who you are messing with do you creep?"

The figure of Mark overshadowed him and he shivered to his very bones. Mark held a ceremonial dagger against Christian's neck. He was sure that this was the end for him, he wasn't going gently. He blacked out again and when he came round he was held on to a massive piece of stone with definite blood draining ducts in the stone. They were placed over the major arterial sites on a human. He hadn't cut them yet but was murmuring a small ancient evil chant with the names of demons and lesser demons. He was preparing the way to Hell for Christian.

The murmuring. the rise and fall as he made the unholy ones signs over Christian's heart. Then silence as he waited for the ancient demons to ascend and show him the first cut to make. Then after about three more minutes of silent chanting the first of his cuts were shown to him and that was the neck on the left side, and it bulged as Christian began to exhale and inhale sharply as his eyes bulged and his major artery popped under the stress of his breathing. Mark pushed his ceremonial dagger, tip into the tension of blood and said artery began to bleed. Then on his right side he cut the man's major lymphatics and it gushed from beneath his armpit. His naked body was bulging as he gave out a cry of terror. These two wounds were only the beginning.

There were several more cuts and he stopped struggling as his blood seeped onto the unholy symbols at the base of the stone slab. This had let a blood demon know his intentions and in turn he had let his blood god know. The blood vanished as if going into a host. The god bled him and bled him good. This was all in preparation for the pure soul, and Mark knew it. The body on the other hand was to be sent to the plague bearers as food. He just had to wait for the opening into the zombie realm. It happened several hours later. And Mark knew he would be well rewarded in the end of days. The times were chaos and death ruled the earth and even heaven would fall to its knees. This had been a thousand years in the making and had been thwarted three times. But Mark was confident he was the only chance his demonic master had at this ending of the world and heaven.

He was a classic guy, as well as ceremonial tables, he had a rack, an iron maiden and various other implements of dark macabre torture, including several ancient knives used in mumification and damning of souls. Sometimes it worked out for the royalty of Egypt, other times they were just meat for the beast. Very unusual times with a lot of praying to both good and evil, they had very little choice with Priests being changeable and some malevolent and some benevolent. They two pretty much walked hand in hand in those days. And Mark was waiting for the sides to be pretty much in the malevolent sides favour. The malicious demons and devils were about to get a foothold into the earth's spirit realm. And then the seizing of the Lords throne and his holy houses will burn in the fires of Hell as its pits and bowers were emptied and the worlds end would follow.

*

The plague bearers dined and dined fresh that evening planning and diverting their energy into the Zombie pits.

Where they would empty as the pure souls life ebbed into Hell, but this of course was a far cry from what the hunters would let happen. Craighton smiled when he returned to the chapel house with the information on Mark Candace. Father Clayton took the file from Craighton and sighed. "So lost so evil," he said and opened the wax seal that held what was practically textbook on the man's life.

Several other Demon hunters had seen and heard of Mark Candace. Several vampire hunts had come up with the identity of a head summoner who had gotten the vampires to safety. The vampires were on the run and Mark had made a damn near impossible move, which was to move them in daylight. He had covered the sullen brood in material and sun block. They were wrapped head to foot and had gathered a small amount of people to feed during the transition phase to the New England, in the land of the brave. They got to the small town in the outskirts of Bentley and hid underground. Knowing that they had just landed in a new set of vampire laws and hunters were predominantly in the lead of the Occult wars.

Clayton read the beginning with a sigh as if he weren't reading the textbook then nobody was. The file asked the question, was he inherently evil or just another flake looking for attention. But his attitude towards the Occult had started young when he had made his first offering to the Old Ones. It was his neighbour's dog, a fluffy scraggly pooch, who he had instantly began to tease and play with the dog. Then on one of the Unholy nights of the blood moon he offered the pet up to Lucifer. He was shocked when he returned and the dead animal was gone. Just the smatterings of blood from the wound that had taken from the stomach to the dog's chest. Killing it, it howled as did the wind out in the wilderness as Mark gave his first offering and he had done well in the eyes of the Satanicus Summoners.

Father Clayton carried on reading the file. The child turned into a teenager and had twisted in the evil magic of the Old Ones. He began an incessant study of the demonic underworld. Every now and then he would sacrifice a small animal, but he was going for the bravest move on his part. He would get one of the local teeny boppers and slit her throat over a virgin candle. He had done so and done so with great pleasure and the powers of hell culminating in him.

He had a group of Summoners whom he had collected over the years and yet still no one could get him. The three summoners that were his prodigy were narking and back biting each other, so Mark used one of his spells and severed their ties with him then sent the three of them insane and into a suicidal rage. They were nothing but a reminder to Mark that it took patience to gain power, especially when his power was indeed the work of the dark ones.

Anyway several children went missing during his later youth. But still nothing could lead them to him. The police were baffled, no corpses, see they were dragged into the Hellish planes where they were taken and dined on by various demons and devils. Mark suddenly rose to the top five of the hunters catch and destroy list. They knew everything about Mark and I mean everything. How once the collector was freed, he would move to England and start his own Occult practice. This would seem bright, holy and superficial. But it was just a front a way to dupe people into what was really his goal to become devil and he would rule over his cultists with an iron hand.

These were his plans and he was well on the way to completion. But it just might have incurred the wrath of one of the other major devils as he flaunted his position in the hierarchy. That didn't sit well with a number of the demons and devils. He was cocky and that just made him even more stronger, the older he got the more sacrificing he did. But the Hunters had been tracking him since his first human sacrifice. A young girl who was intrigued by Marks darkness. He lured her in then knocked her out and laid her in a stone altar. Where he was told by the hellish high winds to deflower the said maiden, then slit her throat over a white virgin candle. He also had the missing pieces of the black Bible, the chapters needed to finish this world and send heaven into dis-array.

"So, you are a source for the Old ones," said father Clayton as he delved deeper into the file of Mark Candace. That meant that Mark had gathered so much evil and summoning powers that he, well he was close to being invulnerable. With much magic and true deathly powers of auto suggestion, as well as various cult ways and magics that were spawned in hell.

He was a tricky customer and had escaped from the hunters a total of five times so far. But Father Clayton kept reading the files. He needed to know what the man was capable of and if he was a devil already, as this was surely his focus his plan. To become a true agent of evil a devil of vast unknown horror, a way into Hell's blistering heat and frenzied feeding of demon, ghoul, vampire and zombie as well as pit fiends and fire elementals.

*

Mark smiled as he washed his ceremonial dagger and smiled as he looked at the stone slab that there appeared to be no trace of Christian. Not blood or anything it had all been sent into the chaos realms of hell where they would dine on the young soul. The denizen of that plane of hell would give more magic to Mark as in all types of offerings if they were appeased, they would empower. And Mark was never short of sacrifices. Now he would have to find a power position to finish off Charles, Elaine and Mary Beth. But he had plans unto which were designed to specifically cause a major ripple in this modern society. A potent powerful spell, this would take a day or so to gather the right material components. So, he began to enchant the wind and moon with spells of fathomless blessing, with wilderness evil and bone evil demon. Who, as Mark chanted, the demons cried into the wind releasing the sorrows of the Hells. He was about to make an example of Charles. And this was done with great concentration.

Marks eyes blackened out and he began to chant and his voice greeted those of the wilderness and they soared towards Charles' house where he was sleeping. He snored lightly as the air blew hot and salty. Mark carried on his concentration, weaving his fingers in the air doing strange enticing motions with his fingers wrapping them around Charles's head particularly his ears and nose. Charles woke to the suffocating feeling in his lungs and head. He coughed then carried on the struggle, then as the spells set in, they were making him a mindless psychotic killer and he didn't have the strength to ward off the demons and all their powers. The spell really worked. He got up growling slightly and walked over to the gun rack and lifted out a pump action shotgun. Then he picked up a box of shells for the gun and headed to his car. He was going to make an early start to that day.

Mark carried on concentrating carried on with his hands twirling and making macabre evil signs. He whispered a canto traxus sidious morticious. He was saying these words faster and faster. The words growing in power and giving no quarter in break or silence. And Charles drove his car to the outer parking lot of the Hospital and began to load the weapon and also fill his pockets with shells. Then he rode the lift to his ward. Then bang, chic, chic, bang chic chic as the shells were ejected, then Bang chic chic, bang chic chic, bang, this went on for seven or eight minutes then the ward was a live running river of blood. Then after the damage had been done, he woke out of his macabre trance and fell into a stage of great grief. Seeing the blood and carnage he loaded the last shell put his lips on the lip of the gun and bang. His head severed then landed with a thump on the floor next to his body. All this and Mark was watching with great concentration, now all that was left were Elaine and Mary Beth.

He smiled at the thought of what was to come. He knew that he had done the most damage with his summoning skills. This was a true test of evil. And his expertise was true to Hells ways. He finished the spell and closed the vortex letting the carnage settle and the demons finished their chanting. Knowing that this was a double curse, not only was Charles a friend to Mary Beth but he was a holy spirit who was supposed to protect Mary Beth. But he and his benevolent guardians had never expected the summoner to be as powerful as he was.

Father Clayton finished the file on Mark Candace, he had a true sense on the summoner and had several ideas on how to deal with him. He turned the telly on and watched the report of the massacre that had just happened a half hour ago. 'The perpetrator was a hospital porter who had shown no signs of stress or mental fatigue. It was senseless and horrific. And no sign of a catalyst. The porter, a Charles Chatsworth, was in his prime with no family or other stressful reasons to send the man over the edge. This made the massacre even more senseless and the gentleman then after the killing spree turned his weapon on himself.'

Mary Beth sobbed as she saw the news. Charles was more than a friend to her, he was a lover and when they made love it was heavenly. Mary Beth started to sob as the news came to an end. Father Clayton took her in his arms as she sobbed and her body racked with grief. Craighton sighed and looked at the disturbed nurse. Knowing that nothing he could say or do would take the pain and grief away from her. Craighton went and prepared some coffee and sandwiches for them.

Mary Beth stopped sobbing and said to Father Clayton, "I've got to get in contact with Clara, Christian and Elaine." Mary Beth settled her sobbing and walked over to the phone. She dialled Christian first and waited until the phone rang out and went onto answer machine. "Christian Sweetheart, it's me Mary did you see the news?"

She then waited and then hung up after a couple of seconds. Then she dialled Elaine's number and waited for her to answer, she was relieved as Elaine spoke, "Hello who is this?"

Mary sighed a sigh of relief. "Is that you Mary?"

Mary smiled and replied, "Yes, it's me Elaine. Have you seen the news".

Elaine breathed out and replied, "Yes Mary Beth I saw the news". She smiled as there was a small sense of relief in the fact that Mary Beth wasn't the only one facing the confusion of such a horrible act of carnage.

Mary sighed again, "Where is Clara and Christian?"

Elaine stifled a sob, "I don't know. I haven't heard from either one in a few days".

Mary Beth went for broke, and she explained the predicament she was in with the hunters, This conversation went on for a good hour with Elaine taking on board everything Mary Beth had to say.

"This is a little hard to swallow," she said as they neared the end of their conversation.

"Well apparently this guy has had his eye on us for some time now".

Elaine stared into nothing, knowing there were no words of comfort she could speak. No, they had a real problem here and the massacre was just the beginning. And her other two friends being missing only enhanced the tale of the summoner Mark, "This Summoner," she said, "is doing this to bring about the end of the world, with demons and devils ruling us".

Mary Beth said, "Yes Elaine".

Elaine stared again into nothing and there was an uncomfortable silence between the two of them. "Where are you, Mary Beth?"

Mary Beth smiled with some sense of relief then gave her the directions to the Chapel House. An hour later they were reunited. Mary and Elaine embraced soon as they saw each other. Craighton smiled and motioned for the two of them to enter the house. They went in and a nun arrived a few minutes later she was there to clean up and help in the small tasks that needed doing. Craighton finished speaking telling the two nurses just what kind of trouble they were in. Father Clayton said a quiet prayer and Father Crufax joined in. They then settled down and Father Cayton gave them the bad news.

"Your other two friends, we have to assume the worst".

Elaine sobbed and Mary Beth stared coldly into the distance. The reality was cold and hard to bear. But it was reality and that was the simple truth. The two nurses could barely swallow the massacre but the thought of the other two friends being dead, well it was a little hard to perceive. Then they discussed and went over the file on Mark Candace. This went on again into the small hours in the morning. They looked at various pictures that they had of the lithe, tall summoner. Knowing that they had hope to save themselves and that they were safe with the hunters. Mark was still planning some way to get the last two nurses into his devilish scheme. He had thought of leading them into a trap, killing the hunters and severing their only hope of surviving the devils moon. Then he would sacrifice the pure soul, Mary Beth and end the life of Elaine, but this was all in the near future. And nothing was certain not right then anyway.

Mark made arrangements with a group of ghouls out in the heart of the city. They were particularly nasty and had been responsible for at least twelve disappearances. But, no police man had even ventured near their lair. The hunters knew the whereabouts of the ghouls but needed to prepare, for the ghouls were known to have a highly poisonous atmosphere, in and around their lair. He spoke calmly to the head ghoul Mattire, who had known about the summoner for quite some time, he had often thought of having some sweet breads with the Summoner, but had never got around to asking, as they only found each other in passing and that was when they were collecting components for various evil spells and curses.

Mark spoke to Mattire and the upshot was they were going to help each other as much as they could. Mark smiled through the corner of his mouth and said, "I need your help Mattire". The ghoul was larger than most ghouls but had that greyish tint about him from eating poisoned human flesh.

Mark carried on, "I need to vanquish my enemies".

The ghoul sat up from his meal. "Yes Mark, I understand that you have a problem in collecting the pure soul."

Mark sniffed and replied, "Yes Mattire. She is with the hunters and is very near impossible to get to".

Mattire sneered and responded, "I have a solution to your problem".

Mark smiled again, he was making progress with the ghoul. "I will see to it that you are fixed with my greatest asset". Mark smiled again, "Thank you Mattire".

Mattire was quick to respond. "It may cost you more than you think".

Mark nodded his head, "Anything my friend".

Mattire grinned a malicious grin, "I need a sacrifice to Asmodeus".

Mark grinned down the phone, "Yes Mattire I can do that".

Mattire gave a dry cough and laughed and replied, "Then we have struck an accord".

Mark laughed and said, "When do you want the sacrifice?"

Mattire laughed at this, "Two, days' time, and it has to be a young child".

Mark knew the very time and it was on a dry moon. He smiled and placed the phone back onto its cradle. Then he began to make preparations to go out and collect a sacrifice for the ghouls. He would have this done quicker than he thought.

Elaine began to read the files on the evil summoner, mostly his case history, psychological reports and methods of the man. He was real stone cold fish he had nothing pinned to him but a lot of crimes attributed to him. But nothing that they could hold him on. And he had a cutting edge lawyer who dealt with all his charges. Beside that the Police were scared of Mark as he really put the fear into them. The first time they had arrested him he had sat in the interview room and barely breathed, the police were concerned that he was compos mentis. That really shook the two detectives, that and the fact he looked right into their souls. No remorse, no guilt, just calm. The dark haired guy so unnerved them that they both went running to church.

This had only made him more untouchable and when he was up for court he was defended by such a good lawyer that he never had to show his face, This had led him to believe more and more about his unholy powers. The Prince of darkness held all the cards with Mark and was often liking to show his power within the judicial system. This basically meant that Mark walking free was an unholy miracle. She carried on reading the list of charges that had been dropped mid-way through their investigations. Serving warrants on the summoner was very near impossible. As somehow Mark's lawyer was tipped off about the search and seizure of Mark Candace.

This was proof that the system which defined a country was rotten to its very core. She carried on reading. It was giving her an edge at least, she hoped it would, Mary Beth smiled at her as she raised her eyes to capture Mary Beth who was sat there staring at her superior.

"Anything I should know?" She asked Elaine.

Elaine smiled at her and said, "When I'm finished, I'll give you a summary."

Mary Beth smiled and sipped some more coffee. It was the third night they had pulled off with very little sleep, Mary Beth was suddenly curious about the grimoire, she was just about to handle the blood soaked book when Father clayton caught her hand.

"It's been steeped in poison," he said, then produced a set of examination gloves for her.

She smiled and put on the gloves and started to work her way through with the pictures of ghoulish ceremonies and deadly wishes and curses. Some in English some in Aramaic. She read and looked at the hideous rites and bleeding rituals all the powers of the Satanicus cult.

Various demons and vampires who were contemplating the Devils moon. Then she read the rite unto which she was part of, The night of the Soul Collector. That night she would be sent from here into Hell which in turn would release the full wrath of Hell onto the earth. She knew that she was in trouble. One part said that the gift of life of the pure soul must be made to disown all the heavens and it's attributes. She would in fact give herself completely to the Summoner. It was all about the hands fate and being in possession of her soul. She thought this sounded ridiculous, as she saw no way that she would give herself freely to the summoner. No, they had time on their side. But that was a matter of minor importance, as they were running out of it. She carried on reading the black Bible. It had her hooked, she read about the lost angel and his halo, she also read about the rites of passage of ghouls and how to summon hellfire in the case of judgement.

This, and a whole lot more, she was fascinated by the evilness, the sinister power that had been around since the dawn of time and how you could bathe in its power, control people and animals with your mind. How the discipline of evil carried with it an enormous burden, a burden that would in fact consume the summoner if things went the wrong direction. She was spellbound, something had happened to her when she had started to read but she ignored it and carried on reading. She made a lot of sense how vampire and ghoul and demon had come to know the evil in them so well. It was calling just like the Clergy. I mean a man must get the choice of whether he is good or evil, at some point he must question whether his faith is strong or wrong. I suppose even a devil must succumb to good at some point, but this was frowned upon by both devil and angel, saint and sinner. I mean, you are after all the product of your up bringing and this book (which she was reading) was a milestone in her Catholic up bringing.

She was fascinated with the whole thing. Not in a bad way but a way in which she felt excited as if she may be able to process something that the hunter's had missed. She was full on engrossed in the book. As she took off her examination gloves and went and got herself another cup of coffee she smiled and went. "Hmmm".

Craighton laughed and said, "What do you expect, they traverse the human body in their job, you think metaphysics and evil are too much for her".

Father Clayton laughed, as it was an excellent point and made a lot of sense as to why she was so engrossed in the blood filled book, Of course she was Catholic and that helped her keep things in perspective, she began her discourse of how and why it couldn't happen to her as she explained the subtlety of what the black Bible was trying to do. It wasn't a strong point but a pure one and Father Clayton was engrossed as she explained the Bible's strengths and weaknesses. How it intended on somehow enticing her into the world of devils and demons, so much so, she would cast down all that she found holy and embrace all that was evil. She laughed as she delved into how exactly they were going to do this. She was smiling at the end of her findings. Like they had just come up trumps with a major piece of the puzzle. Father Clayton was impressed as were the rest of them.

*

Mark snatched the kid right from under his mother's nose. He was quick and the child, well he let out a scream, but was silenced quickly as he resigned himself to his fate. He then tried to beg for mercy but got none.

Mark ferried him away to the ghouls lair. Mattire sent down one of his underlings to acquire the boy. The tall ghoul, who was just after feeding, walked down the stairwell and out into the light of day, Reddick was his name and he relished jobs like this as he always got choice cuts out of meat and they always needed to sacrifice to Asmodeus every dry moon and that was once a month, where angels and devils came together and settled their differences. They were truly blessed this moon as it was at its driest. and the evil got away with more, as good was too long admiring the good it had done. Vanity being the only thing that kept them both in check.

Reddick took the young, limp boy who was in no way getting saved. Mark smiled and said to Reddick, "Tell your master that if he wishes to do further business, he better help me out with the Hunters".

Reddick smiled and replied through a dry cracked voice, "I'll be sure to tell him Master Summoner".

Mark smiled and turned the wheel of the car and headed back to his lair. The tall ghoul took the corpse upstairs and the ceremony began. Mattire produced the ceremonial dagger and cut the young boys jugular from ear to ear. The blood splashed over the virgin candle and the sparks began to form as the devil Asmodeus made his ascension into the earthly spirit world. Growing in strength as he appeared, his eyes of bug-like evil and horned head. He smiled and laughed a great deep, consuming laugh, which would send the Holiest of men insane.

Asmodeus stopped as the ghoul spoke up, "What is my masters bidding?" He asked through a dry cracked voice.

"My bidding, my bidding is to make sure the Collector gets freed."

Mattire smiled and replied, "We are currently involved in the problem of the demon hunters".

Asmodeus smiled, "I take it the master summoner is in true spirit of death?"

Mattire smiled and replied, "Yes master".

Mattire watched as the Devil threw a dark cloak over the body of the child. Then the sparks grew again and both the child and Asmodeus disappeared. Mattire went about eating in the cold icy confines of his lair. He had made a collection of people whom they soaked with poison and began to devour, not hastily, but gently devouring the innards and sometimes the marrow of the bones. They were not greedy, no they served themselves and served themselves well knowing after the Collector was released, they would have an abundance of corpses to dine on as fresh and as often as they wished. They were in the hope of a dark paradise, a sinister end to a world of sickening goodness, they really believed that they had the power to turn the world from heavenly light into absolute evil and malice.

Mattire carried on eating, he was used to the frozen human meat and enjoyed it without gorging and having excess, He was a polite eater. As were the other three ghouls who had come to know Mattire. They never went without and this showed in the way the carried on day to day living. They had nothing to complain about and everything to be glad of. Mattire carried on eating his poisoned liver that crunched slightly as he bit into the cold chilled meat. He was formulating a plan as to how and when to deal with the hunters, he was smiling as he thought of a place where he could trap them, he thought his lair at first but that was too simple. They needed to be somewhere elusive, hidden away with no escape. He thought of various charnel places and unholy covens. But he needed to use somewhere that permutated goodness but was truly sinister. A place where they could walk into feeling safe but change in the centre of it, change into a true pit of a denizen where a denizen of Hell was waiting for them.

He realised that only two places where such things had control over. But he still needed bait. Then he had a brainstorm. A thought of total evil and cunning. A lair where the hunters would go, thinking that they had come up trumps. He smiled he would use a spell of change they would be dreaming when the spirit of Christian would show them into the lair of the Pit fiend. He began to prepare the spell, using a small amount of blood and lighting a black dreamer's candle. He sent the spell directly to all the hunters in the cottage. It was an intense visitation and powerful with colour.

Christian appeared in all their dreams, showing them a beautiful glade and warm sunlight, then he began to tell them why they must come and see it for themselves. As the Gods and the angels are expecting them to be there, so Heaven could gather it strength and empower each of them with spells and exalted deeds. They all woke as fresh as a daisy. And they were truly charmed by the spell. They knew that they were about to change the course of fate, this was just the beginning for them. They got into their cars and followed a beacon of light that hovered and showed them to the glade. Craighton was first to walk into the illusion. He was totally entranced and didn't think anything strange or foul was afoot. Then Father Clayton, he went next then

Robert Crufax then Carlos and together went Mary Beth and Elaine.

They all stood in the middle of the glade with glazed over eyes and awaiting the blessing when everything changed and they saw around them there were bones and rotten meat, as well as blood-soaked stones. It looked as though a nighty battle had been waged there, but no, the truth was harder to imagine. A feasting Dark Pit Fiend was there. And hiding in amongst the rotten flesh and crumbling bones. It was a trap and a very evil and malicious one at that.

Craighton was the first to regain composure and unholstered his Smith and Wesson Colt. "Okay fuckers if this the way you want to play then this be the end of your day".

Robert produced a Mine millimetre Berretta, Father Clayton cracked his knuckles and was ready to go toe to toe with them. But it wasn't them it was a fiery demon that had carved out a hunting ground, a place where it could eat, eat and eat. The more rotten the meat the better. The two women stood in the middle of the pit fiends obvious lair and began to pray. Knowing that they would be helpful to heal and tend to the demon hunter's wounds. Carlos produced a small sawn off double barrel shotgun. The Pit Fiend began to circle the hunters and Mary Beth began to get scared.

Elaine on the other hand showed her nails and spoke. "Okay demon I don't like to get ugly but it's obvious you aren't here to celebrate a holy day". She breathed out and prepared herself for the fight of her life. Then everything stopped and the Pit Fiend began to laugh. Then it charged at Craighton first, knowing that he was the one with the most ability. Craighton saw the thing coming at him and fired the first chance he got. Two shots from his revolver then he moved out the way as Carlos shot both barrels into the things red, inflamed hide.

Then Robert Crufax blasted the thing with three or four shots. That's when the fiend realised that this wasn't the picnic that it had planned. Father Clayton was next; he lifted the thing and began to bear hug it then threw it over his shoulders bursting several ribs and breaking its spine. It howled as it landed on a piece of stone all busted up. The fiend regained composure and started to circle the hunters again, Carlos reloaded his short-stocked shotgun and everybody else prepared for another charge. Craighton smiled and said, "The thing is fearless".

Father Clayton looked at the Hellish creature and said, "As god is my witness, I am fearless, tireless and god has chosen me to deliver his exacting will".

Again, the thing charged at them, again two shots from Craighton, then several shots from Robert then Carlos both barrels. Then Father Clayton gripped its horned head and began to twist its neck. He then ducked under while keeping a grip on its horns and flung it yet again over his shoulder. The muscle's rippled on Father Clayton as he flexed over the limp evil twisted Fiends body. Carlos reloaded his shotgun and blasted its head. Blowing the Pit fiend's skull to pieces. Father Clayton said a small prayer in Latin then sent the Hellish Fiend back to hell. Pouring a small vial of holy water on the demonic corpse. They looked around the area that was an onslaught of murder death and feeding, the hellish fiend had been here by what seemed was years and years judging by the state of decay that some of the bodies were in.

Father Clayton looked at some of the bodies that were in an advanced state of decay and sighed, "How come this is the first we have heard about this Pit Fiend?"

Craighton sniffed defiantly and said, "Well it's obvious that the thing has been hiding behind a glamour, a powerful spell that had everybody fooled."

Father Clayton cracked his knuckles and said, "Well it got the message this day".

Robert kicked some of the corpses over and studied the wounds on them. Throats ripped out with both claw and tooth. He scoffed at the whole situation and how easy it was for them to fall prey to the Fiend. He carried on his little investigation and found the corpses had been gnawed upon. Yep, the thing was defiantly a carnivore. Not necessarily fresh but then again it had done some amount feeding. He finished and walked up to the rest of the hunters who were having a conversation whether or not the Fiend was alone.

Father Clayton looked at Crufax as he came over. "What do you think Robert?"

Crufax sniffed and looked at his feet, "I reckon this thing has been here a little over four years, going by the advanced rate of decay."

Clayton laughed at this in a sarcastic way and said, "See I told you".

Crufax joined the rest of them, "We better leave, as you never know it could have a familiar. Or another Fiend maybe, lurking in the recesses of these woods" They got back into their cars and headed back into the city, they were going to need to rest as they had just survived one of Hells most fearsome creatures and they expected anything to happen, As the major devil who was holding onto the Pit Fiends reigns would not be happy and would need appeased from the ghouls, after all had he known that the Hunters were so skilled he would have gone forth into the lair of the Fiend, waited and dealt with them himself. But the ghouls had managed to dissuade him, as they were optimistic in the dead Fiends abilities. But alas no, the Fiend had fallen foul of the demon hunters and the hunters had dealt with the Fiend with surprising skill and deft timing. It was as if the lord had shown them the way to take care of the Fiend.

They got back to the small church house to find a large feast had been prepared for them. The nun's went into the kitchen and prepared a large meal of finger foods and passion fruits, holy bread and gentle wines that would sit nicely in their guts and aid digestion. Feast and feast they did, Elaine was next to read the grimoire, she snapped on the examination gloves and began to read. The hellish incantations and other curses showed themselves to Elaine who after where they had just been was in a state of perplexity. She smiled and laughed at the thinking behind the ancient curses that led to plague bearers and vampires and ghouls having their way with the pure and the innocent. Taking the holy and the divine down to its last rites. Then devouring. Eat, eat, eat. They had been told, from the denizens of Hell that they would one day rule the earth and the holy and the pure would been slaves to the wicked and resentful. Creatures would emerge from the hellish pits. And the gorging and feeding of flesh and the whips and snares would hold all of Heaven and earth to its own baser ways.

They would be slaves to the hells and hells demons and devils would give no mercy have no compassion, only the strength in sin would keep the devils in check. And that was held in the pure evil spirits of Hell. The ghost the ghoul. The zombie the vampire they would enslave the holy and the pure the sick the lame. The young the old. But the hunters were on top of it. Well, look at the past results. A pit fiend. But who had put the curse on them to show them an idyllic glade. Mattire flung his table ladened with sweet breads and poisonous wine.

"They killed it!" he shouted as the table bounced on the cold floor and the other ghouls hid away knowing that the ghoul Mattire was exacting in his punishment. Reddicks head bowed as he could not look his master in the eye knowing if he did, he would be made an example of. Mattire stood gasping in the air and grew angrier by the second. He breathed in and kept breathing until he struck out and sent the large frame of Reddick across the room with an almighty punch to his chest. Reddick lifted himself of the floor and began to clean up the sweet breads and other things like poisoned blood. He then left the room and joined the other ghouls in the back room. They sneered and hissed at him as though he were to blame for the loss of such an ally. But of course, he had nothing to say in defence of himself. And of-course he knew some day he would be a master of his own group of ghouls. He had plans, plans within plans. Ways that only he knew about. He was seen a couple of times in conversation with a small imp, who was telling him the things that he knew were possible but he had to be careful in the completion of his plans as Mattire was no fool.

Elaine carried on reading the black Bible, realising that knowledge like that could be countered and rendered useless in the world. But it took skill and timing and knowing was only part of the action they could take, no she was seeing a way in which to send the evil forces that were growing in strength back to the pits of Hell. She knew the Bible that she held was incomplete and that worked in their favour. It meant that certain spells and curses couldn't be used. But there was always the chance that one of the demonic forces had acquired the missing pages and there was no way of destroying the evil Bible as it was so cursed that the flames would extinguish themselves rather than consume the grimoire. It was inked in blood and steeped in ancient mystical poisons, as well as the sacrifices that had been made to ink the black Bible. No, it was pretty much indestructible, evil in the most evil of ways.

She carried on reading the thing, reading bits like how to summon plague bearers. How to increase their strengths when in the face of losing a battle. How to replenish strength in the summoning of demons and various other fiends of Hell. But luckily for them they held the black Bible, which gave them a major advantage, especially in the fact of being prepared. But the fact was that there were more of these Bibles, six to be precise, some of which were complete, some in worse shape than the one they had, but still potent and very, very evil. It was a key piece in the corruption of humanity and it was only by luck that Father Clayton, whilst clearing a nest of vampires had come across the thing. He knew what he was looking at the instant he saw the thing. He had gasped in elation, then put on gloves and lifted the thing and put it into a satchel. The vampires he had wiped out in a dawn raid had been sacrificing various virgins, summoning demons and plotting to overrun the world. Father Clayton smiled and said to himself "Jackpot".

He took the item back to his Chapel where he used all his resources to study the evil bloody book and summoning Angels to help him in the way of some of the language. Darius, the Archangel, who was the main angel sent to protect Father Clayton smiled as he knew that this was a major piece in the fight for survival. He and Father Cayton conversed on the subject and how much the artifact would be useful to them in the fighting of demons, wamphyres and ghouls. Elaine smiled as Father Clayton explained some of the books strengths and powers that had, in the very definition of power, been used and released into this world. But hope was not lost, as they had not figured on the various charms and readings of the holy Bible that counteracted some of the evil that permeated from the grimoire.

Elaine smiled and said, "so this is the best way to counteract the evil that comes up from the pits and bowers of hell".

Father Clayton smiled and replied, "Why yes".

Elaine understood that this was a major find in the fight against devil, demon and all other unholy creatures. This book had made a lot of sense in the way the war was being fought.

"But what scares me," said Father Clayton. "Is the missing pieces of the hellish book"

Elaine smiled and asked, "Why Father, what is so important about the missing incantations?"

Father Clayton sat down and responded, "Well you see dear, the Incantations that are missing are important in sealing this worlds fate".

Elaine smiled a small sad smile, "But surely this will work in our favour Father".

Father Clayton laughed, "Nothing is that simple in this war".

Elaine carried on reading and started to take notes on the missing pieces. She had a point that if it wasn't in the enemies, hands then there was nothing they could do to finish off the world. But she saw the flip side, that if they got their hands on the grimoire and had the missing pieces they would get a major foothold in the earth and heaven. Possibly bring about the end of the earth. This was already on the cards with the return of the Soul Collector. But they still needed Mary Beth who was the key to the end of the world as we know it. She was as safe as they could make her, protected by the Holy confines of the Chapel, and the Holy angels watched over her pure soul. She and the rest were truly blessed. They settled into a night's rest whilst Elaine kept up her vigilant study. Of the unholy book.

*

Mark realised that his plan to finish the hunters had failed. Mattire had not bargained on the Hunters being so well coordinated in their onslaught on the pit fiend. He growled slightly at the thought of the Pit Feind being destroyed and this made him nervous. He was in the cold hard fact that the hunters were more powerful than he had thought. They were experts in vanquishing evil and that showed in them as well. They were a powerful conclave of expert demon killers and hunters of the denizens of hell.

Mark lifted his head from the meditation and summoning his Lord of Hell to guide him. The candles in the room flickered and a smell of rotten and cooked human meat wafted into his lair.

He smiled as the voice of the Lord of Hell responded, "You Failed again". It then hissed its breath out.

"It was unfortunate that they were so well prepared my lord," Mark replied.

The voice hissed again, "Well you cannot keep making errors like this".

Mark felt uncomfortable and he was sure that the Lord of Hellfire was just playing with him.

"I'm sorry my lord," He replied.

The devil smiled and said, "Never mind my friend I know a way that you can get at the hunters. And also get the pure soul to come to you".

Mark sneered and looked around his lair. The Lord Devil told him his plan that could very well swing things in his favour showing the summoner an ancient spell that he had used many a time in the rites of sacrifice and the ways to grow in strength and cloak the intentions of the summoner. who was in fact turning more and more into a Devil. But this process took time and the staining of the pure soul was the last rites that Mark could use. He smiled a sinister smile as the Devil chanted and summoned on the denizens in Hell to fill the summoner with unholy curses and other diabolical magic. He kept on grinning as the energies pulsated through the summoner. The whole of hell began to shriek and curse and spit as the Devil made sure the summoner was up to the task of destroying the hunters and also gave him powers of utter chaos and malevolent force. He lay in bed for the next two days spasming and choking on his own breath as if he didn't need air. But this was just the beginning of his journey through the wretched Hells and other fiery chasms. He was enjoying dying and turning evil, dying again then turning more and more malevolent. He was enjoying his change into that of a mighty Devil. Then he saw Hell open up and send the spirits of the damned to circle him with fiery vigour and true evil spirit. He was getting what he deserved and had wanted most of his life but had fallen shy of achieving it. But now he knew it was his destiny; it was the one thing keeping him strong and he was growing eviler and eviler every day.

*

The hunters carried on preparing for the next dry moon then the devils moon would fall hard upon and that was make or break time. They had to guard Mary Beth and guard her well. This was no easy feat. They filled up on Holy Water and loaded pistols, Father Clayton burned sacred incense and blessed each and every one with a prayer and the sign of the cross. He used a little Latin, but mainly prayed in English. He summoned on the spirits of heaven, angels and saints. Craighton loaded his Colt and strapped the Colt 45 bullets around his waist. There were at least forty bullets on the belt. He had never been caught short. Robert loaded his 9 mm beretta and stashed away seven magazines with fifteen bullets to mag. Mary Beth had a first aid kit and a small Bulldog Smith Wesson 38. She liked the feel of the weapon as it was small but at the same time it packed a wallop. Like being hit by a brick. Elaine in the other hand loaded a small Glock 9 with 9 mm bullets, she had seven magazines with eleven in each mag.

Carlos was stood with his serrated machete and short, hog leg, double barrel shotgun. And Father Clayton had a series of throwing daggers and holy knives that had been consecrated with holy water and various other blessings. He was still as strong as any demon, especially in spirituality. He carried on praying as the rest of them bowed their heads and partook of the host. They began to get moving into their cars. It started to rain in the black of that night but what they were about to face was blacker than pitch. Foul odious deeds were becoming more and more common in the world and the more that came the more the hunters had to fight. There were several other teams of hunters but they had their hands full with wamphyre and ghoul and to top it all off the ferrymen demons were back. They had to worship the deathly demon Acheron and they were doing so in blood flesh and bone.

Elaine had read a small chapter on the ferrymen and it had just made her shiver in fear. She couldn't get any heat into herself for an hour or so after reading how they wore their victims skins over their cold and slimy bones. Then she looked at a picture of one of them skinning a young girl and he had done so with the victim being alive and fully conscious. She shivered some more then went and prepared for the nights hunt.

*

Darius was between worlds, knowing his vigilance was a vital part in keeping the world and heaven safe. He smiled and spoke to the hunters, a small sublime pure way that held the hunters charmed and blessed. He finished by reciting the Lord's Prayer. They could all feel the beat of his wings, warm and light and that made them more courageous, more focused. They all smiled as the exited the chapel house and got in their respective cars. And they all headed towards Mark Candace's lair. They knew that he had sussed out the strength of the hunters. But the evil power that was coursing through his body was giving him tremendous power. It was evil through and through and was making him fearless, he didn't need anything other than the power to summon and curse the hunters.

He also had the power of a shade, an evil demon that could fade into the shadows. This had given him the strength and resolve on what to do next. They all parked a couple of streets away from the lair of the summoner. Then walked to his stairwell and began to climb the stairs very quietly. But they had tripped a small rune that alerted Mark to the coming of the hunters. Mark sneered and lifted up a razor sharp sword used in summoning and sacrificing various holy and divine creatures, such as unicorns, fairy folk and day dwellers. He had at one point sacrificed a Lion as his master had desired some game meat. He had fed the rest of the carcass to the pit of zombies. And had been rewarded with a book of sublime dark magics. He was truly an ally to the demons, devils, witches and other pitch as night denizens.

He waited at the side of the door as the door handle turned, he gripped his sword and the first one who came across the threshold it was Craighton, but his muscle memory kicked as the sword swished at the hunter.

Craighton fired a shot in the direction the sword had come cutting from. Then Mark turned shade and vanished into the large confines of his lair. The hunters came over the doorway and stepped gingerly over a blood pentagram. With the severed head of a child being on display. They looked around at the torture implements. All bloodied and stained, with leftover flesh from what must have been at least twenty adults and God knows how many children. They carried on their search and could not see hide nor hair of the summoner. No, he was using his Shade form and magics to escape from them. But before he left, he cast one more curse and that was animate the dead. The corpses of at least twelve adults began to lurch towards the hunters. Each one of the corpses in varying states of decay. some had been cannibalized. Now they were Zombies and hungry for flesh. The hunters didn't give them any quarter they opened fire blasting the heads of the zombies.

It was deafening in the room as they wiped out the zombies. And all they could hear was the laughter of the summoner who as he left shouted, "I shall return hunters I shall return".

He then went to the other lair he had procured for himself. Father Clayton and the rest of them headed back to the chapel to seek sanctuary. As they arrived, they were greeted by the sullen face of a sister superior, who again had made a supper of light bread and fruit juices. They all tucked into the most nourishing meal and that was breakfast. After they finished, they began to discuss the ways in which they could deal with the summoner. They knew it was not going to be easy. As he had acquired the skills and spells of a shade but that didn't bother them too much, they had the ace in the hole and that was Mary Beth.

She knew how vital a role she played in the whole Occult war and she would be damned if she was going to end up in some demonic rite, no not her, it just wasn't on her agenda. She smiled and stretched out on the bed that she occupied. They all fell into a sound peaceful sleep. With Father Clayton watching over them in silent meditation. The day drove on and it was hot and they all waited for the summer breeze to cool their heels and soften their hearts. Again, Darius let his wings beat on them and again they felt the warmth and protection from Heaven. Father Clayton smiled as he could feel the Angel nearby and welcomed its soothing words as it sang a hymn and beat its wings as it came to a chorus. They fell into a gentle light sleep.

*

Outside in the distance, in the cool night there was a brood of vampires that had just come into play, this had happened as Mark had known of their arrival in the City of Bentley. As they were renowned for their fierce fighting and the killing of four teams of hunters. The head vampire, a tall lean blond with evil tattooed all over his body, his name was Claric. And the other two were Kostu and Bevna. They had all been systematic of the killing of four teams of hunters each team having five hunters, which was twenty Clergy and underlings. But Mark had plans that involved the vampires and the unholy ghosts of succubus. Hopefully and if he timed it just right, he would be able to snatch Mary Beth and if that weren't possible, he would grab Elaine and use her a leverage. This actually seemed a better option of the two as he would have a good time torturing Elaine, he thought that if he could get Elaine then Mary Beth would do anything for her friend. It was wicked in its simplicity and even more wicked in the execution of said plans.

He smiled and took a sip of his last victim's blood. Then he set about the task in summoning two succubus. Enough to keep the hunters at bay whilst he grabbed either of the two nurses. And the Vampires would finish off the rest of the hunters. Leaving the summoner with all the aces in his hand. But this plan was reliant on the succubus's taking a major part in the death of the hunters. He began to summon the succubus's, then after the spell finished itself the vampires arrived at his lair. Claric smiled, showing his elongated fangs to Mark.

"So lucky," said the vampire as he looked around the lair with its demonic shrine and various sweet bread knives and saucepans. "You truly are held well in the favours of Hell."

Mark smiled as the Daemon hissed at him. It was a laughing hiss. And Mark smiled a little knowing the power the vampires brought with them. Kostu and Bevna went down the stairs out into the night and into their van where they had fresh victims for them to feed on. The three victims were unconscious and were enough for them to feed on whilst they plotted and schemed plans. They were much satisfied and dined fresh.

"How is Mattire?" Asked Claric.

Mark scoffed and replied, "He's fine but in a foul temper, but that's Ghouls for you."

Claric got ready to bite into the vein of one of the victims, he flashed his teeth then bit into the carotid artery. Mark was much amused by the sight of them dining. It wasn't something or how they dined it was the evil satisfaction that lit up their eyes as they dined. Like hell had just lit a candle for them. It was like fire through their souls. As hot as the pits of hell yet their souls were already damned and had been for hundreds of years. Bevna smiled as he finished of the last drop of blood from his victim. They then cut off the heads of the three bodies and set the remains on fire. Mark then began to tell Claric his fiendish and devilish plan, but they had just under a week until the moon was in the devils blood. And the Soul Collector would be in the prime position to be released. But still they needed Mary Beth and it would take all Hell's treachery to work that spell. But the summoner was confident. And in being so saw a way to get at the hunters. He just had to wait for the succubus's to traverse into the earth realm.

There, screaming shadowy incorporeal bodies were taking shape in the world of the living.

"They will be formidable enemies", said Mark to the three daemons. The wampyre spirit being as it is would have a great advantage over the hunters.

*

Darius smiled again at the way and peaceful rest that the hunters had come to. Then he looked out into the distant astral plane of light and saw the two succubus's beginning to take form into the spirit world of earth. He turned and headed in their direction using the gleam of his sword and rod to guide him towards the evil demonic forms of the succubus's. He had to get there before they fully got their strength. He would lead the hunters into the fray. Darius smiled as he headed towards the incorporeal forms of the succubus.

Claric smiled as he finished off feeding on one of the victims, Mark looked around he could feel the succubus's gathering and growing, getting more and more physical, more powerful the screaming that they did as they gathered form. Becoming more and more audible as they formed, more and more high pitched, the sound stopped briefly and Mark smiled as the voice of the demi-demons began to resonate around the summoner and his guests. Kostu begin to recite a demonic curse of strange and curious power. It was giving him the sight to see into the chapel house, the spell served him well.

The power showed him the hunters as they prepared for the night as they were sleeping during the day. This and the studies of the arcane. They were putting in the time and effort, they were clearly on the spot. Darius visited Father Clayton and told him of the danger they were in. Father Clayton bowed his head and started to pray.

"They have summoned two succubus's."

Father Clayton sighed, "How are we going to deal with them?" he asked the Archangel. Darius said an amen as the prayer finished.

Then he spoke. "He has also gathered a small conclave of vampires. These three vampires are the known killers of twenty demon hunters"

Father Clayton bowed his head and said, "Oh, them."

Darius sighed and carried on, "Yes and it'll take a miracle to see to their end."

Father Clayton smiled and said, "As always we will serve the will of the Lord."

Darius let a small smile shine gently on the hunters and they all felt his warmth. They knew that they had a tough time in the next five or six days. No, they were trying to remain calm and studious. Keep up the silent watchful vigil and search for clues in the texts of the black Bible and also, various other works of dark magics. Father Clayton was reading several pieces on Satanic witchcraft, various spells and incantations. Things that could summon devils and demons, they also had a way in which they could destroy a man's brain, leaving the victim a gibbering useless vegetable. He took note of the various incantations and saw there was a way to guard your thoughts, put up a psionic shield that was a way to destroy the evil that was being aimed at you. It was a mantra from ancient India and could be used to full effect.

In another teaching there was a way to turn the spell around and send it back at the caster. He smiled at this as the light that was shining down into his study was pure and balanced. He was making progress, whilst everyone else slept. He kept a silent watchful eye on the rest of them, making sure they slept without coming to harm from the pits of hell. He was ready but studying at the same time. Every now and then taking a pause to digest and watch solemnly as he read on. He was now reading a passage on making a Shade predominant. This was a use-full charm and all it required was a four leaf clover. He smiled and wrote down the incantation. He would need Davina's help in locating a four leaf clover. Basically, you pronounced the word Shade then blew on the four leave clover. At that point, the summoner would be flung out the darkness and made to face the light. Father Clayton went right to the phone and called Davina. She smiled as Father Clayton told her how the charm worked. She didn't hesitate and came round with five four leaved clovers which she had just picked, Father clayton smiled as he took the piece of silk that was wrapped around the clover. She came into the house and had a coffee. It wasn't too black, but just the right amount of cream and sugar.

*

Mattire finished off his meal of yet another human. Reddick and the other ghouls dined with him but kept their distance as they could tell he was in a very, very black mood. And at any time he wanted he could add their carcasses to his larder, the icy confines of which was full, but still had room. He hissed at the other three ghouls and then scowled at them. But his feeding came first as he began to dine on a piece of lung. He ate and ate heartily as the poison was just right and mixed well in the cold atmosphere. He took his time with a look of anger on his face. He then realised that he had someone watching his every move. Especially since the Pit Fiend was dead, someone from Pandemonium was taking notes on how he lived and how he dealt with incompetent members of his brood. He decided they should starve and when their hunger was at its peak they would go on the hunt for fresh flesh, the thing that was watching him in the shadow was a horned lesser demon and had his orders from Lucifer himself. He smiled under his cowl and wrapped the rest of his cloak around his body. He sighed a little and tittered at the fact that the ghouls were completely unaware of his presence, or so he thought.

Mattire sneered as he cut into the organ of a young woman. Her lung was satisfying his hunger. The Merrick (Poison) was just at the right strength and gave the ghoul all the energy he needed. He could feel the eyes the eyes of the demon on him, Scrutinizing him, making things that little bit more complicated. He would wait until the next moon of summoning then he would speak Asmodeus. His lord. The Devil, that he had to appease in order to keep his life. Mattire sipped some blood out of a chalice then carried on eating. Crunching the salted with poison organ and savouring the taste. He called on Reddick after finishing his sweet breads. "Reddick, I have a task for you."

Reddick sneered at the other two ghouls, knowing that he had just made a path on the right side of his lord and master. "What is thy bidding Lord?"

"You are going to do two things, one a sacrifice is needed in two days, time the other I need one of Father Claytons parishioners. To get information from them".

Reddick bowed at the feet of his Master Mattire. "It will be done Master" He hissed and readied himself for a mission.

*

Darius was studying the two succubus as they began to form and their bones atomised and came together. They were shrieking as they began to form, Darius knew that they were going to be in one Hell of a fight, especially seeing as the three vampires were a force, an unholy force to be reckoned with. Darius knew he would need all his strength and power. And that Father Clayton was looking for counter spells. Spells to ease the evil magics that were going to be aimed at them. Father Clayton was in the middle of noting down several power words and shaping his hand into mystical gestures and in the other hand was of course his cross. He had complete faith in his Lord and needed no encouragement other than his prayers and Latin phrases.

He carried on reading and writing down small phrases in ancient Aramaic. The rest of the hunters woke the next night knowing that they were full on engaged with daemons, demons and other creatures of evil. Father Clayton explained to them what he had just discovered about the shade come summoner. A spell that would force the thing and all its demonic powers into the light. This would give them the advantage as no shade could summon or cast whilst in the surge of holy light. They smiled as he produced the spell component that was a four leaved clover, They, all smiled at the sheer simplicity of the spell. He also told of several other secret hand shapes to protect them against Psionic attacks and various other magic.

Then he explained to them the other news, about the succubus. And he handed out a set of honey and wax earplugs. They all took a pair. "That will counteract the death scream that comes from them. But be aware that the summoner has power that can only be described as 'From the pits of Hell'" He then began to tell them the last piece of news the three vampires Claric, Kostu and Bevna, "All seasoned killers and showed no remorse to the last twenty hunters that they trapped," finished Father Clayton. They knew that this was a difficult undertaking for them. But remained positive in their hopes and faith.

They knew it was Hell to pay. And Hell demanded a Hellish toll. They had a small prayer and thanked the lord and asked for strength in the next week or so.

*

They began their hunt, knowing only that they were going against the powers of Hell and after much discussion they said they would be better to go head on with their skills and their guidance of the Lord. Darius was still watching the completion of the sub-demons. He would hold them back for as long as he could hopefully doing enough damage that the hunters could finish them. But this was just hope and Darius held aloft a curved gladius that Michael, prince of Angels, used in the gladiator games. He smiled knowing that they would try their death scream first. Then he would sever their connection with Hell. Doing so with a small charm he had used to trap plague bearers. This had worked and stopped all kinds of Hellish portals from opening up. He waited as a skull began to atomize and form the shapes of the female demons, he watched as the pure evil that they were made of began its final shape shift. Darius was still cautious though, as these were lesser demons but demons all the same. And he would not treat them lightly. No, he had to do his best to overcome two very evil angels of Hell. They kept on forming into the corporeal state. And all Darius could do was wait and watch.

*

Father Clayton carried on his reading of the evil tome of skin and blood. "We have hope," he said quietly to himself. The rest of the hunters carried on getting ready for the next mission. Mark Candace was preparing a sacrifice knowing he needed as much help from the hellish planes of hell with all its evil and twisted ways. He knew that as a shade he was hard to banish or kill. He rather liked being a shade the power the wickedness that came from living in the shadows. He could summon the very air of Hell that was truly evil and malicious. He felt the heat rise and swirl and enter into him. His eyeballs blackened and his breathing stopped. He was truly cursed and at full of power.

The might of hell was coursing through his body, and he never felt so much power as he did then, the three vampires were stood there stunned, as the energy cracked and pulsated through Marks body. Again, the heat again, the power of hell. He grew more and more in supernatural strength, unholy spells and curses formed in his mind and he felt well, he felt better than anything, more power more malicious energy ran through him. He screamed at the top of his lungs and began to grin. His whole shape changing, turning his once proud human form into the shape of a devil. It had been a long time coming and he had done everything possible to see to it that he was giving the unholy powers of Hell. He grinned at the three vampire, his teeth elongated and like points. This was part of the savagery that was in him. The three vampire's stomachs went cold they felt something that was unusual to them Fear, Mark continued to grin at the vampires. He knew that they were easily dispatched. And the Power that Mark had was ten times the three Vampires. But he decided to give them the chance at destroying the holy avengers. They bowed at the feet of the superior devil. Knowing not only was he vicious but full of ancient evil magic. They were best to do his bidding. And what a mission it was.

*

The hunters were ready and waiting for Father Clayton to finish reading the ancient evil tome. He smiled and shut the book gently.

"We got problems," he said, the rest of them went quiet, and Father Clayton explained the problem of the summoner. "He is destined to do two things" He ran his hand through his hair "One is, summon the unholy, very destructive force, the Soul Collector, the other is change into a major devil, which I think he may already have done."

The hunters were hanging on every word that Father, Clayton was speaking. He carried on, "If he has done this already, it will be all but impossible to destroy him".

Father Clayton took a sip of some tea then continued, "But he still has to sacrifice Mary Beth and well, this aint going to happen whilst I still draw breath". The hunters all nodded at the fact. They only had one more thing on their mind and that was where is he.

*

Mattire awaited the return of Reddick with both his sacrifice and the parishioner of Father Clayton's flock. He waited for a while then he heard the door to the cold, icy meat locker sliding open and in walked Reddick with the small child on one shoulder and the unconscious parishioner on the other. He dropped the child at the evil altar and walked towards Mattire.

Mattire threw back his head and cackled at the sheer malevolence of it. Reddick smiled and spoke through his dry cracked voice box that was constantly being poisoned. "I serve you only Master". he said then let the unconscious body of the parishioner slide onto the floor. Mattire was impressed by the gesture, knowing only slightly that it was a hard task. But first things first, Mattire looked at the young blond parishioner and saw to it that the man was tied to a chair. He had plans for the young man. But when the young man came too, he was smiling and that unnerved Mattire, never in all his days had a piece of meat grinned at him with such defiance in his eyes. An unusual glint in the man's eyes as if he were going to enjoy this. Mattire looked at the young man and thought, 'Strange someone so young and that they were willing to go to their death without a struggle without fear'. The young man looked into Mattire's cold dead eyes and said, "I was given a message for you".

Mattire scrunched up his eyes and replied, "I take it he knows of our existence?"

The young boy smiled and said, "Well hot damn demon, he knew you were behind the Pit Fiend."

Mattire smiled and said, "Well young man you are past the point of no return, shall we continue this over dinner?"

The young blond spat in Mattire's face as he began to gloat in front of the young boy. Mattire just lifted a napkin wiped the spit and laughed at the young man. Mattire began to slowly skin the man alive starting with the back of his hand, The young man started to recite prayers as the evil ghoul began to devour the cold skin of the man.

"I can finish you quick," said Mattire.

The young man sneered at him and said, "That would be pointless. As any information I have you already know."

Mattire gave a dry cracked cackle and started to skin the palm of his hand. "Tell me young man do they have in their possession the full black Bible?"

The young man sneered at him and again spat on the Demon. "You know they do," he replied as the demon wiped his face yet again.

The young man laughed again and said, "You know what you are?"

The ghoul looked at him and the young man carried on, "You are a monstrous pig and you and the rest of your piglike swine, will fail".

Mattire sneered again then with the back of his hand he snapped a slap at the young man. The young man with all the defiance of God's grace smiled and laughed at the ghoul.

"Fucking pig".

Mattire struck him again. The rest well the rest was sheer butchery as he and Reddick dined fresh on the young man. He lasted about three hours and didn't give them jack shit. The whole of Father Clayton's congregation had been well warned of the dangers that now faced them. They were forewarned and forewarned is forearmed. And Mattire knew it. He had done so quite deliberately. His existence was well known but he would pick off the congregation one by one. Or so he thought.

*

The news of the parishioner got to the hunters that very night. And they had a young ghoul in all his glory abducting the young blond man. He had been seen doing the deed. It was an old ford banger that had stopped a little way off from the Church then he had carefully abducted the young blond, then he hunted down a sleeping child, for his sacrifice. The hunters had a registration plate and typed the number into the main frame driving license authority. They got the address of the banged up motor. It was near the outskirts of the city. Where they had encountered the pit fiend. They sat for forty or so minutes waiting for the right time, they knew the young blond was dead and they prayed it was quick. But they had little faith in hope at that time as they were dealing with ghouls probably the evilest of daemons to be around. Certainly, the coldest most sinister hungry daemons.

They were finished with the parishioner and were beginning the sacrifice to their Lord Devil Asmodeus. The hunters listened intently at the door, whilst the murmur of spells was overseen by Mattire, they began to ready the neck of the young child and Carlos went first. He pointed his shotgun at the daemon that was about to anoint the candle with the young boys blood, there was an almighty thunderclap as Carlos fired both barrels at the daemon with the sacrificial knife. His head separated from his body and the head landed on the human fat drawing of the pentagram. Father Clayton entered next and ran into the chilled airy space. He was on Reddick unleashing a barrage of body blows, body blows that you'd think the undead could handle, but no Father Clayton had a set of rosary beads wrapped around his strong right hand. And was delivering him what could only be described as his red right hand.

Craighton pointed his Revolver at Mattire who was still trying to summon his Devil Master. He fired and cocked the pistol and emptied each chamber of the six-shooter. Then he began to reload as the daemon Mattire's chest exploded and his black pumping heart bled the last of his evil, tainted, poison blood. He crumpled into a heap onto the floor. The two nurses knowing only that there was an innocent child who was coming too. They got to him fast and covered his semi naked body with one of their coats. The child opened his eyes and looked into Mary Beths eyes and said with a small whimper, "Are you an angel?"

She smiled and looked back into his eyes and replied, "Of course I am". The child fell back into unconsciousness.

Craighton after reloading his Colt walked up to the dead daemon Mattire and peppered him again with the big bore revolver. After they finished with the ghouls they noticed the partially eaten remains of the young blond churchgoer. Father Clayton said a prayer then made the sign of the cross and they would leave it to the nuns to retrieve and bury the dead, well what was left of them. Well, the nuns and various monks and pastors.

*

Mark Candace felt the grip of evil loosen somewhat, he knew they had just lost a major ally, Mattire and his followers. He then realised that the hunters had gotten on both their feet in the scheme of things. They were now solidly holding at bay the forces of evil. This didn't matter though thought Mark, as they had never encountered anything like him as the evil seeds had turned him part devil. He had unholy writings and ancient incantations. Words of Hellfire and mortal, decay. The evil that his soul swam in was ancient and in bloom in the very pits of despair those pits that had gathered and soaked the sins into the Devil Mark Candace.

The three Vampires went out on the hunt for fresh blood. They would need all the energy they could muster as the hunters were hot on their trail. And fiery as their abilities were, they had underestimated them before and that had cost them dearly. Now with little choice they had to set up some sort of trap that would quash their strength and give them a good advantage. But Father Clayton had sent up a priest's eye of seeing one of the ancient spells that could find the evil vampire without drawing attention to him. He meditated and when he had no energy left Davina followed through with her witches scrying eye. She saw to it the search carried on; she came across two zombie pits and a bone demons lair. This was going to take a while. She mentally noted the two zombie pits and wizard marked the bone demons, lair. This took a lot of strength on her part but she was confident that they would clear them out. The bone demon would be a tough one and the Zombie pits, well you never underestimated a plague bearers work.

She finished hunting through her eye and Father Clayton took over again, she told him of the two pits and the lair that she came across. But still no sign of the summoner or the three vampires. He carried on searching wandering around various patches where people had gone missing. But still nothing,

Father Clayton sighed and rubbed his head as to take away the tension, "I must be missing something," he said out loud, "They must be covering their tracks".

Somehow they had eluded the hunters. "Some sort of ancient curse covering up their tracks". He carried on searching. This went on for three days and three nights. And it was getting close to the Soul Collectors equinox, it's most powerful time and this only happened once every six hundred years.

Mark was in full preparation for the night as it would be the only time that Mark would get to show his true allegiance to hell. The world would be swallowed in darkness. And the pits of hell will empty into the earth. Humanity will bow down to evil of Hell, and they would swarm up from the pits and devour and eat, eat, eat. Until the heavens itself will be washed in blood. The gates, the fields and the flock of holy and the divine turned into slave. With nothing more than the end in being food for the devils, demons, and daemons. The wicked shall own the earth and the pure and the good shall know unholy sacrifice. Mark smiled and gave a small laugh. Then he saw it, the two succubus were nearly ready, but Darius had other plans and those plans were to slow down and preferably stop the succubus from doing too much damage.

They looked through their blackened eyeballs and saw the holy avenger in front of them. One of them spoke, "Ahh holy warrior, you knew why we are here".

Darius scowled at the two demons and replied, "Yes evil ones I know why you are here".

They both laughed a hideous laugh, "You will not get in our way. Holy avenger".

Darius didn't hesitate he attacked the two demons. They fought tooth and claw, And Darius never let up on his swings of the Gladius. He swiped it along one of their abdomen and her guts fell onto the floor. But still she carried on fighting. Advancing on the Holy Angel and getting close enough to claw at Darius's face. Darius swerved the black nails of the demon and retaliated with another slice, this time aimed at the other one's neck. She stepped back and dodged the blow. Darius let his wings beat and beat hard sending the two of them off balance. They quickly overcame the dizzying wind that Darius had sent forth. But he wasn't finished, no, he had a number of tricks up his sleeve, and his wings were just a part of them. The Succubus began to scream, knowing that it would be of no use to them they began to circle the Angel. Flapping their leathery wings against the Angel. Then Darius tried something he shot up between the two Demons and wrapped his wings around himself as he spun sending the energy of their wings back against them. They were immediately thrown away from their target and settling into a steady rhythm Darius engaged again with the two demons, knowing that their next move was to take flight and run from the Holy Avenger. They did so after screaming a large amount of energy at Darius. Darius curled his wings around himself and curled into a ball to protected himself from the demons. They escaped the two of them and went into hiding in the city of Bentley. Darius picked himself up from the ground as he had plummeted like a rock. He smiled and said, "Oh you two will not be able to hide forever".

Father Clayton smiled as he saw the energy of the vampires as they moved easily and stealthily through the back alleys and streets of Bentley. Claric, Kostu and Bevna all three of them in a hunger for blood, waited outside a diner that was a 24-hour free coffee truck stop. They smiled and entered the Diner there were two cops having coffee and doughnuts. And a young couple just finishing off some pie. Claric was first to strike, He gripped the one of the cops by the head and bit deep into his vein in his neck, ripping the flesh and leaving the vein open so as he could drink the blood freely. The other cop reached for his side arm but never got the chance as Bevna was upon him, slicing the cops throat open as he swiped his claws. Kostu was on one of the couple, who were screaming and babbling as the three vampires ascended onto them. The waitress cowered into the corner trying to hide from the sights of the vampires. But this only delayed her life from ending for a short time.

After the three had finished off the diners they saw to it that the waitress was dined upon by the three of them. They ripped her to pieces and drank her blood. Then they walked calmly out the door and back to the summoners lair. Father Clayton followed them as they went back to the Devil, Mark. His Priest's eye just catching the street sign that led to a derelict building on Swampin and Ash a suburb just south of where they were. "Gotcha you sinister fucks".

He then wrote down the directions that came just as his spell was wearing off. Davina looked up she was also reading the evil Bible of the Devils. And making notes as she read. She had come across a possible way to counterattack the spell that was going to be used in the acquisition of Mary Beth. But there was a problem as someone had to chant whilst using a wand of power. That which she would make herself. But the chant was long and you needed to repeat the words over and over. If you fumbled your words the wand would turn to ash and you would be in trouble. It also lit you up like

Christmas and then, well then you would be in trouble every daemon, demon, zombie and ghoul would know you were in the vicinity and would come straight for you.

Then, well you were in a fight and I mean one for your life. You could run but it would be too late. Zombie pits would empty, lairs of vampires would soon know of your existence, ghouls would find you. A blood seal would mark you. A devilish light that made everything in hell focus on you. It could only be removed by the hierarchy of the church. And that meant them to use a daemon exorcism. Davina told Father Clayton the news about the spell and how if done right they would save the pure soul. But if you so much as fumbled, trembled even, the spell would backfire. And all hell would break loose.

"Is it worth the risk?" Asked Father Clayton.

"The spell would be strong enough to stop the Soul Collector coming through."

Father Clayton smiled, "So maybe, there is another way?"

Davina sighed and rested her glasses on the book table. "There might be, but it will take some time to go through all the Aramaic and all the arcane works".

Father Clayton smiled and said, "You got two days".

She smiled and said, "That's time enough". Then she set upon the task of an easier way to stop the Collectors Moon. The easiest was to kill the summoner preferably before he could begin the ceremony. Father Clayton bowed and walked away calmly. Knowing that she was on the ball with the studies of the Arcane. She had been invaluable for years and always came up with answers to the problems that faced the demon hunters. She had been the systematic turning of several fledgling vampires. And getting them back to the folds of the church. She had also been the curator of a mass of unholy and holy texts (She played it neutral) and was always the one to make a quick decision when it came to the Pits and bowers of Hell. She realised that the plague bearers needed only a sacrifice for them to ascend into the Earth Realm, where with much cunning and guile they could start a zombie plague. And this would soon wipe out the majority of the human race. With their seed spreading throughout the world. And the bearers the lizard like creatures spreading the seed. But first they had to be released from their blood-filled sanctuary. And this would only happen if a summoner cast the right curse at the right time. Then Hell would ascend into earth and the plague bearers would be at full strength.

*

Mark smiled and looked at the three vampires as they entered the summoners lair. "You did the deed?"

Claric looked at the young devil and smiled showing his fangs. "Yes summoner"

Mark sneered at the three of them. "You did well".

They sat down and began to rest. The power was still coursing through the veins of Mark, he could taste the crackle of electricity. The power of brimstone, his body was a live conduit of evil and evil through. He sat down to his sweet breads and began to enjoy the meal. He was turning more and more sinister. The powers of hell were changing not just his appearance. But his voice was deepening the more he dined fresh, fresh flesh and various organs were on the table. He dined and dined well. The vampires sat and watched the summoner eat. They thought the act of flesh eating was vulgar and a waste of good blood. vampires were known to squeeze the heart and all other organs of their juices. They did this ritually and that was once a week. They had to dine with the summoner so they usually brought dinner home at least once a week.

They fell into a deep deathly sleep only three more days to go and they had to get the pure soul somehow and it wasn't a thing they could put off until next year. No, this was one in six hundred years to let the Soul Collector free upon the earth and it would ravage and destroy the human race, nothing was in comparison to it, it would bring about the end of days. The world rested in the balance of good and evil and it was tipping slightly in the evil side. They could feel the moons equinox beating the blood down on the worlds, population. Everybody, was feeling the evil and dark forces growing. As the dry blood moon was coming to settle on the earth. And the vampires were languishing in the evil power and Hellish glory. Knowing soon they would be coming out of the shadows and crypts of ancient evil and the feasting and death would come forth into the night. There would be no salvation, no God would be able to save them. No, they would leave the world sodden in blood. The entrails of zombie leftovers would be everywhere. The dead and the dying would stack up and fester and decay on the consecrated grounds of earth they each grinned.

Mark summoned all he could in the way of chaotic energy. The three vampires all bowed as he began to murmur another demonic spell. The forces that were at work were completely evil and sinister. Mark languished in his new lease of the new powers, making him stronger. His appearance was changed but subtly. He was more shade than human he was getting all Hell's powers channelled through to him and now he knew he was an adversary not to be underestimated. His hunger for Sweet breads had grown. But the more he ate the stronger he became. He was constantly feeling the energies crackle through his very essence. He smiled through his black eyeballs and searched the very chasms of hell for more power, more, more, more.

He was readying himself for the final encounter with Father Clayton and his hunters. He just had to wait as he realised they knew where he was located. Now was the time to summon the pure soul to him, a spell of delightful menace. One that could be thought of as a charm, but it wasn't, it was evil through and through. It just appeared as a small glimmer of hope. The one thing that would save humanity and Mary Beth was the only one who could save the world. She was being fattened for the ceremony. The spell would beguile her subtly and send her into the arms of Mark, he carried on chanting opening up a small part of hell that would beguile her, hypnotise her make her one of them, but this was only an illusion. She was being summoned like a lamb to slaughter. Mark Cackled at his newfound power. He realised that the full potential of Hell would be summoned in the next two days. He would be a part of the new order of Hell. The heavens would be drowned in the Angelic blood of the holy and the divine.

*

Mary Beth was listening to Father Clayton as he explained several counter curses that would keep hell at bay. These were necessary and Mary Beth's faith would be tried and tested by the powers of hell. She smiled and relaxed a little as the light of heaven shone on her. She had a positive feeling about this, as though it was just a walk in the park. That's when she heard Darius who was fresh from the fight with the two succubus.

"Hello Mary Beth".

Mary Beth smiled and replied, "Hello Holy avenger".

The Angel smiled and beat his wings. "You are prepared I see".

Mary Beth smiled back into the cosmos of the ethereal plane. A dimension only travelled by the Holy and divine, "Are you ready for the true test of the Lord?"

She smiled and closed her eyes to see the figure of the Holy avenger. "I take it you are still fresh from the fight with the succubus?" she asked.

Darius beat his wings again and replied, "Yes child and no I didn't vanquish them".

Mary Beth was slightly saddened by the news but she knew that the fight wasn't over. She began to say a small prayer to show her loyalty and keep her faith in check. She knew that the holy and the divine power that was through Darius, needed a strength that only mortals have. And their Faith was constantly under pressure. Constantly called upon. Shown in ways like the reflection of the sun. A sun that was shining through all the planes of existence. Giving off varying degrees of light with different strengths and powers. Angels were lucky in the fact that they got to travel these planes freely. Took great strengths and powers from the various positions of the sun. The light being an immortal power point and giving the Angels the strength that they needed.

They were poised over the planes of heaven watching, making sure that humanity was safe in its own complexity and that the test from the Lord God was truly answered and made into heavenly blessings. But they had to keep a lot of things in check, their anger, their lust, their greed and all the other sins that they succumb to. No, the lord balanced a great deal of weight onto the human race. But this was just a test in which the mortals were adhered to, Darius kept the small conclave of Father Clayton's in good standing, knowing that when the time was right and that it was possible for Darius to be there in the fight he would take on that challenge of an Archangel.

The two succubus had retreated out into the lesser planes where they would regain their strength and heal their wounds. They too didn't succumb to the laws on nature. No, they only knew how to cause pain and great destruction but they were out of their depth with Darius as he had become more powerful. As he knelt in the light of the sun saying a prayer of strength the succubus merely thought of it knowing that it was a fair fight between them. Darius carried on praying in the light a light that reinvigorated his strength.

Father Clayton finished his sermon and went about the business of how they were going to have face not only the summoner and the three vampires but the two succubus too. And their main strength was their scream that caused a paralysing death but they had ear plugs made from bees wax. They would also have to rely on Darius fighting them on the other side. He had already encountered them once, and knew they were a force to be reckoned with.

*

Mark smiled as he looked out into the other planes of existence and he saw the two succubus who were healing themselves and growing in strength. He watched as they devoured a young teenage boy that they had grabbed on their way back to the realm of pain and chaos. They smiled as they drank the blood of the thirteen-year-old. They were feasting well in the next dimension; he knew that they would be the pinnacle of his strength. And that they would be the major part of getting the pure soul. They would entrance the young girl, she would be charmed and beguiled into giving herself freely. She would make the victim think they were angels and then by the time they were discovered she would be lost to the hunters, they knew that something powerful and malicious was in a process of something evil.

They would need all their skills to counter the evil that was summoned from Hell's spheres. It was two days until the blood moon when everything cold and malicious would come through into the earth realms. They would empty the pits and bowers into the earth realm then after they finished with God's children, they would swarm all over heaven. With them being helpless to fight off the massive surge of daemons and demons, devils and abominations, monsters, madmen and various other denizens of death.

He cackled into the night air and began to summon. The ceremony would take a night and a day. The day would be filled with energies, evil energies power that the world would never fathom only the feel of death, unholy death the world being summed up for eating and blood and chaos. For things having the chill of evil and death. Mark started to chant and began his offering then with his other hand he began the mystical shapes of Hell sending forth the succubus disguised as holy sweet mothers into the dreams of Mary Beth.

They began to sing to her as they drew closer, she smiled, then with all the charms they could muster they fooled her into getting into a car and driving towards Mark and his devilish conclave of daemons. She left without a trace. Father Clayton was in deep meditation studying counter charms for every curse that Mark could throw at them. She got into the summoners lair and ran deluded into his arms. He smiled and the two succubus revealed themselves to her she knew at once that she had been duped. She grew cold and fell limp into his arms.

Father Clayton woke from his deep concentration and realised that she was gone.

"Ahh dam it ,where did she go?"

He saw that the day was gently fading into night and he knew exactly where she had gone. The rest of the hunters woke to the fact that she had left and was in arms of the summoner. They all panicked at the sheer height of danger they were now in. They knew where she was and they had to stop the blood moon sacrifice. And save the pure soul. It was quite the feat that Mark had just pulled off, to confuse and distract the hunters long enough to be able to prepare for the soul collector. He had only a limited time as the hunters would be no doubt on their way to Mark's lair. They screeched to halt just at the corner of the summoners lair, They checked their firearms and headed straight for the summoners large studio apartment.

They climbed up the stairs and each one of them took a sudden bout of panic.

"Remember the vampires will be at their full strength," Said Craighton. They opened the door slowly knowing after the last encounter with the summoner they had to be prepared for anything. He no doubt had some sort of contingency plan, some dark twisted and evil that had been dwelling in his soul. No, they knew, they knew. The only thing that was in their favour was Darius, but he had disappeared leaving them with little support and no guidance.

Father Clayton scoffed at this in a kind of pure arrogance and he yet again wrapped the rosary beads around his red right hand. Knowing the malice that was surrounding them was not in any way going to stop them. Time was running out and there was no time to stand and ponder. No, they were fast down the rabbit hole and Alice was a devil.

Mark began to lift up his arms and send forth a curse like no other. He would summon the dead again and let loose another fire pit demon. The zombie pits that were just adjacent the building, deep in its basement spewed forth the corpse cannibal flesh eaters, who began to ascend the stairs having suddenly been shown the way to more flesh. Clayton spied one of the vampires drinking from a young teenage boy, well he didn't even see the massive, chiselled out of stone, build of Father Clayton ,who was upon him with his mean hard strength. He began to pummel the thing with his rock hard fists, saying a prayer as he did this.

"And you will know my name is the lord when I lay my vengeance on thee".

The vampire didn't have a chance every bone in his chest was smashed to pieces by Father Clayton with a fury that would have made Mohamad Ali proud. No, he was relentless reciting of the exorcism prayers, banishing the daemon back into the pits of hell. He smashed a hole right through the things chest, sending his ribs through his heart. The rest of them opened fire on the zombies that were encroaching them.

The summoner had Mary Beth chained to a sacrificial table, similar to the one he had used with Christian. The man twisted and changing in form began to chant the very evil way that was making the parallel universe open up and ready the release of the Devil into the human plane. Then the rest of hell would follow. He continued his summoning knowing that there was little hope for the human race.

"Achton murisha wail dae mons hielre". He carried on his chants to pandemonium, the hunters were being held at bay, he was in no hurry. Then the other two vampires decided to have a go. They began to circle the hunters whilst the zombies kept them from focusing anything on them. Robert Crufax was the first one to break the circle. He got through only to be accosted by the remaining two vampires. He snarled as he drew his pistol up and aimed at the things heart. It was as a clean kill as you could get with a vampire. He then went about the task of killing the other one. He pulled a razor sharp machete out of the folds of his coat.

Meanwhile the remainder of the hunters were still dealing with the Zombies. Then out of nowhere came a blinding light that disintegrated the Zombies and Darius was there with curved gladius in hand. He began the task of saving Robert who was just about beaten by the two wamphyre. He sliced one of their heads clean off then set about the task of killing Claric.

This was not an easy job as the vampire who was mature, to say the least, began to turn into mist. He was cowardly in the fact that he had to save his own skin. The summoner on the other hand was about to sacrifice Mary Beth.

"This offering is for you collector of souls!" He boomed these words out and began to prepare the knife. Just as he was about to strike, Father Clayton charged at him and knocked him off his feet and onto the ground. Father Clayton, again with upper body strength began to ground and pound the summoner. But Mark wasn't out the game yet, no he sliced along Father Claytons midriff. Causing a nasty cut, but Father Clayton carried on pummelling the devil. Elaine went through whilst Father Clayton was hammering into Mark and she released Mary Beth, who was groggy and disorientated. Whilst she was releasing Mary Beth Father Clayton again with the rosary beads wrapped around his right hand began to really pound him.

Father Clayton was a force that can only be described as the spirit of the almighty. Darius finished the vampire and Craighton was stood waiting as the air became dry and hot and he could hear the succubus coming through the portal. They descended upon Darius and Craighton. Craighton cast the spell that was meant for the summoner. As he did so the holy light lit up everywhere in the room. Which would hinder the two she demons and cause great pain to the summoner who was already in a world of hurt from the priest.

Craighton then released the spell to counteract the summoners unholy power. The two succubus began to fight with all their might all their hellish strength, but Darius was in a frenzy as the light fuelled his strength and he bathed in its glory. Gathering more strength as he fought back the She devils. Not giving them an inch of advantage; no, the more he carried on the more the power of the holy and divine became strong,

Craighton fired off two shots into one of them then began to charge at the thing with a razor sharp Tanto.

Mark was spitting up all kinds of black blood and his face, well it was pretty much caved in. "Back to hell demonic spawn". Clayton got up and opened up an iron flask and said a prayer then covered Mark in the holy water that instantly scolded and burned the summoner. He was in a world of holy pain and there was no denying it he had failed his Master. No now he would be sent straight into hell and his soul would be destroyed in the pits of the things that he had been worshipping since a child. The light fell on him and he disintegrated into the unholy realm of Hell. The two succubus began to scream as the light grew stronger and more divine.

Darius gave off a huge bellyaching laugh that was when the two she devils felt the true power of good. It had been an eternity since they had felt such pain. They felt how awful goodness was. They began to decay and leave the world that they had hoped to enslave and went back to the fiery pits in which they would subject to their masters wrath. Knowing only there would be Hell to pay. The hunters carried on with their duties that was to cut the heads off of three vampires. And anoint them with holy water. This was a fitting end to them they had finally got their justice. There was no come back, no redemption and certainly no Hell's blessings. They all disintegrated and were nothing but ash and dust. Mary Beth shook off her grogginess and looked around at the dead and the decaying dead.

"I take it we won," she said and they all headed back to the Chapel house. The world was saved and each one of the hunters had played their part.

The End